Cache
of
Corpses

Books by Henry Kisor from Tom Doherty Associates

Season's Revenge
A Venture into Murder
Cache of Corpses

Cache
of
Corpses

Henry Kisor

A Tom Doherty Associates Book
New York

Cache
of
Corpses

"It's in the Dying Room," Jenny Besonen said, voice strained, ample chest heaving. "And it has no head."

Billy Ciric, her boyfriend, sat disconsolately next to her on a bench in the Poor Farm courtyard, staring at the breakfast he had splashed on the rusty flank of Amos Hoskinen's tractor.

"*What's* up in the Dying Room?" I asked. I was a bit breathless myself, having been yanked a few minutes earlier out of the Porcupine City Health Center, where I had been pumping a stationary bike for nearly an hour, and dispatched in the sheriff's department's Explorer out to the scene on State Highway M-38 three miles southeast of town.

"The *body*." Jenny glanced at me almost accusingly, as if I should magically have known the reason for her distress.

"The body?"

"It's a lady. She's wrapped in plastic. And she has no head." Jenny took a deep breath, mending her tattered composure.

"Go on."

"We'd been exploring, and—" Jenny glanced away and hesitated. She wasn't telling the truth. Seventeen-year-old kids are still too immature and transparent to lie convincingly. But it wasn't yet time to insist on the facts, young lady, nothing but the facts.

"Anything else?"

"No. . . . Ah. . . . I don't know."

"Wait here, okay? I'll have a look. Amos, would you keep an eye on Jenny and Billy?"

"Sure," Amos said. He had not moved from the seat of his tractor, but he had kept his phlegmatic calm ever since Jenny and Billy had scrambled, screaming in terror, out the front door of the Poor Farm and told him what they had stumbled across up in the Dying Room. Immediately Amos had relayed their discovery to the sheriff's department on his cell phone—luckily, the Poor Farm lay within the spotty cellular coverage of Porcupine County—and I, the nearest deputy within the dispatcher's grasp, had been hauled to work early and sent to the scene.

A tall, rawboned farmer and stable keeper, Amos was the latest in a succession of owners of the sprawling property once officially known as the Porcupine County Poor Farm and still called that. Looking almost like a brooding red-brick Victorian mansion gingerbreaded with cupolas and turrets—"Hogwarts West," the local children say—the Poor Farm still catches the eye of motorists speeding by on the highway a hundred yards away.

More than a century ago, Porcupine County built the Poor Farm to shelter two dozen or so indigents who worked the rocky, deforested fields in exchange for their survival. For poorhouses of the age, this one wasn't so bad. Daily life there, I knew from the lecture the director of the Porcupine County Historical Society had given a year or so ago, was rugged but not cruel. The unfortunates were expected to help work the land if they could and do chores inside if they couldn't. The Poor Farm had been no Dickensian horror but a lighthouse of modest respite in an unforgiving land where harsh winters arrive early, dig in deeply, and stay long.

From the highway, the place looked sturdy enough to be rehabilitated someday. Closer in, however, a visitor could see that splintered plywood shrouded half the Poor Farm's windows while the glass in the other half simply had gone missing. Doors dangled askew from sprung hinges. Frayed blue plastic tarps, lashed loosely over holes in the roof, snapped in the wind. The two-foot-thick masonry, however, remained solid and mostly unblemished except for the faded five-foot-tall "EAT *more* BEEF" sign whitewashed by a shaky hand on the highway side. The notice had doubtless been posted by some desperate long-ago cattle farmer, perhaps the one who had bought and worked the house and its lands when the state took over care of the poor after the Second World War.

Inside, a large warm kitchen and a commodious parlor once had made up most of the now empty and cavernous ground floor. Shreds of straw left by the hay bales stored there in later years now shared the oaken planks with decades of rodent droppings. Upstairs, men had slept in a large dormitory room at one end, women in another across the wide hall, its door guarded by a stern Cerberus of a nurse. Children had occupied bunks on half the third floor, the highway side. A series of small rooms, used mostly for storage, separated them from the Dying Room, whose face was turned to the fields on the other side of the house.

The Dying Room was where the deathly ill awaited their fate, the thick interior walls insulating their cries and screams from the rest of the house. The arms of two tall men could have spanned the width of the room and almost its length. It had space for just two narrow beds, whose utilitarian steel frames and springs, now broken and rusted, still stood on the floor. Just off the room lay another chamber, little more than a closet, according to legend the coldest enclosure in the house during the winter. There, plain wooden coffins and their contents were stored until the April thaw, when they could be discreetly smuggled down a back stairway and carted to potter's field, where they were often buried in the presence of just two mourners, the grave digger and a minister hired by the county to speed the souls on their way.

Carefully I mounted the front stairs to the third floor, brushing away decades of cobwebs as splintered oaken treads creaked in annoyance. I stepped over the dusty threshold of the Dying Room.

That was the perfect name, for the place itself looked bound for the boneyard. A jagged fissure gaped between the ruined walls and stained ceiling, sagging like a double bed in a cheap motel. Shattered lath grinned from lightning-shaped cracks in the plaster walls. Most of the elaborately carved oaken frieze molding had been pried out and salvaged decades ago.

On one of the bedsprings lay the sight that had so upset Jenny and Billy. A rectangular shroud of thick plastic sheeting, sealed all around to form a transparent but airtight container, encased a yellowish green corpse. The plastic bulged slightly from gas emitted by slow decomposition. A thick scrim of moisture clouded the inside of the soiled plastic, like a dirty shower curtain in a humid bathroom, blanketing a clear view of the contents. I could see enough of the shape within to tell that it was the nude body of a woman, probably young judging by the firmness of the breasts and tightness of the thighs. It had neither head nor hands. Instead of looking like a once living body, it resembled a mutilated life-size statue toppled off its pedestal in a ruined Greek temple.

I stood, picked my way back through the third floor and down the rickety stairs, and strode out into the courtyard. Deputy Chad Garrow, whose patrol area encompasses the Poor Farm, stood talking to Jenny, Billy, and Amos. Chad had been writing a traffic ticket twenty minutes south on U.S. 45, hence I had been called in early to investigate. I quickly filled him in on what I had seen in the Dying Room.

"Shall I radio Alex?" Chad asked. Detective Sergeant Alex Kolehmainen was the local state police forensics investigator and the authority we almost always called in to investigate suspicious deaths. The state police is better equipped for that than are tight-budgeted sheriff's departments in rural counties whose population—and tax base—shrinks by 10 percent every decade. And this at first looked like a homicide, although doubts were beginning to seep into my head.

"Do that," I said. "I'll talk to the kids."

Jenny and Billy still sat on the bench in the warm noonday sun outside the manor house, chatting with Chad. They were both high school seniors, and I knew them. Billy was tall, black-haired in a modified Marine crew cut, good-looking, and muscular. A star football player at Porcupine City High School, Billy was a tight end promising enough for a football scholarship to half a dozen universities. His black sleeveless T-shirt set off his well-cut biceps. Only a bent nose, the product of a hard check into the goal on a hockey rink, marred his sculpted features.

Jenny, the oldest daughter of a dairy farmer, was a sturdy and slightly chubby but winsome and pretty blonde whose loose chambray work shirt, denim overalls, and swampers—rubber-bottomed leather boots—couldn't conceal her abundant womanliness. Her arms and shoulders had been built up by years of farm work, many of them with the heifers that always scored well in the 4-H division at the county fair. Doubtless she had been mucking out stalls that morning, for she smelled cowy, a homey aroma of sweet milk and stale dung whose familiarity comforts rather than repels the country dweller.

Both were nice, hard-working, intelligent kids who applied themselves in school, and both were headed to college, Billy to the University of Michigan and Jenny to Michigan Tech. He wanted to follow his dad into law, and she was hoping to become a veterinarian. I thought both would achieve their dreams—and after graduation probably would leave Porcupine County for good. Jobs are hard to get in a land where the mines have long closed and where most of the tall pines and cedars were cut down more than a century ago, and what jobs there are don't pay much. I just hoped Billy wouldn't get Jenny pregnant, as happened so often up here. Young dreams are so easily ruined by careless rolls in the hay.

Jenny and Billy were laughing with Chad, as if the kids had

forgotten the unpleasant sight in the Dying Room. I was not surprised. Chad, as amiable as he was large, knew how to get witnesses to relax, even to let down their guards so they would tell the truth while being interrogated. He was the perfect good cop who made witnesses and suspects alike think he was on their side.

And now playing bad cop was my job. Jenny and Billy, after all, had found the body, and even in the most remote reaches of the Upper Peninsula of Michigan, those who find bodies are always the first to be questioned, if only to be quickly eliminated as suspects. Despite the astronomical odds against kids like Jenny and Billy having anything to do with the presence of that corpse, I decided to approach them as if they might have. You never know.

I beckoned Billy over to the Explorer, ushering him out of Jenny's earshot so that their stories would be independent of each other's.

"Hop in," I said. "We might as well make ourselves comfortable while we sort this out." I looked back at Jenny, giggling as the beaming Chad, easily ten years her elder, flirted shamelessly with her.

"Okay," Billy said, his expression earnest and helpful.

"Let's start at the beginning," I said. "How did you come to be on the Poor Farm?"

"We were exploring," he said, looking at me with a steady gaze, "and—"

"Exploring?" I interrupted. "Really?" That's what Jenny had said, too, but I didn't believe Billy, either.

"Um—"

"Billy, tell the truth. If you're straight with me and you're in the clear, I'm not going to tell anybody what you were really doing." I was better at playing stern uncle than bad cop.

The kid blushed. "Okay, Mr. Martinez." He looked off into the distance.

"Steve's fine."

"Steve." He slowly tried out the word, as if being asked to call a figure of authority by his given name was another step into adulthood. The invitation was a favorite ploy of mine. Some cops insist on maintaining a dominating distance from those they are interrogating, encouraging a little fear to get them to talk. But casual friendliness often encourages subjects to join me on a mutual path toward the truth. I wasn't chummy like Chad, but I kept the door open.

I waited.

"Well," Billy said tentatively, "Jenny and I wanted to make out, and we thought the Poor Farm would be a good place to do it. Nobody ever comes here. Nobody would see us."

"Billy," I said, "I know as well as you do that there must be a million places in Porcupine County where a boy and a girl can go to *make out* without anybody catching them." I stressed the term to tell him I knew exactly what he meant by it. "Why the Poor Farm, really?"

Billy glanced at me half nervously and half slyly. "Because Jenny and I done it in a million places already," he said.

I had to stifle a smile. But Billy wasn't boasting or playing the smart-ass, just being matter-of-fact. Kids these days approach sex casually, as if it has all the significance of a good breakfast before school.

"We thought the Poor Farm would be exciting. Especially the Dying Room." That he knew the place's history wasn't surprising. Every kid as well as adult in the county did, thanks to the bloodcurdling stories their parents told them every Halloween about the ghosts of the lost and abandoned that wafted out of the Dying Room.

"Did you bring protection?" I asked.

Billy bristled. "You're not my dad."

"No," I said as gently as I could. "But did you?"

"Yes."

"Let's see."

After a moment's hesitation he pulled a foil-wrapped Trojan from his shirt pocket. That the condom was in his pocket, not his wallet, told me he had planned to use it right away, that his intention in trespassing upon the Poor Farm was exactly what he said it was. Besides, I reflected idly, what was there to steal or trash in such a godforsaken place?

"Okay, Billy. I believe you. Put it away." With only a little prompting he related the rest of the story. Shortly after noon, he and Jenny had parked her pickup on the disused dirt road that marked the eastern boundary of the Poor Farm property a quarter of a mile away. They then crept across the meadow, tiptoeing carefully through a minefield of cow patties, to the back of the manor house. They entered it through a doorway whose door was long gone, and enough daylight filtered through the ruined windows to show them the way up the creaking back stairs, festooned with cobwebs, to the Dying Room.

"With some of the seniors at Porky High," Billy finally said, "it's kind of a game to do it in cool places. We try to top each other. A couple of my friends did it in the district courtroom one night. We did it at high noon on the hardware store roof during the Fourth of July parade, and another time somebody used the cab of the pumper in the fire station. We all used the old shipyard building at the end of Main Street."

I remembered that one. In one of the smaller rooms earlier in the year, a caretaker had discovered a mattress, an old microwave oven, a small television and a DVD player, and a couple of porn videos. How long it had been a love nest for teenagers was anybody's guess.

"Once me and Jen used the bridge tender's shelter. The door was open."

I whistled. That tiny cubbyhole atop the State Highway M-64 swing bridge over the Porcupine River must be tighter than the backseat of a Volkswagen Bug. Then I had a thought. "The lighthouse?" I asked. The previous week someone had broken into the old Coast Guard structure, now owned by the Historical Society, jimmying a window and leaving screwdriver marks, but they had disturbed nothing else.

Billy blushed. "Yes. They did it right on top of the pedestal where the lens used to be."

I shook my head, covering a chuckle by saying sternly, "That could be a dangerous game. That was breaking and entering, a misdemeanor meaning ninety-three days in jail and a five-hundred-dollar fine. If they had done anything else illegally at the same time, like swiping something or drinking underage, they could have been charged with a felony—and given a stretch in state prison."

"Yeah, but—"

I didn't tell Billy that Garner Armstrong, the county prosecutor and a man vastly experienced in the thoughtless stupidities of youth, most likely would offer the lighthouse miscreants a plea bargain for unlawful entry of an unoccupied building and a light sentence of a few months on probation and community service. If nothing was stolen or wrecked, Garner wouldn't apply the heavy lumber. To him it wasn't a matter of giving a youngster a sentimental break. He hated to ruin young lives with felony records. Good thing, too. Kids liked to break into deer camps deep in the woods for beer parties and "making out." Usually they were smart enough to clean up after themselves, and only when they left a mess or did damage did the sheriff's department apply its scarce manpower to an investigation.

"So you take each other's word that you've really, uh, *done it* in the places you claim?" I asked.

"No, we prove it with pictures from a digital camera."

I closed my eyes. *Oh, Billy, Billy, Billy.* "That's dangerous. What if the wrong people get hold of the pictures?" I tried to keep the disapproval out of my voice, but I failed.

"They won't. We don't make prints. We keep them on our computers and upload them to each other by email."

"That's not such a good idea."

"Why?"

"Somebody else could get at them. Your parents. Your little brothers or sisters. Believe me, it happens."

"Well . . ."

"I think you and your friends had better think carefully about this game. It could have consequences you never imagined."

I decided to go no farther with the lecture. Too much censure might make Billy clam up. "All right, go on with your story."

Only mildly chastened, Billy related how he and Jenny climbed the back stairs to the third floor, opened the door to the Dying Room, and found the corpse. The gruesome sight, of course, deflated their excited lust. Screaming, they half-stumbled, half-ran across the third floor, down the front stairs, and out into the front courtyard, where, I knew, Billy had vomited on Amos's tractor, barely missing the astonished farmer in the John Deere's seat. Jenny, being the daughter of a farmer and used to the less pleasant sights of animal husbandry, kept her cool—or most of it. In many ways the females of the human species in Upper Michigan are tougher than the males.

Immediately, Billy said—he delicately avoided mention of decorating Amos's tractor—he and Jenny told the farmer what they had seen, and they dutifully remained on the scene while the farmer called the sheriff's department. Teenagers can be both reckless and responsible.

"You never saw that body before?" I asked.

Billy glanced sharply at me. "Of course not."

"Dumb question," I said. "But it always has to be asked. All right. I'm done with you. I'm going to talk to Jenny now, and if what she says backs up what you said, that will be all I need from you, and you can go home. I think you were straight with me, and

I'll keep your secret." Billy nodded, his confidence returning. I could see that he believed Jenny would back him up in the smallest detail.

And so she did, although she displayed absolutely no embarrassment when she told me what she and Billy had intended to do in the Dying Room. She had also brought protection.

"You can't always expect a boy to do the smart thing," Jenny said.

"You think breaking into the Poor Farm was a smart thing to do?" I said, trying to stifle an amused tone.

"You sound like an old fart, Mr. Martinez," she said. "Weren't you young once?"

I didn't take offense. Her words were smart-ass but her tone wasn't. It was just the way many of today's kids spoke, respectful of their elders but not deferential toward them. They had grown up with a directness my generation hadn't.

"All right, you have me there," I said. "I do agree that being prepared is a smart idea."

Conservative pastors in the Upper Peninsula, especially the evangelicals, preach abstinence, which is a perfectly sensible thing to practice but in my opinion hasn't a prayer against the raging hormones of the teenage years. Youngsters in the Michigan backwoods are just as sexually active as those in the cities and suburbs. In the Great White North there isn't much for kids to do in their off hours besides play sports, smoke dope, and make whoopee while waiting until they're old enough to depart for the bright lights.

While I was talking to Jenny, Alex had arrived in his cruiser, returned my wave, been quickly filled in by Chad, and mounted the stairs with his forensics kit to the Dying Room.

"Stay here awhile," I said to Jenny and Billy, and I followed the trooper into the manor house.

"This stiff was meant to be found," Alex announced heartily

as I entered the Dying Room and found him squatting by the body. "But not to be identified."

The lanky trooper rose to his feet like a folding wooden carpenter's rule, rearranging the angles of his knees and elbows until he stood straight, and surveyed the scene. What he said made sense. The plastic-shrouded corpse had been laid carefully on the bedspring, only the closed door hiding it from the rest of the house. But why? Few people braved the place. I suspected months, maybe a year or even two, went by before anyone—usually Amos—opened the door to that room.

"Deputy Sheriff," Alex said presently, addressing me with the exaggerated formality he always adopted when he wanted to insert the needle, which was every other day, "what do you think? If you are capable of thought."

Long ago I had learned not to rise to the bait. Alex is my second closest friend in Porcupine County. Number one is Virginia Antala Fitzgerald, a gorgeous native daughter and the Historical Society director who had given the Poor Farm lecture I had attended. Alex is a master of irony and indirection as well as the owner of an impish sense of humor. We worked together easily, partly because he never lorded it over me like some state troopers who like to treat county deputies like not-too-bright lackeys, and partly because our investigative skills had complemented each other's through several knotty cases.

"Detective Sergeant," I said with equal gravity, "I am not sure we are looking at a homicide."

"And why is that?"

"This body looks pickled."

"What makes you think so?"

"Same color as the embalmed casualties I saw in Kuwait." I had been an army lieutenant after college and criminal justice school, commanding a company of military police during Desert Storm. Now and then my tasks would take me to the Graves Registration

mortuary outside Riyadh where dead American soldiers were prepared for the sad journey home. "No blood at the points of ampu-
tation. Unless I miss my guess, those cuts on the abdomen were
made by a mortician's trocar."

"Hmm." Alex's eyes rose in mock surprise. He knows even
more than I do about corpses. On his way to detective sergeant,
he had been trained thoroughly in forensics and evidence gathering.
He still often did double duty as the evidence technician he once
was, for the tightfisted Wakefield state police post commander
hated to pay overtime to his two busy crime scene techs.

"How long do you think this has been here?" I asked.

"Hard to tell. In a place like this the dust isn't often disturbed
to swirl around and settle on things. But there's only a fine layer,
almost invisible, on this plastic. My guess is probably a month, six
weeks tops."

"Shall we open the—uh—shroud and take a look?" I was kidding.

"No, no, no!" said Alex. "Let the white coats at Marquette do
that. Besides, we didn't bring hazmat suits." The laboratory investigators did most of their work at the state police crime lab in Marquette, 120 miles to the southeast. Carefully Alex photographed
the scene and its grisly contents. "Let's turn her over," he said after
a while. We did so, careful not to tear the plastic shroud on the broken bedsprings. "Looky this," he said, pointing to a soiled white
computer label, an inch high by three inches wide, neatly affixed to
one corner of the plastic. On it was imprinted a bar code.

"Hmm, I don't see a sell-by date." Alex's sense of humor is
sometimes questionable. He photographed the label.

"Maybe it'll tell us where the body came from," I said. "Although I don't think undertakers put bar codes on their handiwork."

"Why not?" said Alex. "It'd speed the bodies through the ce-
lestial cash register." I winced and shook my head. But I knew

that Alex's lighthearted remarks were just a veteran cop's way of coping with unpleasant sights. Police officers may sound callous and hard-hearted, but the truth is that we are as moved as anyone else by the sight of human death.

"Just a sec," he said. He reached under the bedsprings and fished out a quarter and a penny. "These don't look all that old."

"Dates?" I said.

"Nineteen ninety-two on the quarter, twenty-oh-one on the penny."

"Not so old," I agreed. " 'Ninety-two quarters are still in common circulation."

"What do they mean?" Alex said. "Perp drop them accidentally?"

"Probably. Took something out of his pocket, the coins followed."

For a couple of beats, we fell silent. Then Alex said, "Let me show you the back stairs."

We left the Dying Room and walked down the narrow hall to the stairs, carefully keeping to the sides where the joists better supported the rickety floorboards. Alex played his big Maglite on the dust shrouding the topmost treads of the narrow stairway.

"See the tracks in the dust? Three different people came up this way very recently."

"And two of them were Jenny and Billy."

"Who're they?"

"The kids outside with Chad and Amos." I told Alex what they had said, keeping the story brief but frank.

"Hmm," he replied. "Every generation invents its own excitement, I guess."

"What was yours?"

"Oh, the usual kind, beer and cigarettes. We weren't terribly adventurous."

"Speak for yourself." He and I were the same age.

"Here, take this footprint kit and make impressions of the kids' shoes, will ya? That'll eliminate two sets of tracks. That means the third could have been left by the perp. Not that his tracks are likely to hang him, but you never know."

I did so, then said, "What about the front stairs?"

"Let's have a look."

After surveying the scene briefly, Alex said, "No good. Too many tracks and they're too faint and crisscrossed. You, me, Amos, the kids, probably others have gone up and down the stairs—and the wind through the windows and all that blowing straw keeps the dust thin."

In the courtyard half an hour later, Alex said, "We're done here. I'll call the meat wagon."

Afterward, we sent Billy and Jenny on their way, and with Chad's help, Alex and I carried the gruesome package down the front stairs, carefully keeping it clear of rusty nail heads and jutting lath, and zipped it into a body bag. That wasn't necessary to protect the vehicle from the corpse, for the clear plastic shroud was far stronger than a body bag, but we didn't want anyone to have to see what was inside. Then we rolled it into a hearse from the Beninghaus Funeral Home for the trip to Marquette. When it had gone, Alex turned to me and said, "Soon's I hear from Marquette forensics, I'll give you a call."

He didn't have to, but I knew he would. In the small world of Upper Michigan police work, Alex and I are a comfortable old crime-fighting couple. We bust perps together, drink together, hunt together, play golf together, take our women out together, and in general behave like buddies—all activities that many county sheriffs and state police brass disapprove of, because they think deputies and troopers should remain carefully separated in their assigned slots in the pecking order of law enforcement. Hierarchy has its uses.

And, in what passes for Upper Michigan politics, Alex is my campaign manager. Self-appointed and unofficial, of course.

2 "Want to help post campaign signs for Steve?" Alex had asked Chad in the squad room of the sheriff's department the day before, deliberately—and a little cruelly—putting the big deputy on the spot. Chad is the nephew of my rival for the office of sheriff of Porcupine County, the incumbent Eli Garrow, and he got his job partly because of nepotism. Chad is large and friendly, clumsy and eager, but he is no longer a greenhorn with a badge. He has proven his competency more than once, although I try not to get in his way when he's shambling through the office. The cliché is that big men—Chad is six-six and pushing three hundred pounds—often are remarkably delicate with their hands and light on their feet. Not Chad. Just being in his general neighborhood can get you knocked off your feet. In high school, his classmates had called him "Lurch" for his clumsiness, but his speed as well as heft as a center on the football team had won him more than cursory glances from college recruiters. He'd gone to Michigan Tech for two years before joining the sheriff's department.

"He reminds me of a St. Bernard puppy," Ginny once said fondly, "all huge paws and head." She likes him as much as I do, even though, like all women in Porcupine County who have experienced his social graces, she hides the antique chairs when he drops in.

Politically speaking, however, Chad is caught between the devil and the deep blue. I think he secretly hoped I would win the election, but he was also loyal to his kinsman. Alex and I never criticized Eli in front of Chad, though Eli certainly deserved criticism, especially of late. Hiring his own wife as jail matron was bad enough, and so was using the department's newest snowmobile as his personal plaything, but those peccadilloes have been long forgotten. In the poor counties of Upper Michigan, that's as far as political scandal ever gets, and while such niggardly nest feathering could cost a politician an election, it's not worth an indictment.

For a long time, Eli was a first-rate sheriff, but as he aged in the job, he began to treat it as a sinecure, doing less and less work in his office while hanging out in taverns and veterans' halls and deer camps and restaurants with other powerful county old-timers. These days he was bragging too much and drinking too much, often driving with a snootful, and sometimes patting a female constituent farther down her back than was appropriate. Gil O'Brien, a first-rate if overly stern undersheriff, really ran the department, and he tacitly supported my candidacy although he'd never admit it in public. Eli hadn't been in the office since I filed for a spot next to his name on the Democratic primary ballot many weeks ago. Only Chad represented the family, and when he was in the squad room, he and the rest of us avoided the topic of the election as if it were a turd on the doorstep.

But the county's prosecutor and commissioners considered Eli an increasing embarrassment, and they had asked him to stand down for a new sheriff. They'd promised him a big retirement dinner at the best restaurant in the county with fulsome speeches of praise, but Eli refused the bait. As soon as he learned that I had filed a nominating petition for sheriff, he stormed out of his office, slammed the door, and said he was taking a few days off for a rest. That few days had grown to several weeks, then months. In the beginning he had called in now and then to consult with Gil over departmental matters, but for quite a while he hadn't bothered.

Gil is as competent an administrator as he is a cop. He could have run for sheriff, but having neither taste nor talent for politicking, he had stood aside when Garner Armstrong, aided and abetted by Alex and Ginny as well as a couple of the commissioners, tapped me for the task. Why I accepted the challenge, I'm sometimes not sure. Though I was still a deputy in my early forties, I loved the job as much as I love Porcupine County, where I washed up long ago, another stick of human driftwood, after a broken romance. Being a deputy was never dull. It got me out both among people and into the woods. But to complete his life a man needs a little ambition, a willingness to use his talents to the fullest. I'd had some luck solving a couple of celebrated cases, but now maybe I needed to move on.

Still, politics complicates a life. Unlike Eli, I wasn't born to be a pol. For one thing, I am shy. I'd rather have an ingrown toenail removed than get up before a crowd to talk. Pressing the flesh at church suppers and the VFW Hall got old the first day I tried it. I like talking with individual folks at length on the sidelines, getting to know them, not exchanging one face for another every few seconds as a temporary center of attention. The self-aggrandizing insincerity of professional politicians nauseates and repulses me. If I can't be candid, I tend to shut up, and taciturnity is fatal for an office seeker.

But somehow I had persuaded myself that Porcupine County needed me. In the middle of the night, at the tiny hour when a man lies naked to his deepest secrets, I have to admit that holding such an idea is an act of ego. Admitting this was not easy. For one thing, although I was adopted as an infant from the Lakota Sioux reservation in South Dakota by a visiting missionary and raised in upper New York State as a good white Methodist, I still retain an Indian tendency to hide my light under a bushel. Indians hate to make a fuss, which historically has hurt them with politicians, who tend to grease the squeakiest wheels. Modesty is a cultural imperative for Indians brought up in their own traditions. But the roots of my diffidence might also lie in my white upbringing. My adoptive father, a devout and strong-willed preacher, raised me to be humble and polite. Which the chicken and which the egg? Which the wound and which the bow? It doesn't matter. I am what I am, never mind how I got to be that way.

But my Indianness definitely colored the campaign. People in these parts are annoyed by what they consider the double-dipping of Ojibwe from Upper Michigan reservations into casino money *and* government welfare. Why them and not us? the whites ask. We're poor, too, and nobody's looking out for us. Three hundred years of nearly genocidal history doesn't matter much to anybody, white or otherwise, struggling to survive in the here and now. True, I'm Lakota and not Ojibwe. To the majority culture, however, members of minorities look alike, and they tend to lump Indians together. I won't say Porkies are bigoted any more than rural Americans anywhere, but some of them are, and in a tight race their votes can make the difference.

The trouble with all this is that I'm a cop as well as an Indian. Is a citizen's averted gaze or hesitant handshake evidence of deep-seated prejudice against Native Americans, or merely the usual citizen's skittishness in the presence of the law? Who can tell?

Politics is always complicated. Not only is Eli Garrow a likable fellow and a superb campaigner, but his family all but owns the southern reaches of Porcupine County. The Garrows arrived from Cornwall and set up camp on the shore of Lake Superior during the copper boom of the 1850s and went forth and multiplied, intermarrying with the Irish, Croatians, and fellow Cornish who followed, then with the Finns in the early twentieth century. Half the South Porkies, it sometimes seems, are descended from Obadiah Garrow, a mining engineer who wrested a fortune in high-grade copper ore from a mine, now long shuttered, deep in the Trap Hills, which bisect the two halves of the county. And the rest of the population seem to be close cousins. Some mean-spirited folks claim incestuous relationships among certain Garrows, but I don't know about that. Every Garrow I have ever met has just five fingers on each hand. All the same, I could swear the eyes of some of them are set suspiciously close together.

Porcupine City, on Lake Superior, holds more than half the county's population, and since I was so visible in town—my daily beat covers the north and west of the county, Chad's the south and east—I was strongest there, Alex thought. The farther away from Porcupine City I stood, the less appeal my name held for voters.

"Maybe that's because townspeople are more sophisticated than country dwellers?" I once asked him.

Alex shook his head. "Not in the Upper Peninsula. Yoopers are Yoopers."

But our very rough polling technique—casual questions asked of a few passersby—suggested I wouldn't do better than 60 percent in town. If Eli had 80 percent of the smaller number of people in the south, he'd beat me in the primary.

Unlike many other states, Michigan holds its primaries the first Tuesday of August, three months before the general elections in November. Eli and I were both running as Democrats, unchallenged by any Republican. Upper Michigan is solidly Democratic so far as voting is concerned, although many—possibly most—Yooper voters are deeply conservative in cultural matters. They favor hunting and gun rights and are family oriented, antiabortion, and suspicious of gays and lesbians—but often they depend on financial subsidies from the state for their daily survival. Hence they send Democrats to the state house as well as the U.S. Congress and Senate, although they often split their tickets and vote for a Republican president.

For the most part, however, personality, not political ideology, drives local elections in Porcupine County. That's what made running for office such an uphill climb for the likes of me.

"You've got to go campaign outside town, especially in the south," Alex declared, and he was right.

And so on my off hours, I'd drive to Ewen, Bruce Crossing, Trout Creek, Paulding, Paynesville, and Coppermass, saying a shy hello at the Elks and American Legion wiener roasts, and speaking a few words if I was invited to the microphone, which wasn't often. I fared no better at the church suppers, except for the Catholic potlucks. Thanks to the Black Robes, the French Jesuits who explored the region in the seventeenth century, most Indians in these parts are Catholic when they are not traditional, and evangelical congregations tend to look askance at Catholics. The evangelicals probably thought I used to be a papist, although I was brought up Protestant, and, like so many preachers' kids, I left the church in a youthful act of rebellion. To many born-again southern Porkies, faithlessness is worse than being Indian and heathen. But I wasn't about to join a congregation and become a campaign Christian, like some politicians. I dislike in-your-face religiosity from the sincere and cannot abide it in the insincere.

On the way to an event, I'd stop by a few roadside homes and walk up, uniform cap in hand, to ask if I could post a campaign sign in the front yard. "Sorry, we're Eli people," most home owners said, although a few—Porcupine County residents are not rude—did invite me in and hand me a glass of lemonade. Some of them even said, "Sure thing, be our guest." I had a lot of campaign signs, most of them financed by a couple of benefit dinners Alex had organized, as well as by a couple of friendly county commissioners and Garner Armstrong, the district attorney. My political war chest, however, was probably one-tenth the size of Eli's. His cousins contributed en masse, partly because Eli was shameless in using his influence to find them jobs with the county and the state. And he saved money by reusing his campaign posters from several previous elections, while I had to start from scratch.

And now he was rubbing my nose in my tiny budget by buying

full-page ads in *The Herald,* the county's weekly newspaper, almost every week, even though the primary election lay two months away. I could barely afford a four-inch-high notice in the paper once a month. What's more, Eli was now engaging in what passes for hardball politics in Porcupine County, dealing in subtle innuendo.

"ELI GARROW FOR SHERIFF," today's full-pager said. "BORN AND RAISED IN PORCUPINE COUNTY." That was Eli's way of saying "Steve Martinez is an outsider," and no local could miss the point. I arrived in Porcupine County shortly after Desert Storm and have been a resident and a property owner for only a decade and a half, a blink of an eye in the long memories of homegrown Porkies, whose roots often go back four and even five generations.

"A CHURCHGOER ALL HIS LIFE." That appeal to the religious underscored the fact that I am "unchurched," as the Episcopalians politely say. Many people in the Upper Peninsula measure a man's character by his public as well as private commitment to the Lord.

"MARRIED 47 YEARS." I had been keeping company with Ginny Fitzgerald, the Porcupine County Historical Society's director, for three years. Until very recently, we had been happy in our arrangement, choosing to put off the topic of permanence until some vague time in the future. Though we often shared the nights, we lived in separate homes, I in a rustic cabin on the lake shore six miles west of Porcupine City, Ginny in a log home she'd financed with an inheritance so considerable nobody knew about it but me. But some voters, especially elderly women with nothing more important to condemn and even less to keep themselves occupied, considered such an arrangement "living in sin," and they occasionally told me so.

"A FAMILY MAN." Eli and Dorothy had seven children, who themselves had large broods, and the photograph displayed forty-seven Garrows of three generations at the family's umpteenth reunion the previous month. And those didn't count the hundreds, maybe even thousands, of first cousins, second cousins, cousins once removed, and cousins by marriage who also showed up at the VFW Hall. And me? I was a bachelor without a family. Bachelors are always suspect. We haven't put down biological roots, sowed our seed in the land. We could pull up stakes at any time and disappear for greener pastures. We haven't committed. We're untrustworthy.

"ONE OF US" said the headline next to a large photograph of Eli beaming before a large knot of maybe three dozen Porcupine Countians, every last one of whom was white. Unsubtle. "Eli's getting desperate," Alex had said after the latest ad had appeared. I wasn't so sure. It felt more like getting piled on by the entire defensive line of the Packers. All I am is a good cop with a decent record.

And that arrangement with Ginny had arrived at a crossroads.

3 "Hello, Mr. Martinez," said Tommy Standing Bear with grave courtesy, gazing without blinking into my eyes as I arrived at Ginny's place the morning after the incident at the Poor Farm. Tommy was twelve years old, mahogany skinned and black haired like me. Ginny had become his foster mother just two weeks before. He had been a ward of the tribe on the Ojibwe reservation at Baraga.

Tommy had had a hell of a life. His parents had been unemployed alcoholics, and they had both died the previous year when their pickup spun off the highway south of Baraga and struck a tree. Edgar Standing Bear had been driving under the influence. An unmarried uncle who was a logger and a sergeant in the National Guard had agreed to take Tommy into his care, but he was deployed to Iraq before the paperwork could be completed. The boy had been shunted into the reservation's foster home system until his uncle could return.

I had felt an uneasy sense of déjà vu when Ginny introduced me to Tommy. My birth parents on the reservation at Pine Ridge had died of alcoholism, and a drunken driver had killed my adoptive mother and father. My heart had immediately gone out to the lad, but Tommy still wrapped himself in a carapace of subtle mistrust. Not outright hostility, for he was too polite for that.

It would take a while to get through to him. But we Indians are nothing if not patient. Patience is one of the few weapons we still have, whether we are traditionals or steeped in white culture.

"Hi, Tommy," I said. "Where's Ginny?"

"Kitchen, Mr. Martinez," he said. Ginny was too warm and loving to want to be called "Mrs. Fitzgerald" and too realistic to suggest that he call her "Mom," a term frowned upon for a foster mother anyway, for the foster relationship always begins with the understanding that it is temporary. She hoped that he would, in time, call her something more than "Ginny" if she showed him lots of love—and patience. White people need to have patience, too, and Ginny had more than her share. Maybe it came from hanging out with an Indian, rubbing off from me. That's what I once told her, anyway. She just chuckled and waved away the notion. She doesn't think Indians are much different from white people, although I do my damnedest to persuade her otherwise.

In the last few months I had paid several visits with her to Baraga to do the paperwork, to be vetted by the state children's services social workers and lawyer, and to meet Tommy. Ginny was the sole foster parent, but I went along to lend moral support and to help persuade the social workers of Ginny's moral probity and financial responsibility.

"Wear your uniform," Ginny had said. "That makes you look respectable."

"I don't look respectable in civilian clothes?" I had demanded.

"Oh, you do," she had said hastily, "but the star on your chest speaks multitudes."

I had thought Ginny would be given an infant or, at most, a two-year-old, but the social workers had other ideas. There were just too many older children needing temporary homes. When we arrived, Tommy had stood up from his chair in that gravely polite fashion Indians have with strangers and had gazed at her with an unsettling calm. In its own way, it was love at first sight, at least on Ginny's side, and I have to admit I was struck by a similar feeling.

"He's got that indefinable something," she said, "just like you."

"Me?" I said in puzzlement. "What's so indefinable about me?"

"You'll never know," she said with a giggle. "Indefinable is indefinable."

In the middle of my woolgathering in Ginny's living room, Tommy returned to his computer to surf the Internet, looking for songs to download and transfer to the iPod Ginny had given him as an offering of welcome when he arrived at her house. Tommy is an intelligent lad, a whiz at math, scoring several grades ahead of his age in tests at the Baraga reservation school. As soon as he arrived in early June, Ginny enrolled him in a special summer algebra class. Summer school had long been a thing of the past in cash-poor Porcupine City, but so many freshmen had flunked algebra that winter that the school board decided to offer the course to meet the requirements of the No Child Left Behind Act. Partly to make retaking the course less embarrassing to the flunkees, it was opened to any interested kid.

"It'll give him something to do," she said, "and it'll give him a chance to make some friends before school starts in the fall."

Tommy was also mature beyond his age. He was not sullen and uncommunicative, as are so many adoptees from troubled backgrounds—just quiet, polite, and guarded. He could laugh, especially at a joke, but he still kept everyone at an emotional arm's length, including Ginny. He was still sizing us up, determining how we would fit into his world and how he would fit into ours. That is a very adult thing to do, and I felt deeply sorry that Tommy had been robbed of the carefree childhood all youngsters deserve.

He was slowly making friends among the kids in town. Small for his age, he was still quick, wiry, and athletic, and though he could barely hit the ball out of the infield, he did so with remarkable consistence. Porcupine City's Little League team was happy to have a dependable new leadoff batter and second baseman. When school started in the fall, I felt sure, this Indian boy would mix well with the third- and fourth-generation Finns, Irish, and Croatians, descendants of the miners and woodsmen who had settled this remote land. People up here are almost entirely white, with maybe one or two African Americans and Mexicans wanly peppering the salt, and though, like large white majorities everywhere, they tend to be suspicious of people who do not look like them, they are still familiar with Indians. Their children tend not to care so much about human differences. Even in the boonies, diversity today finds a better reception among the young than it does among their elders. Ginny worried that Tommy's size and skin color might lead to a confrontation with a schoolyard bully, but I told her I didn't think there were enough kids in Porcupine County anymore for that to be common. Early on they all learn to look out for their neighbors, just like their parents. It means survival in a harsh land.

"You're just being sentimental," Ginny had said. "There are bullies everywhere, even here." I didn't argue. She's a native Porky and I'm not.

When Tommy and I had met at the orphanage, he looked me in the eye and said candidly, "You're Lakota. You used to be enemies of the Ojibwe." The Ojibwe of Baraga evidently knew all about the Native American lawman in the next county.

"Yes," I said, "but that was a long time ago." Almost three centuries, in fact. But today, Indian kids on the reservation learn their tribal histories early. That had been denied them for a long time by the missionaries and the Bureau of Indian Affairs, who for more than a century had wanted them to worship the white man's god and practice the white man's ways.

"Yes," Tommy said with a shrug. "It doesn't matter anymore."

"No. Times change."

He nodded. Ever since that day, he had continued to treat me with cool formality whenever I dropped by, still calling me "Mister" even though Ginny encouraged him to call me "Steve." He was just beginning to call her "Ginny" instead of "Mrs. Fitzgerald." I couldn't understand why he hadn't fallen in love with her at first sight, as I had. Or maybe he had but didn't want anybody to know. As for me, I didn't know whether he was cool because I was a stranger, because I was a rival for his foster mother's heart, or because I was a Lakota. Sometimes you just can't read the wandering trail a kid's mind takes. Sometimes he can't, either.

I was still learning to read Ginny's, even though we had been lovers for a long time. Originally Ginny, who had been feeling the biological imperative, had wanted to adopt outright. As a woman in her forties, she had not wanted to risk the potential complications of having a child naturally. When she first brought up the idea of adoption, I had thought she was peremptorily nailing the banns of marriage to my forehead, and that scared me for a bit. But I came around, as does just about every man sooner or later, to the idea of commitment. Still, Ginny wanted a child for herself. "I hope you'll be in the picture, Steve," she said. "Every child needs a father. But I'm going to start my family whether or not you're ready. The door is always open. You know that."

But Ginny hadn't walked through that door just yet herself. For a single person, adoption is difficult, for social services prefer families with two parents, not one. So she decided to test her maternal skills first by fostering a child.

And God knows I couldn't enter that door of parenthood, foster or otherwise, just then. Running a political campaign had taken up almost all my free time, as I had known it would. For Tommy, I decided, being his foster mother's busy and often absent boyfriend was better than being a busy and often absent foster father. A boyfriend has fewer obligations to a child, and the child knows that. But at some point after the election, I intended to go to Ginny and Tommy, hat in hand, and ask to be formally sworn into the partnership. I told Ginny more or less as much, without quite using the word "marriage"—that word, for some reason I can't explain, frightens me—and she nodded and said calmly, "All in good time."

That's not just patience. That's forbearance. That's one reason why I'm nuts about her. There are so many reasons. She is a very wealthy woman, but lives modestly, though tastefully. She does not lord it over the people of Porcupine County, nor does she play Lady Bountiful, but shares her considerable fortune with them in absolute secrecy. She knows very well that money alters the way people look at a person, and she does not want anyone to know she has it. As a trained historian, she is a gifted researcher, able to smoke out the most obscure facts about the most ordinary people, and that is a boon to a boyfriend who is a law enforcement officer. She is sweet and funny. And, by the way, she is also very well-shaped and good-looking in her early forties. She is, in short, a hell of a redhead.

I walked into the kitchen, grasped Ginny about her slim waist as she stood at the sink, and breathed in the scent of her hair. As I picked up a plate and a dish towel, feeling loving and helpful, the phone rang. Ginny, her hands full, leaned over and elbowed a button on the speakerphone. She likes to chat while cooking and doing the dishes.

"It's Alex," the voice said. "I'm calling from Marquette."

4 "Tewk?" Alex said.

"Tewk?" I echoed.

"Short for Two Crow."

"That's not gonna fly. My name is Steve, goddammit."

But I wasn't really pissed off. Alex is comfortable enough with my Indianness to make genial fun of it now and then. He thinks I'm oversensitive. I guess I am. But I know Alex hasn't a malicious bone in his body.

The smart-ass preamble surprised me, though. On the phone Alex is usually peremptory, not bothering with the polite noises of social lubrication. I don't think he's picked up a receiver and said "Hello" for decades. Ginny blames his long bachelorhood.

"It's a cadaver," he said.

"Yes, I know," I said, thinking Alex was again setting me up for a one-liner. Through the doorway, I could see Tommy gazing at the screen of his iMac, hands unmoving over the keyboard, head cocked toward me, listening. Kids don't pay attention to their elders when you want them to, but they always do when you'd rather their interest lie elsewhere. Nothing escapes a kid. Especially Tommy, I was learning rapidly, and he also knows how to think about what he hears. I tried to be discreet whenever he was within earshot, especially when talking about police matters. Hard as I tried, I usually failed.

And on this occasion, I failed big time. I completely forgot Alex and I were on a speakerphone. Brain fart.

"No, a *cadaver* cadaver," Alex said. "You're right. It was embalmed. But not for burial."

"What, then?"

"Medical school, probably, the forensics guys said. It contained industrial-strength quantities of phenol, formaldehyde, alcohol, and glycerine. The hands and head had been removed with surgical saws. The intestines had been sucked out."

"So I was right about the trocar cuts." Embalmers use trocars, sharp-pointed hollow needles an inch or so wide, to vacuum out the innards of the corpses they prepare, either for medical study or for funerals. The absence of gas-producing entrails slows down decomposition and keeps the body fresh for a longer time. "But what about the hands and head?"

"Harvested. These days the majority of medical cadavers aren't dissected as entire specimens in anatomy classes but are cut apart and the pieces distributed for specialist study. Sometimes the harvested items aren't embalmed but kept fresh on ice for transplants. Plastic surgeons practice on heads, and hand surgeons on hands. I suppose belly button specialists—"

"Enough, please, Alex," I said, trying not to gag. "I haven't had lunch yet."

"Well, that shoots down my idea that the hands and head were cut off to prevent identification."

"It does. Convenient, though, isn't it?" I said. "What about that label with the bar code?"

" 'Frank's,' " it said. " 'One dollar and seventy-nine cents a pound. Sell by December thirty-first.' " Frank's is the local supermarket.

"You're disgusting."

"Aren't I? Anyway, we came up empty on the code. The numbers and letters resemble no commercial bar code anybody's ever seen."

"Could it be a private code?"

"Could be."

I sighed. "What's forensics going to do with the case?"

"Ice twice."

"Come again?"

"Put it in both the cooler and the cold case file."

I winced. "Aren't we clever?"

"Aren't we?" Alex can be so smug. "Eventually they'll just cremate the remains. No point in keeping them around."

Ginny slammed the silverware drawer. "You're creeping me out!" she declared. "Tommy, let's go out on the beach and hunt agates and leave the policemen to their business."

The lad stood up obediently from his computer and strode with Ginny out the back door, but not before shooting me a speculative look. I was sorry I hadn't kept the conversation with Alex more private. Kids don't need to hear that kind of stuff. *I* don't need to hear that kind of stuff, either.

"Well, I'm glad we're not looking at a homicide," I said presently. Alex and I do enjoy the thrill of chasing a killer now and then—a rarity in the sparsely populated Upper Peninsula, where murders are few and far between—but, like most U.P. lawmen, we really prefer the comfortable routine of police work, burglaries and thefts and traffic stops and the like. Routine is easier on the head as well as the emotions. You get more sleep that way, too. "What charges, exactly, are we looking at?"

"Illegal transport of human remains. A felony."

"That's all? What about desecration?"

"If the amputations were done legally, by licensed embalmers for a legitimate reason, it's not desecration."

"Hmm. Probably a worker in a mortuary or cadaver lab sold the body to whoever planted it in the Dying Room," I said. "What's the penalty for that?"

"Up to ten years in prison and a five-thousand-dollar fine."

"What about the guy who carried it away and dumped it?"

"Same ten years and five thousand. I looked it up. Michigan is one of the few states that by law limits the privilege of the final disposition of human remains to funeral directors."

"Yeah. The Tom Rooney càse." Three years before, a farmer in Coppermass had wanted to bury his dead mother in the family backyard without the intervention of a funeral director and had fought round after round in the courts with the State of Michigan, the stories about the dispute entertaining readers in *The Herald* all winter. His mother had requested the unusual means of final disposition in her will, and he had suffered sticker shock at the funeral home. The law is the law, the judge said. Tom was adamant, standing on principle and even refusing a local mortician's offer of free services. For months, Mama languished in the Porcupine County Hospital refrigerator. Finally, when the judge ordered the hospital to hand over the body to an undertaker for burial in potter's field, Tom caved in.

"The Full Employment for Michigan Funeral Directors Law," Alex said with a contemptuous growl.

I fell silent, thinking. Why would anyone *want* a cadaver in the first place?

"Alex."

"Yes?"

"No sexual evidence?" I had never read Krafft-Ebing's *Psychopathia Sexualis,* but I knew about necrophilia, as every police officer does, and perhaps some of the kinkier necros liked to use medical cadavers for their jollies. I said as much.

"No sexual evidence," Alex echoed. "Nothing at all. It wouldn't matter, anyway. Michigan isn't one of the eleven states that criminalize necrophilia. In fact, Tewkie boy, it's so rare that it wasn't illegal anywhere until 1965, when a female Oregon funeral-home worker got caught serially abusing the customers and the press had a field day with it."

"My name, goddammit again, is Steve. And your deep knowledge of the weird and obscure never fails to amaze me."

"It's just the company I keep," he said. "Breakfast chat at the Marquette morgue, you know. Pathologists and forensics investigators like to talk about their work. You ought to hear them on Halloween."

I returned to the subject. "But why?" I asked. "What was the perp doing with a body missing its head and hands? Why would he go to the trouble of sealing it in heavy plastic and depositing it in an old house where it was bound to be discovered sooner or later? Why not just bury it in the backyard?"

"Or perps?" Alex said. "Maybe it took more than one person to hump that stiff up the stairs to the Dying Room. Even without head and hands, it and that plastic sack still weighed a hundred thirty pounds."

"I don't know. A fellow in good shape could have done it. Remember all those ten-mile marches with seventy-pound packs in army training?"

"All right. Then where did they, or he, get the cadaver?"

"Coulda been anywhere."

Alex was right. Whether they are disassembled or not, there are never enough cadavers to feed the demand in medical schools and transplant hospitals, and so there's a thriving black market in fresh new bodies. A crooked crematory worker might fob off an urn of animal ashes on the bereaved and sell the human corpse to a broker, or a hospital morgue attendant might pass an unclaimed body to a trusted ambulance driver to peddle to a cadaver lab, no questions asked, and doctor the record to hide the transaction. Cadaver labs, too, aren't always careful with the stream of corpses that flow in every day from hospitals and big-city morgues. Sometimes there's a bit of shrinkage in the warehouse.

"Illegal trafficking in organ transplants?" I suggested. In a celebrated case recently, a body snatcher working for a shady

New Jersey tissue-harvesting lab had strip-mined the corpse of Alistair Cooke for his bones, even though the cancer that killed him had spread to his skeleton. Cancerous transplants can cause malignancies.

"Don't think so," Alex said. "Far as I know, they're not transplanting whole heads and hands. And nothing else was taken besides the entrails. All the other organs were intact."

"Yeah," I said. "And you would think ghouls like that would make sure today that the corpses were cremated afterward. Gets rid of the evidence." In the New Jersey case, a buried body had been exhumed and discovered to be missing half its organs even though the former owner had never given permission for harvesting.

I could hear Alex rubbing his stubbly jaw.

"It still doesn't make sense," I added.

"Everything will make sense when we know the facts."

"A brilliant remark. So where do we start?"

"Beats me."

"*Should* we start?"

Alex grunted.

By simultaneous but unspoken acclamation, we trundled the Poor Farm corpse into our mental cold case file and rolled it shut. Why bother? Sometimes a mystery is best left a mystery. Especially in these remote and budget-conscious parts where the law is stretched thin. We do that all the time. We have to.

"See you tomorrow," I said.

"You've forgotten," Alex said, sharp accusation in his voice.

"Forgotten what?"

"The open wedding dance."

"What?"

"Not yours, numb nuts."

"Whose?"

"Jerry Muskat and Adela McLaughlin."
I groaned. Now I remembered.
"Duty calls."
"Damn."

5. In much of backwoods America and especially in the Upper Peninsula of Michigan, people often celebrate weddings and anniversaries and birthdays that end in a zero by renting a hall, buying a keg or two, and then publishing an ad in the local weekly newspaper inviting all and sundry to come share their happiness, even if they might be strangers or merely passing through town. Open celebrations are one way the members of a dwindling population hang on to one another. Attendees often bring potluck dishes to pass around on folding tables lined up along one side of the hall, for the party givers are usually too pinched to afford much more than the communal beer and the small fees charged by the operators of the halls, who make their profits at the cash bars.

These blowouts foster a sense of community, a feeling of we're-all-in-this-together, and showing up is a way of saying, "Here we are. We exist. Appreciate me, and I'll appreciate you, for we may not be here tomorrow."

I enjoy these shindigs immensely. Once in an off-duty while, I will work an event as the lone hired security, wearing my deputy's uniform although usually not my revolver, unless a township official requests it. I'm not out to arrest people, just calm them down and make sure they're not driving if they've had a snootful. Often they have, and the trick is to judge when a fellow is just having a hell of a good time or is about to cross the line into noxious behavior. When that happens, I quietly usher them to the nearest door and tell them to find somebody to take them home. Often I have to ask, sometimes all but order, someone to volunteer for the task, and they usually say okay.

On the few occasions when someone gets pig drunk and belligerent, there's always an off-duty deputy or state cop in civvies to help frog-march the lout to a patrol car for a ride to the sheriff's department lockup, where we'll allow him to post bond or spring him loose in the morning with a headache and a lecture. In either case, when the court date rolls around, the prosecutor will usually drop the charges as not worth the county's time. Of course, if someone throws a punch and it connects, that's misdemeanor battery, and we'll ask the connectee if he wants to press charges against the connector. Usually he doesn't, and often he can't remember the connection anyway.

Most of the time I attend these hoedowns not as security but as a member of the crowd. I like to stay on the sidelines, nursing a beer, chatting with friends and dancing with Ginny, who is indefatigable on the dance floor and wears out half the male population of Porcupine City, young and old, before she calls it a night. At Jerry and Adela's celebration, however, I had to be present as a political candidate, and I didn't look forward to that. At all. Ginny sent her regrets—she was taking Tommy to a movie in Houghton—and I knew I'd miss her.

I wore civilian clothes, jeans and a new Packers sweatshirt. Ginny thought I should wear my deputy's uniform, reminding people of what I was running for, but I was in a contrary mood. As I parked my battered Jeep in the lot of the cavernous old clapboard-sided town hall of Coppermass on the eastern side of Porcupine County, I walked by a brand-new cherry red BMW two-seater bearing a City of Chicago sticker and the Illinois vanity plate REBEMER. *That must be a pun of some kind,* I thought, although the car easily cost fifty thousand dollars and needed no fancy plates to set it apart from the muddy pickups and SUVs in the lot, sporting mostly dented Michigan plates.

Out of long habit, I fished a notebook from my shirt pocket and jotted down the Beemer's plate. Doubtless the car's owner was a rich summer person from the big city slumming with the rubes, but I like to make notes of unusual sights. You never know if they might come in handy someday. Both my glove compartment and my desk at the sheriff's department squad room are stuffed with dusty, stained notebooks that went back years to my rookie days.

"Hiya, Camilo," I said as I approached the town hall door, "how's it going?" I stuck my hand out. Sergeant Camilo Hernandez looked at it in surprise. He is a tribal police officer for the Lac Vieux Desert Band of the Ojibwe Nation at Watersmeet in Gogebic County, and Jerry and Adela had hired him as security for the party. It didn't matter that Camilo was well out of his jurisdiction, though he wore full uniform except for his sidearm. Enough Porcupine County deputies and Michigan state policemen attended these things as civilians to make official arrests if needed. Those were rare when Camilo was doing security. He almost never needed our help, for he is a persuasive fellow.

Camilo is a Tex-Mex mestizo who hails from El Paso and is mostly Apache. I know him well, regularly losing part of my paycheck to him at poker. We don't need to shake hands any more than one would shake hands with one's spouse in the morning. He is short, wiry, bowlegged, and fast as a rattlesnake, but full of smiling good humor. I have seen him take down large and powerful drunks with only a nightstick and without losing his grin. They never see what's coming.

"Ah," Camilo sighed in sudden understanding. "Politicking, eh?" He grasped my hand and shook it elaborately. "You have my vote," he said in a voice meant to carry. People looked at us and

I colored. Everybody knows Camilo doesn't vote in Porcupine County, but in Gogebic County.

"Get your ass in there, Steve," Camilo said. "Pat people on the back and shake their hand and ask about the family. That's what Eli does and it works for him."

"All right, all right, I'll do my best."

Just as I entered the doorway, I turned back to Camilo. "See who was driving that red Beemer?" I asked. BMWs are rare in Upper Michigan.

"Yeah." With his chin, Camilo pointed inside at a tall, slim, and dark-haired young man. I couldn't have told you the name of his tailor, but I knew he was expensive. So was his barber. The sleeves of his Hugo Boss shirt were rolled up, the better, I thought, to display the Rolex on his tanned left wrist. The young man stood talking quietly with a knot of others along one wall, all of them Porkies in their twenties well known to me. He shifted from side to side on his feet, glancing about nervously to see if people were watching. I noticed that his conversations were brief, one or two words with locals who showed little interest in him. There was nothing arrogant about him, just the shyness of wanting to belong. He looked utterly out of place, and he knew it.

I was not surprised. Many of the well-educated, well-to-do young Chicago suburbanites who summer at their parents' expensive vacation homes on the Lake Superior shore are swaggering, supercilious young punks who like to lord it over the rubes, insulting waitresses with paltry tips. "FIBs," the waitresses call them. "Fucking Illinois bastards."

But some of them, often misfits and loners at home, seek acceptance among Porkies of the same age, admiring the locals' skills with their hands and their craft in the woods. If a young Porky thinks a city boy means well, he'll take the greenhorn under his wing. That happens with older summer residents, too. We don't mind summer people so long as they treat us with respect. Those are the best kind, for sometimes they fall so much in love with the people and the country of the Upper Peninsula that they move up here permanently, often to retire, and they modestly expand the suffering local economy.

Not so long ago, I had experienced the lad's feeling myself. I turned away, but not without sympathy. It's always tough to be an outsider.

I steeled myself and went into campaign mode, working the outskirts of the crowd. "Hi," I said to everyone whose attention I could catch. "I'm Steve Martinez and I'm running for sheriff. Here's my card. Call me if you'd like to talk about it. I'm hoping for your vote."

Scores of people, perhaps a hundred, sat at folding picnic tables, scarfing potluck barbecued pork, butter-slathered corn on the cob, fruit Jell-O, and Finnish cakes and pastries, while the speakers at the edge of the rickety stage played soft rock tunes. When sober, Porkies are polite and deferential. Gravely, most of the men shook my hand noncommittally, took the card I proffered, and quickly lost themselves in the crowd. A few looked me in the eye and turned away. Some made sure they weren't in my path as I approached. Several smiled, grasped my hand warmly, and whispered into my ear, "You've got my vote, Steve. Go get 'em."

They whispered because they didn't want to get on the wrong side of Eli Garrow, who had arrived and was glaring at me from the far corner of the room. Unlike me, Eli was resplendent in full uniform, including brilliant white shirt, gold-encrusted garrison cap, and Glock automatic pistol at his waist. Behind his back we called him "The Target," because his bright finery would have attracted the bad guys' bullets if he ever got into a firefight, an unlikely prospect in quiet Porcupine County. I caught Eli's eye, nodded, and waved politely. "Defer to him," Alex had said during one of our campaign skull sessions. "Be courteous and respectful. It'll piss him off." And so it did. I bowed slightly and saluted Eli, who turned away, a dark cloud wreathing his face.

The speakers in the corners suddenly boomed with the voice of Charlie Yarema, the mechanic at Syl's Garage in Coppermass who moonlighted as a disk jockey. "Yo, gang," he crooned. "Let's start with everybody's favorite!" The unmistakable piano introduction to Bob Seger's "Old Time Rock and Roll" washed over the growing crowd, and couples twirled from the supper tables to the dance floor. Spectators, including me, swayed and snapped to the music, and I had to remind myself I was on a mission. For the next hour, I worked the crowd, keeping mostly to its outskirts but now and then plunging in to the edge of the dance floor when I spotted somebody whose hand I hadn't yet shaken.

I stopped once to watch Camilo skillfully edging a boisterous logger out the door, one hand in the small of his much bigger subject's back, and the other gripping an elbow right at the painful pressure point we called the "come-along nerve." So swift and efficient was the smiling Camilo that the overserved lumberman barely had time to protest before the door shut on him.

The place jumped. Everybody was having a noisy good time, especially when Charlie put BTO's "Takin' Care of Business" on the player, and half the crowd fell laughing to the floor to dance the alligator, limbs flailing. Then it was time for a couple of polkas—Charlie always made sure the older folks enjoyed their favorites—followed by "Proud Mary" by Creedence Clearwater Revival, the band Yoopers most adore.

"Dollar dance!" Charlie shouted over the din.

One by one, the celebrants popped a dollar bill into a hat Charlie held, then danced with bride or groom for a few seconds before the DJ motioned in the next. The lines were long for Adela McLaughlin, a cute freckled redhead who waitressed at O-Kun-de-Kun Restaurant in Lone Pine, and her new husband, Jerry

Muskat, the M-64 bridge tender. As the noise level rose out of sight, so did inhibitions, and soon women were dancing with Adela and men with Jerry. The hat overflowed and Charlie had to stuff bills into his shirt pockets. Afterward, the purse would go to Jerry and Adela, defraying many of the costs of the evening. I thought they might even make a small profit.

I felt a hand on my shoulder. It was Alex, dressed in a cowboy outfit. His tooled leather Western boots and fringed buckskin jacket would have made a Houston oilman jealous. Alex loved country-and-western music.

"Havin' a good time?" the trooper shouted over the din.

"Nobody can hear me," I shouted back. "I'm just shaking hands now!" Alex grinned, then grunted as he bumped into Eli Garrow, who had been working his way through the crowd from the opposite end of the room.

"Didn't know you were working security," Alex yelled to Eli, nodding toward his uniform. "Times are that hard, eh?"

"Fuck you, Kolehmainen," the sheriff growled, loudly enough for heads within a ten-foot circle to turn and stare at Eli's angry red face and clenched fists.

"Tsk." Alex turned away, grinning. One more second and Eli, old and slow as he is, might have tried to throw a punch. Alex not only is a master of the needle, but he knows just how far to thrust it without provoking his opponent to violence. Had Eli exploded, not even Camilo could have stopped the brawl that would have ensued—and Coppermass being Garrow territory, Alex and I would have come out a very poor second best. Besides, cops aren't supposed to get into fights. We moved away before hostilities could escalate.

Soon Charlie took a break, and the din settled down to a dull roar as people left the floor and fell upon the desserts. I had just taken a bite of nisu, the sweet Finnish pastry, when a heavy hand landed on my back and a drunken "Hello!" burst into my ear. I turned to see who it was. It was Harold Garrow, a ne'er-do-well and sometime beneficiary of his brother Eli's nepotism. Eli had steered a couple of county road patching contracts to Harold, who screwed up the jobs so badly they had to be redone. Among other things, Harold was suspected of having impregnated a niece, who left the state and was never heard from again. He looked just like Eli. Both men were short and broad, bullet headed and mustachioed. Harold was not one of my favorite people. And he was loaded.

"God, Shteve, I'm happy to know ya!" he drawled through a cloud of peppermint schnapps, wavering on his feet and thrusting his ham-sized hand in my general direction. I grasped it. It was wet and greasy. God knows where it had been.

"Ya really done ya people proud!"

Here it comes again, I thought, *the patronizing.* Some folks just don't believe Indians can solve crimes all by themselves. After a recent drug case in which Alex and I pooled our talents to catch a bunch of dangerous felons, the whispering started in certain hostile quarters: the Injun was only fronting for white brains. He was Garner Armstrong's boy and did what the prosecutor told him to.

"But ya know, ya had help from that trooper. He really ran things, didn't he?"

I held my temper. "We work as a team, Mr. Garrow," I said.

"*Sure* you did," he said. "Ya know, when Eli wins, you're gonna hafta find another job. I can always use a strong back on my trucks."

Harold spoke without irony. He was technically wrong. I was a union member and couldn't be fired for political activity. But if Eli won, he could make life miserable enough for me to look for another job somewhere.

Bile rose into my throat, but I held my tongue, took a deep breath, and said evenly, "Nice to see you, Mr. Garrow. Excuse me." As he lurched away, I turned on my heel and nearly knocked down the tribal police.

"Want me to shoot him?" inquired Camilo, who had heard the exchange. He was still smiling, but his grin bore a ragged edge, like a knife sharpened with rocks. *He doesn't like Harold, either.*

"No," I said quietly, "but feel free to cut his heart out and feed it to the wolves."

"Tsk. You Lakota are *so* bloodthirsty."

"Bullshit," I said. "We both know what Apaches did with fire ants."

"Yeah," said Camilo. "But you have to admit that didn't leave so much mess."

"Like hell." I was chuckling now. Camilo always makes me feel better.

By this time, the party was beginning to wind down, the crowd slowly trickling out to the parking lot and departing in cars and pickups, only half of which, I suspected, had designated drivers. Jerry and Adela saw them all off, friends and strangers alike, hugging and kissing, shaking hands and waving. It had been a happy evening for everyone. Almost everyone.

I needed to pee, and I strode back inside, looking for the men's. I opened the wrong door, the one to a storeroom, and I walked in on the throes of passion. His slacks were down, her denim skirt was up, and they were coupled together over a countertop like a locomotive pushing a caboose uphill. He was the young man who had arrived in the BMW, and he was lost between the billowing thighs of a beefy blond filling-station attendant from Lone Pine easily ten years his senior. They both looked ecstatic, oblivious to the world around them. They did not even glance my way.

"Excuse me," I whispered needlessly, swiftly closing the door.

It looked as if tonight the lad had found a big welcome in this part of Porcupine County. I was glad one of us had.

6 Gazing into the bathroom mirror, I fretted over the premature bags under my eyes that Ginny says make me look like a younger Iron Eyes Cody, the imitation Hollywood Indian who wasn't born a Cree/Cherokee, as he had claimed, but was actually the son of Italian immigrants. But my hair is still genuinely thick and black, with the beginnings of gunmetal gray at the temples. Indians, thank goodness, don't get bald unless there's a honky in the woodpile, nor do most of us need to shave. Our cheeks just don't grow hair. Speeds up the morning toilette. Then a few loose ends that had been pricking the back of my brain wormed their way into the foreground of my thoughts.

Loose ends bother me, as they do any conscientious cop. One reason we become cops is that we want to know the answers to everything, no matter how trivial. Were those fresh screwdriver marks on the garage window jamb left by someone trying to break in? Or was a home owner just trying to get the window open so he could paint it—and did he simply forget a few weeks later that he'd tried, calling the sheriff when he noticed the gouges? It happens more often than you'd think, especially if the home owner is elderly and beginning to lose his short-term memory.

Of course, police officers can't afford to spend much time thinking about such minutiae. We have real crimes to solve and crooks to catch. Still, that cadaver at the Poor Farm had been bothering me. Some kind of misbegotten prank? Probably. Was a crime committed? Obviously. It's against the law to leave dead bodies lying around. But was anyone injured or even offended? Probably not, except for that amorphous and abstract lump we call Justice. Sooner or later, the Poor Farm cadaver would slide of its own accord to the back of my mental cold case drawer, perhaps to be resurrected sometime in the distant future as a fleeting wisp of memory. But now it still lay fresh in my mind, poking insistently at my consciousness.

Later that morning, the curtains slowly began to part. The first break was the sort of coincidence you can't believe when it happens in second-rate mystery novels but to a real-life cop is a vital part of solving crime. Investigations are full of coincidences. The trick is discriminating between the trivial and the significant. This one came two weeks after Jenny Besonen and Billy Ciric had sneaked up to the Dying Room for a little extreme whoopee. I had just come from lunch at Merle's Café on River Street, the main drag of Porcupine City, when I saw Phil Wilson across the road, descending a short slope underneath the big wooden sign that said: "BEGINNING OF U.S. 45: PORCUPINE CITY TO MOBILE, ALABAMA."

Phil, a big, beefy fellow in his late fifties who sports a lush white Santa Claus beard, is the co-owner of Wilson & Simon's Ace Hardware on River Street. His people go back several generations in Porcupine County, Ginny once told me, to the earliest days of the copper mines. A grandfather had been mayor of Porcupine City and his father had founded the hardware emporium. Phil grasped one of the six-by-six legs of the sign, bent down, and retrieved a tiny object from the concrete base holding the six-by-six. He straightened up, examined the object, and made a prying motion on its top. Out of it he drew a long coil of what appeared to be film. Curiosity got the better of me.

"What in the world are you up to, Phil?" I called.

He didn't answer.

"Phil?"

"Geocaching," he called back.

"Geo what?"

"Caching."

"Oh yes," I said as I walked up to the sign. "I've heard of that. Orienteering with a GPS, isn't it?" Handheld Global Positioning Satellite receivers are everywhere these days. I use one while flying the sheriff's airplane and often carry it with me into the woods to pinpoint the precise geographic locations of crime scenes. Knowing roughly where you are is pretty, but knowing *exactly* where you are is gorgeous. That makes it much easier to dispatch a rescue squad to an injured hiker or a recovery team to a crime scene, or just return to a lovely spot you discovered in the woods.

"Sort of," Phil said, his face reddening as he spoke. For him, conversation took a major effort. Vietnam had changed him. The once ebullient boy had become painfully shy. He never married, never attended social events, and ran his store from inside his tiny office, allowing his clerks to wait on customers. When he had to interact with others, he treated them with polite deference and with as few words as possible, never looking them in the eye. They liked him all the same. They remembered what he had been and were sorry about what war had done to him.

"Tell me," I coaxed.

"This here's a minicache." He held up a plastic thirty-five-millimeter photo film can painted the same color as the signpost, a tightly wound roll of paper, and a tiny nub of a pencil.

"Yeah?" I said.

Suddenly the old Phil poked through the fog and the words tumbled out. "See, Steve, people who locate the cache with their

GPSs write their name and the date to prove they've found it, then put everything back like it was. Couple days ago, the twenty-second name appeared. Not too bad for a cache. that's only six months old."

He bent down and replaced the film can at the foot of the post. "There," he said. "You'd never spot it."

Talking about a private passion sometimes parts the curtains of hurt, and what Phil said interested me for its own sake. I had to admire the handiwork, too. From ten feet away, the film can looked like the head of a bolt holding the post to its base. As Phil said, unless you were looking for it, you'd never notice it.

"You put it there six months ago?"

"Right."

"And how do people know it's there? What do you do, put an ad in the paper with the latitude and longitude of the spot?"

The words flooded out. "No, I post the information on the Internet. There's a bunch of Web sites devoted to the sport, and I used www.geotreasure.com. People see the name of the cache and a clue to what it's all about—this one is called 'Where the Road Begins'—and the coordinates, and go hunt it up and sign their names. This is an easy one. I designed it for beginners."

I stood up and smiled. If the game of geocaching could bring a little happiness to this sad man, I approved of it.

"Okay, Phil, that's fascinating. Have a good day." And I strode to the sheriff's Explorer to return to patrol. As I got in, I looked back. Phil was watching me, his eyes on mine. He raised a hand in good-bye. I wouldn't say he smiled, but he looked a little less melancholy. I waved back, my heart lightened by the encounter. We cops serve and protect in unusual ways sometimes.

On my way west to Silverton on M-64, the idea slowly began to grow in my mind: could that corpse in the Dying Room be somebody's idea of a geocache? Maybe that was only a coincidence, but it fit. The body was put where it could be found, but you had to know where it was to find it. Swiftly I wheeled around the Explorer and headed for Ginny's a few miles back toward Porcupine City.

7 "What do you know about geocaching?" I called as I swept into Ginny's sprawling log home on the lake and nearly tripped over an Oriental rug that hadn't been in the foyer before. Genuine Persian, I could see at a glance, for I hadn't washed down my idle hours in the bars of officers' clubs in Kuwait and Saudi Arabia, but had gone out into the markets and learned a little about the fine carpets and jewelry of the Middle East.

Ginny doesn't live flashily—like most women in Upper Michigan, she wears shorts and T-shirts in the summer, Levi's and Pendletons in the winter—but she furnishes her roomy log home with the elegance of a woman fortunate enough to be tasteful as well as educated and wealthy, although she chooses not to show that side of her life to anyone except a handful of trusted friends. She has truly returned home to Porcupine County, where she was born in more than modest circumstances as the daughter of a university-educated mining engineer who believed his children ought to earn their places in society and respect others who also had. She never lost that legacy of modesty and regard for others, even at Wellesley and later as the bride of a wealthy businessman who left her his considerable fortune when he died. She is a well-respected and well-liked citizen of Porcupine County, and that sense of belonging, not her money, her house, or its furnishings, is her most beloved possession.

"For goodness' sake, Steve, can't you say hello first?" Ginny called as she skipped down the stairs past a pair of Helen Frankenthaler drawings on the landing wall. I knew they were not prints, but originals. "Haven't you ever heard of foreplay?"

I blushed, because Tommy Standing Bear was gazing at us from the kitchen where he was doing his homework at the counter while watching MTV, a form of multitasking I have never been able to understand. He looked at me shrewdly. You never can tell what's going on in a youngster's mind, but I was sure a lot was going on in his. I knew from his small smile that he had not only heard what Ginny had said but also knew what it meant. Kids learn so early these days about intimate relations between the sexes. Among them, too.

"Hi, Tommy," I said.

"Mr. Martinez," he replied with his usual courteous nod, the smile still on his face.

"Steve," Ginny prompted for the umpteenth time. "He likes being called Steve."

I didn't say anything. "Mr. Martinez" was better than "Tewk."

Tommy just nodded politely. I knew he demurred, but he was too circumspect to argue. I admire that in anyone, especially a kid. Smart kids like to challenge adults on the spot. Very smart kids know how to bide their time. Tommy is one of those.

"You said something about geocaching?" Ginny said.

"Yes," I said, and, in my eagerness forgetting about the boy, I told her about Phil Wilson's little cache, his sudden blossoming, and the "Eureka!" moment it had spurred while in the Explorer. "I think that corpse at the Poor Farm may have been left there by geocachers."

Too late, I remembered Tommy's presence. At the kitchen table, his eyebrows had risen.

So had Ginny's. "Now that sounds like a possibility," she said. "Let me see what I can find out about geocaching."

The sources of Ginny's gifts as a historian are twofold. One, she never forgets a fact, and can pluck it in an instant out of the high-speed memory chips of her mind. Two, she is an expert researcher, especially in library databases and on the Internet. I love her for many things, including her warm heart and shapely person, but it is her nimble mind that is most invaluable to a boyfriend who works as an underpaid law enforcement officer in an impoverished rural county.

She stepped over to the computer she keeps in an office nook off the kitchen. It was, I knew, connected to the high-speed network that runs along the lake from Porcupine City to Silverton thirteen miles west. I have my laptop hooked up to a slow dial-up connection, all I can afford on a deputy sheriff's salary. Ginny, however, never settles for anything but cutting-edge technology. "Saves time," she often says. As a girl, she learned that good tools were always worth their cost.

Tommy had followed and was standing behind her as she logged on.

"Let's see what Google tells us," she said. "Ah, it's a biggie. More than a million hits. Let me winnow them down."

A few minutes passed as Ginny, with Tommy helping by pointing to likely sites, worked her way through the World Wide Web.

"Found a site that explains it simply," she said. "You ready?"

"Sure," I said.

"Quote. 'On May first in the year 2000, the military stopped degrading the accuracy of the GPS navigation system, a series of two dozen satellites in low Earth orbit that continuously broadcast their positions, allowing receivers to triangulate on the signals and determine their location on the surface of the Earth. Suddenly handheld GPS receivers were accurate to within thirty feet instead of three hundred feet. On that day the game called geocaching was born.

" 'The concept of geocaching is really quite simple. Someone hides a stash—usually a Tupperware container filled with assorted small trinkets, such as Monopoly game pieces—in an interesting, out-of-the-way place, and records the exact geographical coordinates with a GPS receiver. These coordinates, along with a few helpful hints, are posted on one of several geocaching Web sites. The stash seekers then use their GPS receivers to find the treasure. Each person who locates the container adds an entry to a logbook included within, takes a trinket and replaces it with one of his own, then puts the container back where he found it. Sometimes a cache includes a disposable camera so that the finders can take photos of themselves for the cacher to put on a Web page.' Unquote."

"That's it?" I said. "Somebody would pay two or three hundred bucks for a GPS receiver just to trade a few trinkets? Sounds like a bunch of gadget heads hunting for each other's junk." For a moment I forgot what the game had done for Phil Wilson.

"There's more to it than that," Ginny said. "Listen to this: 'Knowing the location of a cache is only part of the goal. Getting there often is an adventure. You might hike for miles through the woods toward a cache, only to discover that a deep chasm lies between it and you. There's always more than one way to approach a cache.'

"And besides," she said, "what's wrong with promoting a little exercise in the fresh air?"

"What else?" I asked.

"Quote. 'Geocaching has its roots in the nineteenth-century British orienteering sport called letterboxing,' " Ginny continued. " 'Its practitioners secreted a container with a one-of-a-kind rubber stamp inside it somewhere on a moor or a heath, then posted in the local newspaper a PERSONALS notice giving either the location's map coordinates or a coded message telling how to find it. Those who found the container used the rubber stamp to mark logbooks they carried with them. Sometimes the containers held clues to other containers located elsewhere, and often letterboxers spent days and even weeks hunting down the next treasure trove.' End of quote."

"Are there rules to this game?" I asked.

"Oh, yes," Ginny said. "Just a couple. The first rule is to trust everyone. Not only do cachers trust finders to put everything back as it was, they also trust people who happen upon the caches by accident not to plunder them."

"And the second?"

"No drugs, explosives, ammunition, pornography, or food," she said. "Kids might find them or animals might dig them up."

"Anything else?"

"There are all kinds of caches. Microcaches, like the one you saw in town today. Multicaches, in which the cache seeker is sent from location to location until he finds the final cache. Offset caches, in which the posted coordinates take the hunter to a location where he must continue by using map and compass to find the container. There are event caches, where a whole bunch of people get together in a park to find stuff, like a high-tech Easter egg hunt. And there are virtual caches that aren't really caches at all but a spot on Earth where you can stand and look for something, like an unusual road sign, and report back to the cacher on a Web site what you saw. Those are popular in national parks where the rangers don't want people trampling sensitive areas."

"I'll be damned," I said. "I had no idea that geocaching was such a big deal."

"There's more," Ginny said. "The caches are rated for difficulty. Some, like the one Phil Wilson planted, are really easy, little more than a Sunday stroll in the park. Then there's extreme geocaching, in which you need to be a rock climber to find a cache at the bottom of a ravine or be rich enough to afford a helicopter to reach the summit of a steep peak. One cacher put a container on the bottom of the Red Sea."

"That's it?"

"Not quite. Here's a reference to 'rogue geocaching.' That's putting caches in places people shouldn't go—sewer systems, abandoned mine shafts, fences at maximum-security prisons, the White House lawn, et cetera. Or putting things in caches that shouldn't be there, like rusty nails or moonshine."

"Or cadavers," I said. "Yeah. That's what we've got. Can you print out all that stuff for me?"

"Sure. Tommy, would you take care of it?" Eagerly, the lad filled the printer with paper and began the job. *Wise of Ginny,* I thought. Nothing reaches a youngster's heart more than a simple gesture that tells him he is of value.

"May I borrow your phone?" I asked Ginny.

She nodded. I dialed Alex's cell number.

He listened. "Be right over," he said.

"Ask him if he'd like to stay to dinner," Ginny said.

I did. The answer was as I expected.

I don't believe Alex has ever had supper all by his lonesome. As a bachelor with a host of female friends, he never lacks for invitations. One reason he is so popular is that when he calls on a woman, he leaves his smart-ass self at home. Rather than scoring points off her tender sensibility, the way he does with mine, he solicitously asks how she's feeling and offers approving comments on a new hairdo, piece of jewelry, or sweatshirt. A new embroidered sweatshirt often passes for haute couture in the Upper Peninsula, where harsh weather dictates fashion. Woolrich is far more common than Donna Karan, and Timberlands outnumber Manolo Blahniks.

Alex always amazes me. He's quick to spot the smallest alteration in a woman's appearance or the slightest change in her emotions and casually mention it. Ginny once claimed that's because he's genuinely sensitive and observant, a true gentleman, but I replied that the truth is nothing more than that he's a smart detective highly trained to spot things other police officers might miss.

"You have no imagination, Steve," she had retorted.

Maybe not, but I learned long ago never to argue with her assessments of my mental capacity, which usually were generous when she wasn't herself trying to score a point off my hide. After a round of Molsons and cheese curds on Ritz crackers, a common Yooper hors d'oeuvre, I turned the conversation to business.

"You think that cadaver is somebody's idea of a cutting-edge geocache?" Alex asked, disbelief in his voice.

"What else have we managed to come up with?" I replied.

"I guess you may be right," said Alex. "But I can't imagine a corpse as the object of a high-tech scavenger hunt. Why not something else? Why do people do the things they do?"

Alex is very good with women and hard evidence but less imaginative when it comes to motive.

"Look at 'Folsom Prison Blues,'" I said. "Johnny Cash sings that he'd 'shoot a man in Reno just to watch him die.'"

"What's that mean?"

"Just what it says. People do the damnedest things for the damnedest reasons."

"If you say so." Alex didn't sound convinced.

"Why'd Hillary climb Everest?" I asked.

"Because it was there."

"Exactly."

Alex's dubious expression didn't change. I decided to try another tack. "What'd the forensics guys make of that bar-coded label on the plastic shroud around that cadaver?"

"Not a lot. They ran it through a standard bar-code reader and got this." Alex pulled out a typewritten sheet. It said:

J D G I J I H 2 G J A I A F D 1

"A cryptogram?"

"Maybe," Alex said. "We thought it might be a simple substitution code, letters for numbers, the kind amateurs think of. To start with, we assigned the letter A to mean the numeral 1 and B to mean 2 and C to mean 3 and so on. We came up with"—and Alex wrote the following on a sheet of printer paper:

0 4 / 9 0 9 8 ? 7 0 1 9 1 6 4 ?

"We don't know what the numbers 1 and 2 in the original alphanumeric sequence would stand for, though," he added. "That's why the question marks."

"Maybe North and West?" I asked. "See, there are enough alphanumeric digits in that line to add up to a geographical location. For instance, right here on my GPS"—I took out from my knapsack the handheld Garmin I used on both the ground and the air—"the coordinates where Quarterline Creek next door enters the lake are N 46 50.631 W 89 26.682. That's 46 degrees 50.631 minutes North latitude, 89 degrees 26.682 minutes West longitude. Sixteen characters, leaving out the decimal points. That sixteen-character bar code could be a geographical location."

"Looks like it might be," Alex said.

"But what we've got doesn't look like one," I said. "Break that line in half and assign the letters N and W to the halves, and finally put in the periods. Now we've got 04 79.098 N, for latitude, and 70 19.164 W, for longitude. See, the N and W letters follow the numbers in the old way geographers used, rather than preceding them in the modern manner.

"But this doesn't work. If those numbers 7 and 0 after the first question mark mean degrees West, sure, that could be a longitude reading, but we have a problem with the latitude numbers. North 4 degrees is okay, but 79.098 minutes is impossible. Minutes don't go higher than 60. And even if that was actually 59.098 minutes, the coordinates would put us in eastern Colombia."

We stared at the sheets of paper for many minutes, hoping the key to the code would leap out at us. But neither Alex nor I are professional cryptographers, though both of us have worked simple newspaper cryptograms.

It took a twelve-year-old Ojibwe math whiz to divine the meaning.

"Try looking at the numbers backwards," Tommy said.

Alex and I jumped. So concentrated had we been on the

sheets of paper before us we hadn't noticed that Tommy had come downstairs and was standing by us at the table.

"Uh, Tommy," Alex said with a gentle but firm tone, "this is humdrum police work. It's not very interesting. I think you'd find something more fun on television or on the computer." Alex may be an ace with women, but not with kids.

Tommy Standing Bear may have been only twelve, but he knew when he was being patronized. He shot Alex a wounded glance.

But suddenly Alex shouted, "The boy is right. Look!" With a pencil he wrote in reverse order the digits taken from the letters on the bar code:

?4619107?8909740

"If the first question mark stands for longitude and the second for latitude," Alex said in an excited voice, "and we apply North to the first and West to the second, we get North 46 degrees 19.107 minutes and West 89 degrees 09.740 minutes. Ginny, where's your map of the U.P.?"

Ginny—who had come in from the kitchen where she was fixing a pilaf from raisins, almonds, and wild rice, her Upper Michigan variation on an old recipe she had brought home from a visit to Pakistan with her late husband—pulled a rolled topographical chart from a cabinet drawer and handed it to Alex. He spread it open on the dining table and with a ruler pinpointed the location.

"Five miles northeast of Watersmeet! We're in business! Dollars to doughnuts the corpse in the Dying Room was a—what did you call it?—a multicache? When one cache sends the finder to another?" Alex had suddenly become a believer.

"Damn right," I said. I turned to the boy and said, "Tommy, thank you very much. We apologize for doubting you." I glanced at Alex and held his gaze. "We" meant "he," not "me."

A grin began to curl at the corners of Tommy's mouth. "That's okay, Mr. Martinez," he said.

I stuck out my hand. Immediately, Tommy grasped it and shook it gravely.

That moment was, I would recall much later, the real beginning of the bond between Tommy and me.

"Ginny," he said, "maybe I could have a GPS for my birthday?"

She looked at me and we both nodded. A simple but capable hiker's GPS costs a hundred dollars on Internet retailers and can be had used for less than half that on eBay. Such a device would be a more than suitable gift for an intelligent twelve-year-old who lives in the country.

"Let's call Camilo," I said presently, looking back at the map on the dining-room table. "That spot near Watersmeet is in his bailiwick." The tribal police, who were cross-deputized as Gogebic County peace officers with full privileges of arrest, covered mostly the eastern reaches of the county, although their jurisdiction extended all over it. Sometimes speeders on U.S. 45 were startled to be pulled over by a tribal police cruiser and handed a ticket from a mahogany-skinned officer well away from the tiny Lac Vieux Desert reservation. Camilo's polite but stern cop manner cowed almost all of them, but once in a while an out-of-state driver would protest, "We're off the reservation! You have no jurisdiction!"

"Want to bet?" Camilo would say, removing his Serengetis and flashing his victim a shark's smile. "Double or nothing on the fine?"

They always gave in.

Speaking of Camilo, he wasn't in, or on duty. Gone to Rhinelander for dinner, the dispatcher said. That was more than an hour southwest of Watersmeet, but the Upper Peninsula has so few decent restaurants that Yoopers think nothing of driving sixty or a hundred miles into Wisconsin for a good meal. Camilo would overnight there, the dispatcher added, and return sometime the next day.

"Time to hit the air," I told Alex. "We'll fly over that spot with my GPS and see what there is to see from above."

"Hold your horses, Steve!" Ginny said firmly. "Time for *dinner*. And let's not talk about this subject at the table, shall we?"

We didn't. The pilaf, superb even for Ginny's sophisticated kitchen, kept our minds off cadavers. And we didn't have to drive a hundred miles for it.

The Porcupine County Sheriff's Department Aviation Division—that's me—operates a new Cessna 182 Skylane, a trade-up from a threadbare old 160-horsepower Cessna 172 Skyhawk. Actually, the Skylane isn't exactly new, having been manufactured in 1981, but it's in much better shape than the smaller and older Skyhawk, with an almost new paint job, a freshly overhauled engine, and a refurbished interior. It carries four people, like the 172, but the 230-horsepower engine of the 182 enables the department to ferry the pilot, an oversized prisoner, and a large escort deputy all the way to Lansing at better than 150 miles per hour with a full load of fuel, and its big wing tanks allow us to loiter miles out on Lake Superior during long searches for overturned boats. As the chief pilot—actually, the only pilot—of the aviation division, whose decidedly unluxurious six-by-ten-foot office occupies one greasy, cluttered corner of the communal county hangar at Porcupine County Airport, I count among my tasks the job of exercising the Skylane for an hour a week to keep engine and controls limber and corrosion free. I earned a pilot's license on weekends in the army and as soon as he discovered that, Undersheriff O'Brien, a master at manipulating grants for expensive police equipment, fished for and landed the Skyhawk. That airplane served us well for several years, but when it eventually proved less than adequate for some tasks, Gil wheedled and lobbied and pulled strings until the State of Michigan agreed to finance the Skylane. However, the 182 being considerably more expensive to operate than the 172, Gil made me justify every drop of fuel the larger plane burned. I wouldn't think of going lollygagging in her, boring aimless holes in the sky like a weekend pilot with nothing better to do than brush up on his flying skills.

But when I took the airplane up on official duties, I secretly shed my land-bound self and became my middle name, Two Crow, mounted Lakota warrior at one with the hawks and eagles, married to Sun and Wind. I never told anybody about that. My friends wouldn't have understood, except maybe Camilo and a traditional Ojibwe or two. One of these days, I vowed, I would take Tommy Standing Bear up in a rental airplane from Land O' Lakes and introduce him to the exhilaration of soaring with the birds. He, I thought, would not only understand my feeling, but also embrace it. I was beginning to feel proprietary toward him, ready to share with him the tiny link I occupied in the great chain of being.

Today I was alone. Alex had other duties, and I suspected he was secretly delighted. Alex hates small planes, although he is brave enough to swallow his fear when duty calls. He makes a terrible passenger, sweating and clenching his teeth and fists and yipping in consternation whenever the airplane hits a patch of mild turbulence. I have to keep up a steady stream of soothing chatter to placate his white-knuckled demons.

Doc Miller, one of the internists at Porcupine County Hospital and my personal physician, waved from the hangar where he kept his Cessna Bird Dog, a lovingly restored Korean War–era army spotter plane the same size as the Skylane. "A warbird on the cheap," he called the meticulously maintained old airplane, but I knew that keeping half-century-old aircraft flying is anything but cheap. And Doc, as a physician in the boonies of Upper Michigan, is not handsomely paid. But he is a bachelor with only one expensive obsession, that Bird Dog, and nobody gainsays the money he spends on it, often taking local children for rides in the sky. And I am glad for his frequent help during air searches for lost hikers in the woods and overturned boaters on Lake Superior.

As the Skylane roared skyward from the runway, I gently banked her into a climbing turn south toward Watersmeet, a crossroads town of a thousand people fifty-six miles south of Porcupine City at the junction of U.S. 2 and U.S. 45. In less than thirty seconds, the plane had clawed its way to five hundred feet above the treetops. I leveled off, set the throttle and manifold pressure for cruising speed, and watched the numbers unroll on the screen of the handheld GPS receiver I had Velcroed to the instrument panel. Southern Porcupine County is mostly second-growth forest interspersed with open land, some of it cropped by cattle but most slowly being overrun by brush and scrub. Dirt roads still used by pulp loggers snake across the landscape, now and then disappearing under the forest canopy that in many places grows higher and thicker with every passing year. Soon the rocky outcrops of the copper-bearing Trap Hills and the Victoria Dam and Impoundment on the Porcupine River passed below, as did the crossroads of Bruce Crossing, and the open, flat, forest-and-lake lands of Gogebic County approached through the whirling propeller. Ecologically, this area of the southern Upper Peninsula looks like neighboring northern Wisconsin, sparkling ponds and lakes scattered across the dark boreal forest like diamonds on a jeweler's velvet.

At almost the precise spot reported on the bar code tag stuck to the shroud of the Poor Farm corpse, I looked directly below. A tiny, almost circular clearing of tanned grass and low brush not more than seventy yards wide, a small pond in its center, appeared in the forest canopy. *It figures,* I thought. Tree cover blankets and fuzzes the line-of-sight transmissions from the GPS satellites far out in space, and it would make sense for a geocacher to stash a treasure at the edge of a clearing where a handheld GPS can lock on to several satellites for an accurate fix. I dropped down farther to two hundred feet above the treetops, holding the Cessna in a tight circle above the clearing. Through the edges of the trees I could see the twin ruts of a Forest Service dirt road leading to U.S. 45 three miles to the southwest. It would be easy to hop in an SUV or jeep to reach N 46 19.107 W 89 09.740, and I knew exactly what we would find there.

10

"Almost the same," Alex said as he, Camilo, and I gazed with distaste at the plastic-wrapped, naked torso that lay just behind and under a downed log five feet thick, just a hop, skip, and jump through the brush off the Forest Service track through a corner of the tiny Lac Vieux Desert reservation and out onto public land just outside the national forest. It had taken us ten full minutes to locate the corpse after stopping at the exact coordinates given by the tag on the Poor Farm cadaver. A GPS may be accurate within twenty or thirty feet of a given point, but in heavy brush, a circle of twenty or thirty feet in diameter can conceal a lot. Ten minutes seemed like hours in humid ninety-degree July heat with no-see-ums and blackflies buzzing around our heads, swathed in beekeeper's muslin, and Alex kept up a running mutter of salty terms, mostly variations on "fucking bugs," as he stumbled into trees and over brambles, head down as he watched the numbers unroll on his GPS. Had we been searching for a geocache in the city, he would have walked into a lamppost.

I cussed a few times myself. Camilo, who had spent much of his professional life searching for clues through tropical heat in thick East Texas brush, chuckled at our discomfiture.

It was a clever place for a geocache. From the Forest Service track, the log was barely visible in the tall grass and brambles, and only when the searcher was standing directly on top of it could he see the shallow depression slightly behind and under. From every other angle, the geocache couldn't be seen.

Like the Poor Farm cadaver, the body was missing its head and both hands. This time, however, putrefaction was well established, the gases of decay plumping the plastic shroud seemingly to the bursting point.

"Almost the same," I said. "But not quite."

"Not quite how?" said Camilo, who had not seen the corpse at the Poor Farm.

"The body at the Poor Farm was a well-embalmed medical cadaver," I said. "I don't think this one is."

"And this one is old," Alex pointed out. "See the wrinkled skin, the gray pubic hair? The other one was young."

"So?" Camilo said.

"Medical cadavers are almost always of the young or early-middle-aged and are in good physical condition," Alex said. "Medical students need to learn about anatomy from those and the specialists need to practice on the healthy. But this is an old guy, probably sick, full of arthritis and prostate cancer and God knows what else. Not the sort of thing an anatomy student dissects."

"Look at the decomposition," I said. "I'll bet my next paycheck this body was embalmed for a funeral, not for study." Morticians prepare corpses to look fresh only for a few days, just to last through the end of a funeral service and make it to the cemetery. Anything more would be gilding the lily, wasting talent and materials. Funeral directors appreciate economic efficiency as much as other businessmen.

"Then why would the perp cut off the head and hands?" asked Alex. He knew the answer, but somebody had to say it, and I did.

"To prevent identification," I said. "In this case, only that."

"Come again?" Camilo asked.

I explained how the Poor Farm cadaver's head and hands probably had been harvested for specialist study, but not this one.

Camilo nodded in understanding. "But if you're right and this stiff was embalmed for a funeral, wouldn't an undertaker somewhere be short a customer?" he asked. "Wouldn't he report it missing—and couldn't we identify it that way?"

"Yes," I said, "but it could have been earmarked for cremation after the funeral, not before. If the mortician was crooked, he could easily have sold the corpse to our perps and delivered an urn of dog ashes to the mourners."

"God," Camilo said.

"Jeez," Alex said.

Both men were offended, not by what I had said but by its implications. Cheating the bereaved is high on the average cop's scale of evildoing, not quite in the league of homicide but not far from it either.

"What do you make of the coins?" Alex asked after a while.

Five American coins—a dollar, a half dollar, a quarter, a dime, and a penny—sat on the plastic-encased chest of the corpse. So did a shilling coin.

"My best guess," I said, remembering Ginny's lecture on geocaching, "is that these are tokens left by the geocachers who found the location, left to prove they were here. Each geocacher would have a coin assigned to himself."

"Or herself," said Camilo, not so much in political correctness as in keeping an open mind about the perp or perps.

"Does that mean one of our suspects is a Brit?" Alex asked.

"Maybe," I said, "but not necessarily. There are six coins in common American circulation, and if more than six geocache hunters are involved in this, they'd need some other coins to identify all of them."

"There were a quarter and a penny at the Poor Farm cache," Alex said. "But not the others."

"There's no nickel here," Camilo said, voicing what we all had noticed.

"Gentlemen," I said, "maybe that means that Mr. or Ms. Nickel hasn't found this cache yet."

"Could be," Alex said thoughtfully.

"We oughta get to the bottom of this," Camilo said. "Once is a stunt but twice is a crime."

"Ya think?" Alex said dubiously.

"Yeah," I said.

"We could set up a stakeout here," Camilo said. The tribal police's resources, augmented by the federal Bureau of Indian Affairs, are modest but still far greater than Porcupine County's. "I can deputize a bunch of reliable guys to sit in a car all day and all night on U.S. 45 and report every vehicle or person who goes up this road. Not many do. We can check them out pretty easy."

"All right," Alex said. "Your catch for now, Camilo, but when things happen, the state police will be happy to help."

By that, Alex meant that the troopers were ready to take over if the case turned out to be too much for a tribal force or county sheriff's department to handle, or if the crime spanned more than one jurisdiction. In a murder case on an Indian reservation, the FBI would take ultimate responsibility, although these days the feds were slow to do so, being up to their ears in antiterrorism chores. Often, the FBI would ask the state police and sheriff to investigate as far as they could, and the G-men would take over the case when the bulk of the work, sometimes all of it, had been done. But though the tribal cops were in charge for the moment, the clearing wasn't part of the Lac Vieux Desert reservation. No need to notify either the FBI or the U.S. Forest Service Police, who would have been called in if the corpse had been on national forest land.

"All right, let's turn him over and see what's underneath," Alex said.

Gingerly, careful not to tear the plastic, we rolled the body over on its front. And saw nothing on the underside. Not even a bar code.

"Hmm," I said. "Maybe this was the last cache in a series of them, and maybe the one we found at the Poor Farm was the first—or even the second or third or God knows what."

"Lordamighty," Alex said. "This *is* a puzzle. It makes my head hurt."

"Let's look around," I said. "Maybe there's some other kind of clue." An hour's search turned up an old fishing creel and a few tattered twelve-gauge shotgun shells.

"Ain't nothing here," Camilo said, "other than a few tire ruts, and we've already taken casts of them."

I believed him. Apaches make some of the world's best trackers. Nothing escapes their notice.

"All right, we're done here," Alex said. "Let's call a taxi to take this fellow to Marquette."

The taxi turned out to be a muddy Chevy Suburban belonging to the state police, and Alex turned out to be the reluctant cabbie.

11

I was sipping coffee at my desk under the grimy green concrete block walls at the sheriff's department and chasing overdue paperwork around a cracked china mug emblazoned with "TAKE A MYSTERY AUTHOR TO BED TONIGHT" when Alex called, jolting me from my reverie about the source of the mug. It had come from an itinerant wannabe whodunit writer from Chicago who had stopped in one day to check a few facts about police work and was never heard from again, at least not at the department. I wonder if he ever managed to publish a book.

"Just as we thought," Alex said. "Yesterday's stiff definitely was a short-term embalming, the pathologist said. A quick dip in the juice and a bit of makeup to look good in church."

"Just as *I* thought, you mean," I said. Sometimes Alex needed to be reminded who came up with some of the brilliant ideas.

"All right, all right. Well, the pathologist also said the hands and head were hacked off with a cleaver or an ax, not surgically removed. The bone ends were shattered, not sawn."

"You know what that means," I said.

"You tell me."

I sighed. Alex likes to play dumb. "That means it wasn't a professional who did the dismembering," I said. "I think a pro would insist that head and hands be removed before he sold a corpse—if it ever was identified it'd get back to him—but he probably watched while the guy he sold it to did the job, just to make sure it was actually done and the buyer didn't take the parts along with him. The pro probably saw to it that the head and hands were cremated along with a dead deer or whatever was available, so there would be enough weight to the urn and the family wouldn't suspect a thing." Car-deer accidents are so plentiful in Upper Michigan and northern Wisconsin that a crooked crematory worker on his way to the office could easily gather a carcass from the side of the road and throw it into the back of his car or pickup.

"Yeah," Alex said. "So we can add desecration of a human body to the charges when we catch the assholes."

"*If* we catch them," I said.

"You don't sound so confident."

"I think these perps are smart people. And I think they're playing with us. I think they're from outside somewhere, and they think we're a bunch of Barney Fifes, and that's why they've picked us for their game."

"From outside?" Alex said. "Why?"

"I don't know. Fooling around with dead bodies doesn't seem to be the sort of thing a Yooper would do. It's such a . . . a . . . a *jaded* thing to do." There it was. I just didn't want to believe anybody in my adopted bailiwick was so bored with life that he was capable of playing sports with corpses.

"Hey, Yoopers have committed all the other crimes in the book," Alex said. "Why not this one? Besides, it's so unlikely that a casual visitor would've known about either of those two places where we found the bodies. It's probably a whole bunch of people playing this game, and one or more of them could be local."

"Don't forget the Internet," I said.

"Internet?"

"Yes. You would be surprised what Web sites can tell you. There's a Web site for every county in Michigan, and the one for Porcupine County has a page on the Poor Farm. In fact, Google brought up no fewer than forty-six hits on it. If I were looking for a place to stash something like a cadaver, I'd start with the Web."

"Now what?"

"I guess we wait and see if anybody shows up at the stakeout."

"Right."

I hung up and pursued a few more forms around my desk.

"Deputy Martinez!" Gil's gravelly voice thundered from his office.

"Sir?"

"Come in and sit down!"

I relaxed. The invitation to plant my butt in a chair meant the undersheriff wasn't going to grill me about the cost of the latest oil change on the Cessna. He did his chewing out while his victims stood before his desk at attention, sweating. Gil liked to do things the military way. He had been a drill instructor in the army for four hitches before deciding upon a new career of tormenting rural deputies.

"Shut the door!"

I did.

"Have you seen this?" He shoved a *Herald* across the desk at me and thrust a massive index finger at a front-page article. "CHANGES NEEDED IN SHERIFF'S DEPARTMENT" the headline said. It was an "interview" of Sheriff Eli Garrow—actually, it was an op-ed column he had written himself in third-person format and disguised as a news story. I could tell Eli's voice by the awkwardly folksy language—the kind a cop uses when he doesn't want to sound like a cop—as well as shaky grammar and questionable spelling. *The Herald* would print just about anything handed to it, and it often did so without the polish of an editor's pencil. That gave the letters and amateur-contributed articles a certain just-folks authenticity, but sometimes the authenticity was so great the result was nearly incomprehensible. That was, I thought, unnecessarily cruel to the writers. Semiliterate doesn't necessarily mean stupid. People who can barely read and write are often smart in other ways.

"Can you believe this shit?" Gil demanded.

Among other things, Eli wrote, if he were reelected, the department would keep two deputies on road patrol twenty-four hours a day, seven days a week, in addition to the dispatcher. These days, with cutbacks in state and federal funding, we'd had to furlough two of our nine sworn deputies and spread the rest thin. Only during daylight hours did we have two officers on patrol, and at night we had one based at the office to be sent out as needed. On Friday and Saturday nights we had one or two other deputies on call if barroom disputes escalated beyond the duty officer's ability to handle them. It wasn't a great way to police a big county in the middle of the wilderness, but it was all we could do with our scarce resources. Grants could bring in new equipment, but we had to pay our personnel with funds from the increasingly undernourished county coffers.

"Where's Eli going to get the money for that?" I asked.

"Doesn't say," Gil grunted. "Pie in the sky."

We stared at the newspaper for a few minutes. Then what passed for a smile distorted Gil's face, usually as composed as a pressure cooker just short of the bursting point.

"The only way Eli could do that," he said, "would be to talk the county into raising taxes. A lot."

In Upper Michigan, economic times are never good—they're just variations on bad and worse. The voters are sensible. In the last elections, they voted Yes on a proposal to raise the millage just a tad for the county public library and the county public transit, both highly popular services. But two or three more full-time deputies and their benefits would cost a lot more than that.

"Deputy Martinez. You are hereby ordered to campaign on the fact that Eli's proposals would hike our taxes. Is that clear?"

"You can't order me to do that!" Gil may be the boss of me as a deputy, but he's not the boss of me as a politician.

"Of course not," he said, in a tone about as placating as he ever gets. "But be sensible. Eli thinks he's gonna fool the voters, but they're gonna realize what he'll cost them. You've got to point that out to them."

"Yeah. But I'll be damned if I do it the way Eli's doing it."

"You don't have to. Just go out there and shake hands and let them know what happens if you don't get elected."

"All right."

"Now get out of my office." Gil turned to the file cabinets behind him in dismissal.

In encouraging me, he was committing an act of insubordination. Eli was still the sheriff in name, though he hadn't been in the office for weeks, ever since Garner Armstrong had told him his days were numbered. The undersheriff's first loyalty is always to his boss. If it ever got out that Gil was giving me campaign advice, Eli would fire him on the spot, for the undersheriff serves at the sheriff's pleasure and is not protected by a union, as we deputies are. And that would kick up an enormous fuss in Porcupine County, for Gil is a highly respected if not exactly cuddly police officer.

I'd keep my mouth shut. But I could see my task clearly: to commit dirty politics, or what passed for dirty politics in Upper Michigan. I had to. My opponent was doing so—in more ways than one.

Shutting my desk drawer and grabbing my ball cap from the hat rack, I started for the door.

"Stick around a bit," said Joe Koski from his dispatcher's desk. "Chad's coming in with an interesting pinch."

"What? Who?"

"You'll see."

When I was halfway through my second cup of coffee, the big deputy rolled in, pushing two grizzled and unkempt men in their forties ahead of him like a monstrous border collie nipping at the heels of a couple of raggedy sheep.

"What do we got?" asked Joe, the booking officer as well as dispatcher and town gossip. Soon all of Porcupine County would know what we got.

"Caught 'em pulling up and trashing campaign signs," Chad said, "from both public and private property. They had a couple dozen signs in their car trunk, too."

I blinked. Gil came out of his office and glared at Chad. Messing with campaign signs is a third-class misdemeanor, about as serious as public drunkenness or disorderly conduct. The fines would barely pay for the deputies' labor. Some laws are just not worth enforcing. Had I been in Chad's shoes, I'd just have read the riot act and made the perps put the signs back.

Chad saw my blink. "Just doing my job, Steve," he said, calmly and not at all defensively.

Joe asked the question we all wanted answered. "Whose signs were they?"

"Martinez's," Chad said.

"Mine?"

"Just doing my job," Chad said again. Gil turned on his heel and without a word strode back into his office.

"Names?" Joe asked.

"Jim and John McCulloch," Chad said. "Residence, Two-thirty-three Stover Road, Bergland." I recognized the names. The McCullochs are first cousins to the Garrows.

"Eli put you up to this?" Joe asked.

Neither of the unshaven men responded.

"Eh?" Joe asked again. Both men just glowered.

"Stay right here," Joe told them. "Chad, let's talk." The two deputies walked into the empty sheriff's office and conferred for a couple of minutes. Then they returned unsmiling to the squad room.

"We're booking you on misdemeanor malicious destruction of property," Joe told the men. "We'll send you a court date in the mail. Meanwhile, sign here, and we'll release you on your own recognizance."

I shot a glance at Gil in his office. His head bobbed slightly in approval. Fifty-dollar fines wouldn't begin to pay for the labors of the deputy, the dispatcher, and the magistrate, as well as the paperwork, but they'd send a clear message to the forces of Eli Garrow.

As for Chad Garrow, I now knew where his loyalty lay. Not to Eli, not to me, but to his badge and to the law. That was enough for any man to ask.

I got up once more to leave, and Gil stuck his head out of his office again. "Deputies," he said, "henceforth we will enforce the campaign-sign laws. For *everyone.*" He shot me a glance. I could have sworn he winked, but with Gil, that was not only unlikely, but probably physically impossible.

In Porcupine County, as in just about any Michigan locality, campaign-sign ordinances usually are honored in the breach. Cops have more important things to do than pounce on technical infractions of the election ordinances. But now I'd have to look sharply at my own signs. At least three I could think of were maybe five or six feet too close to the road. But that was all. I didn't have one-third the number of signs Eli set out. Couldn't afford them.

"Put it on the order board for everyone to carry tape measures on patrol," Gil told Joe. "Make sure those signs are at least sixty-six feet from the center lines of all two-lane highways and that the sight lines at all road intersections are clear. And if any campaign signs violate the law *in any way,* confiscate 'em."

I couldn't keep my eyebrows from shooting up. That meant maybe half of Eli Garrow's signs were technically illegal, not just because they were posted where they weren't allowed, but also because they didn't clearly state who had paid for the sign, as the law required. The Ewen graphics shop Eli used for most of his signs didn't have the proper equipment to do small-size lettering, and so they left off "The Committee to Reelect Eli Garrow" from their products. Most everyone in the county had noticed the omission, and a few had even clucked in disapproval, but the infraction not having the gravity of, say, bank robbery, we all had forgotten about it.

As I passed by Gil's office, he looked up at me from his desk. "Just doing my job," he said. He did not smile.

12

Sure enough, by midafternoon, the entire county knew what had happened that morning at the sheriff's department. Joe Koski had gone out to lunch at Merle's and told a few folks, who told a few folks, and soon the news had been carried far and wide. Out of habit, Joe had also broadcast the order to all cars, even though both deputies on patrol that day—Chad and I—had been in the office. Up until that spring, the Porcupine County Bush Telegraph would have picked up his transmission. That was the old unofficial network of radio scanners most everyone kept on the kitchen table and many illegally carried in their cars and pickups, tuning them to the various government bands—police, fire, ambulance, hospital, highway, even the bridge over M-64—keeping track of what went on in the county. That way the news would have spread instantly throughout coffee shops, garages, and taverns all over Upper Michigan.

But the bush telegraph suffered a heavy blow when the new eight-hundred-megahertz radio system was adopted by all the Upper Peninsula police forces as well as the state police. For technical reasons, scanners tuned to the police frequency have a hard time picking up broadcasts, so no longer does everyone in the county know when Joe dispatches an order to the deputies in the field. The new system not only allows us to keep a better handle on security, but at last it covers the many dead spots all over the county that the old line-of-sight radio technology couldn't reach. No longer do we have to try our cell phones—themselves hobbled by huge dead spots—or stop at someone's house and ask to use their landline phone.

Also, I knew that as soon as I left the squad room, Joe would call Horace Wright, *The Herald*'s only reporter, and that next Wednesday a small front-page story would appear about the arrest of two Bergland residents for malicious destruction of campaign signs. *The Herald* wouldn't mention their names, not until a sentence had been passed—if it ever was, because the district judge often dismissed trivial offenses as not being worth the court's time. But Joe, who spent half his off-hours at Merle's Café, would make sure those names got out into the sunlight where everyone could hear them. Rough justice, but justice nonetheless.

Before Joe had had time to spread the gossip, I was on my way out of town on M-64, heading west to start my patrol by delivering a civil court summons, when I decided to stop in at Ginny's for a quick hello and a cup of her first-rate Colombian coffee. I knocked, she called "Come in!" and I found her sitting at the kitchen table gazing gloomily at Tommy, whose head was bowed so that I couldn't see it.

"Good morning," I said cheerily to both.

Ginny nodded, but Tommy didn't look up.

"S'matter?"

"Tommy was in an altercation after school yesterday," Ginny said. "He doesn't want to tell me about it."

Altercation? What's wrong with "fistfight"? Women are so dainty with words, as if a prettier one softened reality.

"That so?" I asked Tommy.

He looked up. A large mouse discolored his left eye socket, and his upper lip lay split and swollen over the lower.

"Who did that to you?"

Tommy shook his head.

"I'm talking to you as a friend, Tommy, not as a cop."

Tommy nodded but kept mum.

"May I see your hands?"

Slowly he brought them out from under the table. Cuts and bruises lathered with antiseptic ointment covered his knuckles.

"Looks like you gave as good as you got."

Tommy nodded.

"What was it about?"

"Nothing."

"That's a lot of something on your face and hands for nothing," I said.

"Tommy, talk to me," Ginny said. "Maybe I can help."

"Thanks, but I don't need help." Tommy said the words politely, without rancor or sullenness. His calmness unsettled me.

I looked at Ginny and nodded. She shrugged, as if what was happening at her kitchen table was a hopelessly male thing and utterly beyond her power to understand, let alone influence.

"If you do," I said, "let us know, okay?"

"All right, Mr. Martinez."

"The bus is almost here, Tommy," Ginny said. "Better run." Visibly relieved to be let off the spot, the lad grabbed his book bag and dashed out the door, sprinting up the short distance to the highway. Through the trees I could see the flashing strobe light atop the approaching school bus. He'd just make it.

"What do you suppose the fight was about?"

"I don't know," Ginny said. "I'm afraid some bully attacked him."

Ice knifed into my heart. Was it because Tommy is an Indian?

"Maybe it was just a bully," I said. "Maybe not. Boys get into fights for all sorts of reasons."

"I don't know," she said, hugging herself. "But he came home last night bleeding and barely able to see out of that eye. He let me give him first aid but he refused to say what happened. He went to bed right away."

"Hmm. How's he doing in algebra?" The summer class had begun three weeks earlier.

"Quite well," Ginny said. "Jack Queeney said he's picked up algebra so fast he's actually helping teach the class."

"Hmm. Lots of remedial students in it, aren't there?"

"Most are from the high school."

"Wonder if some thug resents a smaller kid being smarter than him." Smarter, maybe with a different color of skin, who knew?

"I don't know. Maybe."

"I have an idea."

"What?"

"I'll find a reason to be at the school when the class lets out later this morning. I'll see if there's another kid with battle scars."

"Don't push it too hard, Steve. Tommy is a very proud boy. I wouldn't want him to think we were going to come running every time he had a problem. He needs to be independent."

"He *wants* to be independent," I said. "There's a difference."

"You'll be careful?"

"I'll just do my job."

At one minute before noon, I stopped by the junior high to consult with Jack Queeney, who coached the Little League team and taught math at the high school, including algebra and the summer class. The new baseball jerseys we deputies had chipped in to buy had arrived at the sheriff's department, and it was the perfect excuse to pay Jack a visit.

As the bell rang, I waved to Jack and strode into his room with an armful of uniforms while the two dozen pupils filed out. I nodded to Tommy, who looked at me quizzically, and said hi to a few of the youngsters I knew. One of the last boys to file out was a big, overstuffed towhead with scuffs and bruises on his chubby cheeks and a lip even fatter than Tommy's. He outweighed Tommy by at least twenty pounds, maybe thirty. He had the weight and the reach but not, I thought, the speed.

"Who's that kid?" I asked Jack when they had gone.

"Teddy Garrow, from Matchwood. He's fourteen, and it's his second time around in this class. He'll never pass."

If Jack had noticed that two of his students bore the fresh marks of a fight, he didn't let on, and I didn't mention it. But it looked as if the campaign for sheriff might be trickling down into places where it didn't belong. I hoped not.

13

As I was broiling on the big kettle grill a freshly thawed walleye I'd caught a few weeks earlier in Lake Gogebic, the phone rang.

"Steve? Camilo."

"What's happening?"

"We just had a visitor at that stakeout."

"Tell me."

"Remember that rich young guy in the red Beemer at the dance last week? That was him. He turns in and parks just out of sight of the highway, looks around behind him, goes up the road. Billy Bones saw him from his pickup and followed him in on foot."

Billy—actually William Bonham—was an Ojibwe, a retired tribal police officer in his midseventies who often filled in at the shop when Lac Vieux Desert cops called in sick or went on vacation. Billy had been getting forgetful lately, and one of the things that often slipped his mind was his concealed carry permit for his huge and old-fashioned Colt Peacemaker .45. Issued long ago when he first joined the force and renewed regularly since, the permit wasn't good outside Michigan. The tribal police and the Gogebic sheriff's deputies often had to rescue Billy from indignant Wisconsin and Minnesota law enforcement officers who had been alarmed by the bulge in his Windbreaker. Amazingly, no one had confiscated the weapon. It was only professional courtesy, but I think sometimes that can be taken too far.

Still, Billy was a peaceable and competent unofficial reserve officer, a man of widely known reliability, and he was one of the first Camilo had enlisted for stakeout duty at the Watersmeet cache.

"The Beemer guy didn't see Billy?"

"Steve, Billy's an *Indian*. What do you expect?"

"Not all Indians know how to hide in the woods anymore."

"That's all Columbus's fault, you know." Camilo, who could become one angry Native American on the subject of the manifold sins of the white man, would orate at the drop of a hat on the incompetency of the European explorer "who didn't know what he'd found but wrecked the neighborhood anyway." Then he would start in on Coronado and Pizarro and De Soto and the rest of the Spanish invaders who despoiled the Southwest looking for El Dorado, and we always had to stop him before he had worked up too much of a froth. We'd heard it all anyway, and even if we agreed with him—as I did—there wasn't much we could do about it. Way too many conquistadors and cavalrymen in the forts.

"Never mind, Camilo. Go on."

He sighed in irritation, thwarted from his soapbox. "The subject was carrying a GPS, and at about the spot where we found the corpse, he stopped and tramped around for ten or fifteen minutes, searching for something. When he didn't find what he was looking for, he cursed loudly enough for Billy to hear him, then ran back to his car and took off south on Forty-five. Billy not only got his plate but also his face with a telephoto."

"Excellent."

"What now? Alex is downstate in Lansing." The case had begun in my bailiwick, and Camilo was deferring to me as the unofficial senior investigator. Such deliberate politeness was how cops in differing jurisdictions got along, and we in the U.P. were especially careful about it. We needed each other.

"What was that license plate?"

"Illinois. One of those cutesy vanity things. 'Rebemer.'

Whatever that means. Also a City of Chicago sticker and a neighborhood parking permit."

"Camilo, we're in business," I said. "If you'll contact the Illinois DMV for the owner of those plates, I'll pay a young lady a visit."

"What young lady?"

I told Camilo what I'd seen in the storeroom of the Coppermass Town Hall at the wedding dance of Jerry Muskat and Adela McLaughlin, mildly editing the story in the interest of PG-rated decency.

"Hoo boy," Camilo said delightedly, slapping his thigh. "Dead bodies and sex. We haven't had such a combination in years."

It *was* a break in the routine.

"Pervert," I said primly.

"Sure."

"Camilo, let's not tip the guy off too soon. There are probably others involved in this, and we don't want to spook them just yet. Let's just find out what we can about him from Illinois and Chicago law enforcement."

"All right, call you later."

As the sun sank into Lake Superior an hour later, I pulled up at the Mobil filling station and convenience store on M-64 just north of Lone Pine in the western reaches of the county. Luck was with me. The beefy blonde I had seen locked in embrace with the Beemer guy was on duty. Two suspiciously young men strode out to a pickup as I entered, calling as they left, "S'long, Sharon." They carried a couple of six-packs of Bud, but I decided they were old enough and left them alone. Other things occupied my mind.

"Aren't you a handsome one now, Deputy?" Sharon said lightly as I took a Slim Jim from a rack and plunked down a five-dollar bill. She wore extreme-low-rider Diesel jeans and a yellow T-shirt two sizes too small. The effect would have been knockout sexy had she weighed twenty pounds less and had her heavy perfume come from elsewhere than the Dollar Store. As she placed the change in my hand, she stroked my palm with long fingernails. I gently pulled away and said just as lightly, "Sorry, honey, I'm spoken for."

"Well, ain't that my tough luck?" She spoke flirtatiously and without anger, but there was a wistful note in her voice. Many unmarried and no longer dewy women in rural northern Wisconsin and the Upper Peninsula are like her, high school dropouts who grow up there or drift in from elsewhere to work in dead-end minimum-wage jobs, barely keeping their heads above water, until they become single mothers supported by the state. Many of their younger sisters depart for the big cities aboard Greyhounds and are snared by enterprising pimps shadowing the bus stations for new blood. In the country, a surprising lot of these women have no families and only a tiny circle of friends. With them, they spend their equally tiny disposable incomes in bars on the weekends, often waking up with a hellacious hangover next to a man they met the previous night. They eat a cheap, high-carb diet and turn to fat rapidly, often shedding teeth but never seeing a dentist. Sharon, I thought, probably had been pretty when she was a teenager, but hard lines had settled into her face and a roll of fat had started above her hips. Within a year or two, she would cross the line into obesity and flirt with diabetes.

"Maybe it's *my* tough luck," I said. I leaned my forearms flat on the counter, hunching my shoulders and ducking my head, and looked up from under the brim of my ball cap with an encouraging crinkle of my eyes. Ginny once called that a devastatingly irresistible posture, and it does seem to work with women and small children.

"Sharon, isn't it?" I asked.

She nodded hopefully.

"Sharon what?"

"Sharon Shoemaker."

"I'm Steve Martinez."

"I know, Deputy. Seen you around lots of times." She had a faraway expression on her face, as if she was trying to remember if she had ever slept with me, and if she had, whether I had been any good.

"Actually, Sharon, I'm here for another reason. There's a guy I'm interested in, and maybe you can tell me something about him."

"Who?"

"Don't know his name. But I saw you with him a few nights ago at that party for Jerry and Adela in the Coppermass Town Hall."

"Huh?"

I looked at Sharon carefully. It did seem that she was honestly drawing a blank. So many men, so many nights, who could keep track?

"Tall, rich looking. Drove a Beemer."

The light of recognition dawned on her face. "Yeah," she said, as a slow smile that spoke of remembered delight crept up her lips. It must have been good, really good, that encounter in the store-room.

Then her grin faded. "Did he do something bad?"

"I'm not sure," I said truthfully. "Trying to find out. What was his name?"

"Artie. Arthur. Clyde, no, Kein, no, *Klein*," Sharon said. "He said he was from Chicago."

"What happened afterward?" I said. "I'm sorry, but I have to ask. Did you go home with him that night?"

"Oh, *no!*" she said with mostly mock indignation. "I'm not that kind of girl!"

"Didn't say you were. But do you remember anything about him?"

"Not much. He didn't call after."

So there were limits to Artie Klein's acceptance by the community—limits he himself had drawn. I was not surprised. A rich kid from Chicago might help himself to a little ice cream, but he wasn't going to take over the freezer. A classic one-nighter—and maybe not even that.

"Did he say what he was doing up here in Porcupine County?"

"I'm trying to remember," she said. "Yeah. He said he was looking at property on the lake, maybe going to buy it."

"Did he say what he did for a living?"

"Some kind of investor."

"Did he say what company he worked for?"

"Fiddler something."

"Fidelity?" A shot in the dark.

"Yeah! That's it!"

"He give you an address, a phone number?"

"He wrote down a number. But it turned out to be a laundry, a dry cleaner's. Yeah, I called it."

"What'd he write the phone number on?"

"A business card he got out of his wallet."

"Do you still have it?"

She hesitated a moment, then said, "Yeah, I think so." She turned and squatted to pick up her purse, hidden behind a filing cabinet. Her short T-shirt rode up and her low-riding jeans rode down, and just atop the cleft of her doughy buttocks peeked a small tattoo of a Teutonic cross. Maybe she had once been a biker bimbo. Germanic symbols are popular in that culture.

She rummaged in her purse and found the card. "It's not his, just an old one he used to write the number on the back."

I took the expensive pearl-colored pasteboard. BEAR STEARNS AND COMPANY it said in raised copperplate engraving. ANDREW MONAGHAN. Under that, the phone number, with a 212 prefix—Manhattan. Nothing else. Not even an address. Utter simplicity, as bespoke the card of an employee of one of the country's richest investment firms. On the back was scrawled a phone number.

"Did you call this number, too?" I asked, tapping the front of the card.

She hesitated almost imperceptibly, then shook her head. I let it go. A blind phone call from an unknown woman in the middle of nowhere never would get past a secretary at a New York investment house. Very likely she didn't want to admit she'd been rebuffed. People have their pride.

"May I keep this?" I asked. As it had for Sharon, the card probably would lead to a dead end for me, but then it might not. Possibly Mr. Andrew Monaghan was just an acquaintance in the industry, but it was equally possible that he was keeping nefarious company with Mr. Arthur Klein. You never know. You always have to check.

"Sure," Sharon said. "It ain't doing me any good." Then, a beat later, she finally asked the obvious question: "What did he do?"

"That I can't tell you at this time," I said. "We're not sure. We're still investigating." That was the truth.

"Oh."

"Thanks for your help, honey," I said, flashing her my most winning smile. "Bye for now."

"Uh, Steve," she said as I turned to walk out.

"Yes?"

"If you find out anything about him, could you let me know?" The fretful expression on her face suggested she remembered something else. Perhaps Artie hadn't used protection during their unscripted encounter and she worried that she was pregnant.

"If I can, I sure will. Thanks again for your help."

"Thanks." She came out of her station behind the counter and stood in the doorway, the pool of light from a single bare bulb above outlining her sad and lonely face as I drove away into the night.

14

I had just moved one of my own roadside campaign signs two feet farther into legal territory when the radio call came from Joe Koski.

"Steve, we got another," he said.

"Another what?" I asked, wearily knowing the answer.

"Stiff. Looks like it may be a homicide this time," Jerry said. "Hiker called in and said he found a body in a cave just off the North Country Trail about two miles west of Norwich Road. Says it's real ripe, just lying there uncovered. I took his statement about an hour ago."

"Alex back from Lansing yet?"

"He's on his way, but won't be here till tonight."

"All right. I'll swing by and get the bug and safe kits and a body bag." I had been sent to Lansing not long before to be trained in the basics of forensic-evidence gathering on the rare occasion when a state trooper with those skills wasn't available, and Gil had used his grant-writing skills to promote a bit of sophisticated crime-scene equipment, including a forensic entomology outfit and a couple of personal protection kits for cases involving hazardous materials. "Call Chad and tell him to meet me at the parking spot by the trail at Norwich," I added. "Have him bring a stretcher. Where's that hiker?"

"Right here in the department."

"I'll take him along to show us. Is he okay?"

"Sure. A little green around the gills, but willing." Thank goodness for concerned citizens.

"I meant did you check out his story?"

"Yes," said Joe. "He's clean. So is his gal. I've got their particulars in case we need to talk to them again."

After I'd gathered kits and hiker and we were on our way, I asked him to talk to me. He was in his early thirties, fit and athletic, and dressed in sensible but not in-your-face-expensive outdoor gear.

"Can I see some ID?" I asked.

He showed me a Wisconsin commercial license that entitled him to drive eighteen-wheelers. I handed it back.

"What were you doing on the North Country Trail?"

"I already told the deputy at the department," he said. "Do you need to hear it, too?"

"The deputy hasn't had time to fill me in," I said. "Do you mind going through it all again?" If what he told me matched what he told Joe down to the last detail, chances were he was on the side of the angels and could be scratched off the suspect list.

"Oh, nope," he said. "Let's see. I'm from Green Bay. My name's Dan Kowalczyk. Me and Katie, she's my girlfriend, we drove up yesterday to walk the North Country Trail and do a little camping."

"Where's Katie?"

"In the Porcupine City Motel," he said. "She ain't feeling so good. Not after what she saw."

"We might need to talk to her later, but we can do that when she's feeling better. Go on."

"We parked our car at Victoria yesterday and pitched our tent at a campsite near there last night and were making good time on the trail this morning when I had to take a dump. I decided to climb down into a ravine below the trail and go behind a tree.

When I got down there, I smelled something awful. I recognized that smell. I was in the army in Iraq."

No soldier who has ever crossed a fresh battlefield can forget the cloying odor of human putrefaction. There is nothing else like it in the world. It sticks to your clothes, it sticks to your skin, and it sticks to your soul.

"I know what you mean," I said. I'd experienced it a little more than a decade before, and in the same part of the world.

"Katie and I looked around a little, and found a shallow cave under an overhang. Right inside it there was this body, all bloated and purple and stinking. It had no head and it had no hands. The noise from the flies was awful."

"What did you do then?"

"Me and Katie walked back up the trail to Norwich Road and waved down a car. It was almost an hour before one came along. The driver brought us to town. I put Katie in the motel and went to the sheriff's office."

"Thank you, Dan. You did exactly the right things."

"I hope so." He took a deep breath.

So did I. "Do you have a GPS?" I said.

"No," he said calmly. "I don't get lost in the woods very much. Maybe sometime I'll get one. I know they're handy and can save your life, but I don't need one, and anyway it's more fun to do things the old-fashioned way, with a map and compass."

"Bet you drive a stick shift, too."

"How'd you know that?"

"I'm kinda retro myself. Prefer the good old tools, like this revolver." I patted the .357 at my waist and chuckled.

Dan smiled wryly but didn't laugh. He wasn't one of our geocachers.

Presently we arrived at the almost hidden entry to the North Country Trail on Norwich Road. A wooden U.S. Forest Service sign marked it, but if you weren't watching, you'd speed right past the small hole in the forest wall. Chad was waiting on the verge of the road with his equipment, and we changed into heavy canvas brush clothing before starting off with Dan. I filled Chad in as we began the hour's hike west along the ridges of the Trap Hills. It was slow going. The North Country Trail is not a well-tended national park path pounded flat by hundreds of thousands of feet a year, but a sometimes all-but-invisible track land-mined with roots, loose rocks, and mud holes. In spots, only the metal blazes nailed to the trees, their paint fading under the elements, showed us the way. The faint path took us through heavy brush, down rocky screes, and up steep slopes. Often we had to climb over dead trees that had fallen over the trail. Blackflies and brambles plucked at us everywhere, and in spots the humming clouds of no-see-ums were so thick we had to tie bandannas across our faces to avoid breathing in the tiny insects. We sweated piggishly.

Fortunately, before starting back to Norwich Road, Dan had had the presence of mind to mark the spot where he had stepped off the trail for his call of nature. He had tied a red handkerchief around a branch overhanging the trail. He must have been a competent soldier, I thought, probably a noncom.

I recognized the niche in the rock where the body lay. It wasn't a natural cavern, but one of many mine entrances in the high ridges that were started but never finished during the first frantic copper boom of the nineteenth century. Prospectors had hacked away at the rock for a few weeks before giving up on their hope of finding a vein of copper, leaving behind man-tall gouges six or eight feet deep and ten or so feet wide. This one, just above a pretty brook bubbling at the foot of the ravine, had been a favorite spot of campers for a long time before the Forest Service set up a string of official campsites along the trail. Once, during a cloudburst on a weekend hike, Ginny and I had taken shelter at that very spot.

The smell staggered me, causing bile to lurch up my gullet

and my eyes to water. Chad gagged, stepped off the trail, and vomited. Quickly he wiped his mouth and returned.

"Shouldn't have had that anchovy pizza for lunch," he said calmly. Tender tummy and all, Chad was not a wuss.

"It's right there," Dan said, pointing.

I stepped over a log and saw it through a buzzing cloud of flies.

Even with the gaseous distortion and discoloration, I could see that it was the body of a young woman. As Dan had said, there was no head and no hands. The body lay mostly inside a torn plastic shroud that was much like the others we had found, but made of a much thinner material. Animals had been feeding on one leg.

"Dan, if you want, you can move up the trail to a spot where the air's not quite so foul. But I'd appreciate it if you stuck around for a while. We might need you to answer questions."

The ex-soldier nodded quietly. He knew his duty.

"Chad, let's dress up." Up the ravine at a healthy distance away from the corpse, we broke open the hazmat kits and donned disposable Tyvek coveralls, hoods, and booties, thin neoprene gloves, and respirators. It was a warm afternoon, and I began to sweat as soon as I took the first step toward the corpse, but the respirators cut the stink to almost nothing. There wasn't much we could do about the swarm of flies.

For two hours, Chad and I worked, first photographing the corpse in situ from several angles. Multiple knife marks on the torso, both shallow slashes and deep stabs, suggested the cause of death. There was no blood, meaning that the woman had been killed elsewhere and her body cleaned before it was carried down the North Country Trail. Both her nipples and her navel were pierced by silver rings an inch in diameter.

"Look at those needle tracks, Steve," Chad said. "She was a junkie."

A trail of purplish punctures surrounded by bruised flesh walked up the inside of the body's left elbow.

"Might have been a prostitute," I said. "If semen's present and the medical examiner finds the DNA of several sexual partners in it, that'll all but clinch it. Hey, look at the bone ends. They're crushed and splintered, not cleanly sawn. This lady wasn't dismembered by a mortician, like the Poor Farm corpse. She was butchered, like the one near Watersmeet. If embalming fluid was used at all, the job was botched. This is the work of an amateur."

We plucked maggots from the teeming flesh of the corpse as well as the soil around it and popped them into specimen jars. Those might help the forensic entomologist at the central state police crime lab in Lansing to pinpoint the time of death. Flies frequently lay eggs on a corpse within an hour after its owner is killed, and the times of the developmental stages of the resulting maggots, even their internal temperatures, can be measured accurately.

"We're done, Chad. Let's zip her up."

Gently we slid the body into the bag and onto the aluminum stretcher. With a roll of duct tape, I sealed the zipper, hoping the smell wouldn't leak from the bag but knowing it would.

"Hold it," Chad said. He bent down, scratched in the gravel where the body had lain, and pointed. "Look."

A shiny nickel, head facing up, glittered from the dust.

"Stand aside," I said, stepping forward to photograph the coin where it lay. Then I scooped it up, examined it carefully, and dropped it into a ziplock bag. "That wasn't there before the body was laid on top of it. It's brand-new, right from the mint. No weathering at all."

"What's it mean?" Chad asked. He hadn't been with Alex and Camilo and me down by Watersmeet, where we had discovered the array of coins atop the cached corpse.

"Maybe nothing," I said. "But it might be a link to the other two bodies."

I explained what Alex and I had speculated about the existence of coins at the cache sites. Skepticism and puzzlement wreathed Chad's face.

"Let's get going," I said.

"Give you a hand?" Dan called from up the hill. I nodded.

It took two hours for the three of us to make our way back with the bagged body down the rocky, winding trail to Norwich Road, and I was grateful for Dan's help. When we arrived, we slid the stretcher half crosswise into the back of the sheriff's Explorer, over the folded rear seats. We drove back to Porcupine City with all the windows open and the intake fan on high against the noisome mess in the back.

After dropping Dan at the motel and telling him we might need to be in touch again, Chad and I drove the two hours to the lab at Marquette and delivered the corpse and most of the evidence we had gathered, but FedExing the maggots to Lansing. At my cabin that night, I showered for twenty minutes, lathering up heavily and scrubbing vigorously, then fell into bed and into a fitful sleep, the stench of corruption still heavy in my nostrils.

15

Two days later, we held a war council in the sheriff's squad room. Garner Armstrong, as prosecutor and chief law officer of Porcupine County, presided. Gil, Chad, and I were present as duty officers on shift, Alex represented the state police, and Camilo Hernandez had driven up from Watersmeet for consultation since one of the bodies had been found in his bailiwick. Joe Koski took notes.

"Here's what we have," Garner said. "Three bodies. One a fully prepared medical cadaver, one an old guy embalmed just enough to last through his funeral, and one a woman, probably a prostitute, stabbed to death elsewhere and left to rot in our county." In the last case, the medical examiner had confirmed the cause of death and discovered the DNA of four different men in semen samples taken from her vagina. The victim had been a longtime heroin addict, common among urban streetwalkers. The entomological evidence showed that she had been dead for eight days. Embalming fluid, but not enough to have done much good, leaked from her tissues. As for the other two bodies, the forensic experts' best guess was that they had been stowed away for three to six weeks. More tests were needed to narrow down the times of death, although knowing those probably wouldn't help in the first two cases, for they weren't homicides.

"So what ties them together?" He answered his own question. "GPS coordinates link the second one to the first. A nickel links the third to the second—maybe. That could just be a coincidence. But all three are missing their heads and their hands. Maybe in the case of the medical cadaver there's a good reason for that, but not in the other two."

For the record, Gil said the painfully obvious: "Those bodies were meant never to be identified."

"But they were also meant to be found," Camilo said. "Maybe even by us. They were hidden in plain sight, if you know what I mean."

"Kind of like a message in a bottle," I said, surprising myself.

"Explain," Garner said.

"You know," I said. "You write a message with your name and address and put it into a bottle and throw it into the lake. Then you wait for somebody to find it and write you that it was found. There could be a million reasons to do that. Maybe a young couple is just curious about the chances for a reply. Maybe a teenage girl sends a message she hopes a boy will find. Maybe a church lady puts in a passage from the Bible and hopes it will touch somebody's soul. Maybe somebody's shipwrecked and wants to say, 'Help me.'"

"We looking for a freak?" Alex said. "Or maybe freaks?"

The room fell silent. Then Chad spoke. "What about missing persons?"

"Nobody's reported either a lost cadaver or a missing body prepared for burial so far as we can find out," Alex said. "And who's going to report a missing hooker, especially a junkie? They come and they go, and nobody cares. What's more, the hooker being a homicide victim may have nothing to do with her being a cached corpse. Maybe she was just the closest thing on the shelf at a funeral home, hadn't been embalmed yet, and was sold as is to the guy or guys who cached her."

"DNA?" Chad persisted. He may be ignorant about some things, but he knows how to educate himself. He's not afraid of asking questions some people might consider inane—he thinks the only stupid question is the unasked one.

"The examiner took tissue samples from the vic for that possibility, but he's not going to run a full DNA test unless there's some DNA to compare it with, like a relative's," Alex said. "Complete DNA tests are too expensive and take too long unless there's a good chance of getting a match. And when nobody's reported a relative missing, what's there to compare DNA with?"

Chad wasn't satisfied. "What about the DNA in the sperm?" he said. "Possibly her last john killed her. That would link killer and victim."

"Yes," Gil said patiently, "but the mere presence of sperm doesn't mean the owner of the sperm did the vic, just that they had a business relationship."

"It's circumstantial," Chad said, "but it *is* evidence." We all looked at him. The lad was learning fast.

"Again, what do we have?" Garner cut in. "Three dumped bodies. One of them clearly a homicide, but probably committed elsewhere before being brought to Porcupine County. Why 'probably'? For one thing, we don't have heavy-duty professional hookers like that up here. Not enough customers. She's got to be from one of the big cities. And she isn't exactly the kind of victim most police departments want to break their backs for." He sighed deeply.

Garner was just being honest. Like the rest of us in that room, he values human life and wants whoever had the evil effrontery to take it to pay for the crime. But he is also a practical man and knows that the resources of a financially pinched county will have to be allocated where they can do some good. We are forced to practice a kind of legal triage.

"So what can we do?" he asked.

"We can go deeper on that guy with the Beemer," I said.

"You have his name," Garner said.

"Arthur Kling," Camilo said, checking his notebook. I nodded. That was close enough to Klein, the name Sharon had given me during our tête-à-tête at the Lone Pine convenience store. She had had a snootful and couldn't remember clearly.

"Illinois DMV gives his address as Twenty-two ten North Remington Avenue in Chicago," Camilo continued. "That's a gentrified old neighborhood, the Chicago cops tell me, full of rehabbed condos popular with young professionals getting ready to settle down and raise families. But the cops have no sheet on him. He's clean."

"And all we have him on is being present at a place where we had found a body earlier."

"Not quite enough," Garner said. "We don't know that he was there at the same time the body was. Matter of fact, he probably wasn't, not if he was looking for a geocache. Only way to find out is to ask him."

"Yes, but grabbing him up for questioning might spook the other perps," I said, "so we've decided to move slowly on him."

"You sure there are others?" said the prosecutor.

"I think there has to be at least one other," I replied. "Those bodies are heavy. And there might be as many as seven perps, if those coins left on the body at Watersmeet mean what they might mean."

"Be that as it may," Alex said, "one of the perps just has to be local. I just know it. Yeah, it's possible to Google good hiding spots on the Internet, but even with that, the Poor Farm isn't the sort of place outsiders are likely to know about. That one is probably an inside job. Hell, it's got to be."

"So what now?" Garner leaned back in his oaken swivel chair. It squeaked.

"I'll go talk to Phil Wilson," I said. "Maybe he knows other geocaching fans in the county. Maybe one of them is our guy."

"I can check out Arthur Kling," Alex said. "I'll call in a marker at Chicago Homicide." The Chicago police automatically would send an investigator to question Kling if we asked, but a detective who owed a favor would try harder on an out-of-town request.

"You know any profilers, Alex?" I said. "If these are freaks we're dealing with, maybe a profiler can help us figure out what's going on in their heads."

The others glanced at me dubiously. Criminal psychological profilers are favorites of pulp fiction writers and television dramas, but many detectives in the field have doubts about them. They're not often much help catching perps, although they're terrific at shrinking their brains afterward. True, they have had successes, like psychics who divine where a body is buried. Cynical cops, however, argue that profilers and psychics come to their conclusions only after other people have done all the shoe-leather work, eliminating the impossibilities and leaving nuggets of truth for the shrinks and mediums to divine. I keep an open mind about them. So does Alex.

He nodded. "I'll talk to a good friend at Lansing who's a profiler. She's a pretty good psychologist and might have some ideas for us."

"Okay," said Garner. "We'll meet back here when somebody has something solid."

As the gathering broke up, Alex cornered me on the way out.

"Ten days to go," he said.

"To what?" I was just playing dumb, but Alex missed the joke.

"The *primary*, you idiot."

16 The moment of truth—at least the one about the election—was almost upon me.

"In Bergland last night," Alex said, "Eli was holding forth on WPRC"—the local FM station, devoted to country and talk—"about the three bodies that've turned up in Porcupine County that the deputies can't seem to identify. He said that if he was in charge that wouldn't have happened."

"The bodies or the identification?" I asked.

"He didn't say. He didn't have to."

"Not good."

"Not good. So you're going to have to tell Horace why Eli's wrong." With his chin Alex pointed to the *Herald* reporter, sitting patiently outside the sheriff's squad room, notebook in hand. "Good luck."

As Alex left, I beckoned Horace into the squad room and sat him in a chair next to my desk.

"What's on your mind?" I asked the reporter.

"You know perfectly well what's on my mind, Steve," said Horace, who actually is quite friendly toward me and never misses a chance to make me look good. Eli has offended him several times, more than once in a humiliating way. Horace is a dapper fellow, affecting colorful bow ties and suits in a place where the latter are worn primarily to funerals. Horace also fulminates against gays in the right-wing editorials he writes, but his dress once caused Eli to call him an "old queen" on a radio show. Whether or not Horace, a retired Milwaukee newspaperman, is that or just flamboyant, I don't know and don't care. He tries hard to be unbiased in his reporting and sometimes succeeds, but I am glad that when he fails, it is usually in my favor. But he had not endorsed me for sheriff in the colorful and highly conservative op-ed columns he writes when his dander is up. He knew that if Eli won, he'd have to get along with the old sheriff, so he tried not to offend him needlessly.

I did know what was on Horace's mind, but I played it coy. "Tell me," I said.

"Those bodies. You know. Last night Sheriff Garrow all but said you were incompetent."

Eli hadn't, not quite. Election etiquette in Upper Michigan doesn't permit direct attacks of that kind. But he had left the possibility dangling unsaid on the air where everybody could hear it. And Horace was running with that possibility, like the good reporter he is.

"Well, Mr. Wright," I said—I call him Horace most of the time but "Mr. Wright" when we're dealing with each other professionally—"you know very well I can't comment on an ongoing investigation. All I can tell you is that we have discovered three human bodies where they should not have been."

"I've heard they've been mutilated. How?"

Joe Koski may be a gossip, but he is a careful one. Most likely the information had come from a blabbermouth at the crime lab in Marquette. It happens. But the exact details hadn't gotten out.

"That will have to remain confidential for legal reasons," I said. That could be true, but the most important reason was that we didn't want the perps knowing we knew what we knew.

"Name one."

"*Mr. Wright!*" I had to laugh. Horace was a persistent cuss.

"All right, all right."

"But I can tell you that we believe that although the bodies were dumped in Porcupine and Gogebic Counties, the deaths took place elsewhere."

"So it is not a murder investigation?"

"I can't comment on that."

"Can you comment on what Sheriff Garrow said last night in Bergland?"

"Exactly what did he say?"

"Quote. 'If they hadn't run me off, I'd have got to the bottom of this long ago.' Unquote."

"All I will say about that is I'm surprised Sheriff Garrow thinks he was run off. He said he was taking a few days off a few months ago after the prosecutor asked him to stand aside and let somebody else run for the office, and he never bothered to come back. The rest of us go to work every day and do our jobs."

"Thanks, Steve," Horace said delightedly. "There's my lead." All I had voiced were facts that everyone knew—but facts neither candidate had articulated up to now.

And Horace's would be a good story, I was sure. He is an old pro. People would be clucking with excitement when the front-page leader was published the following Wednesday. What I had said was Porcupine County's version of a savage political counter-punch. It might even win me a few votes.

As Horace left, Joe Koski looked up, grinning, and gave me the thumbs-up sign.

17 Ginny and I were sitting in her kitchen that evening when Tommy bounced downstairs from his room in his Pony League uniform.

"Hello, Mr. Martinez," Tommy said gravely.

"Evening, Tommy. What've you been doing?"

"Surfing on the *wiinindibmakakoons*."

"And that is?" I said.

"*Ojibwemowin* for 'computer.' Means 'little brain box.'"

Ojibwemowin is the language of the Anishinaabe, the Ojibwe word for themselves. *Anishinaabe* means "Original People."

"I've heard something like that," I said. "An Ojibwe medicine man who once visited my cabin called my laptop a *windibaanens* and said that meant 'little brain machine.' I guess that means *Ojibwemowin* has more than one word for many things, just like English."

Tommy shot me one of those maybe-the-old-guy-isn't-as-dumb-as-I-thought-he-was looks the young of any culture often display when surprised by their elders.

"Find anything interesting?" I asked.

"Yes, an Anishinaabe story." Like most large surviving Native American tribes, the Ojibwe have committed much of their history and their culture to the World Wide Web. "It's the story about how the dog came to the Anishinaabe."

"Tell us."

Tommy scratched back a chair on the kitchen floor and sat down at the table. This would be a long story.

"Two Anishinaabe in a canoe got lost in a storm on the lake and were blown onto a strange beach," Tommy began, with the same faraway look I had seen in the eyes of all kinds of Indian storytellers. He recited from memory, not from a computer printout. This lad had been taught the traditions of his people and he knew how to repeat a narrative. His voice had subtly changed from a boy's to an Ojibwe storyteller's, almost a singsong, with inflections and colorations that added subtle meanings to nouns and verbs. Back on the reservation, he must have listened to the old ones tell the ancient tales, and their style clearly had made an impression on him. Maybe he would become a storyteller himself, one in much demand at powwows. I began to feel both envy and pleasure at his rootedness. An orphan Tommy may be, but he has a greater sense of belonging than I do. His links to his origins have never been broken.

"When they saw huge footprints on the beach, they were frightened," Tommy continued. "Soon a giant with a caribou hanging from his belt like a rabbit came walking down the beach. The giant told the Anishinaabe he was a friend and to come home with him. They were tired and hungry and had lost their weapons in the storm, so they followed the giant to his lodge.

"That night a *windigo* snuck into the lodge and told the Anishinaabe the giant had hidden other men away to eat them. The *windigo* pretended to be their friend, but he was actually the eater of people."

A *windigo,* I knew, was an evil spirit analogous to the demons of Christian teaching.

"But the giant would not give him the two men and grew angry. He took a big stick and turned over a big bowl with it. Out jumped an animal the Anishinaabe had never seen before. It looked like a wolf, but the giant called it 'Dog' and told it to kill the evil *windigo*. Dog shook himself and began to grow huge and fierce. He sprang at the *windigo* and killed him. Then Dog shrank down and crept back under the bowl.

"The Anishinaabe were so happy with what happened that the giant gave Dog to them, although he was his old buddy. He said Dog would take them home. They went to the beach and the giant gave Dog a command. Dog grew bigger and bigger until he was almost as big as a horse. The Anishinaabe held tight to the back of Dog as he ran into the water and hung on while he swam and swam for a long time.

"Many days later, Dog saw a part of the coast the Anishinaabe knew, so he headed for shore. As they came close to the beach, Dog shrank back to his normal size, so the Anishinaabe had to swim the rest of the way.

"When they reached shore, Dog disappeared into the forest. When the Anishinaabe told their tribe what had happened, the people thought the men were lying. 'Show us your little mystery animal,' the chief said, 'and we'll believe you.'

"A few moons rose and fell, and then one morning Dog returned to the two Anishinaabe. He allowed them to pet him and took food from their hands. The tribe was surprised to see the creature, and pleased. And Dog stayed with them.

"And that, as the Anishinaabe say, is how the dog came to the Earth to live with man."

"I love that story!" Ginny said, looking a bit confused. "What's the moral, though?"

"North American Indian stories don't necessarily have obvious morals, or even points, in the sense that Western European stories do," I said, unable to keep a touch of academic loftiness out of my voice. "But they're rich in irony. You have to think about them, let them sink into you."

Tommy nodded and glanced at me with another you're-not-as-stupid-as-I-thought expression. He was, I thought, putting me through some kind of a test. Or maybe the spirits were using him to send me a message about the growing mystery of the three corpses. There was a lot more to this lad than met the eye.

"I'm sure Lakota have a story very much like that," I said. "Maybe someday you can show me how to find it on the computer."

"Sure," Tommy said, and smiled. He was smiling at me more and more these days. I thought I was getting somewhere with him.

"Almost time for the ball game," Ginny said as a honk resounded from the driveway.

"See ya later!" Tommy said, suddenly a little boy again, and he dashed out the door to his ride.

When he was gone, I turned to Ginny and said, "There was a reason he told that story, but I don't know what it is. I had the distinct feeling I was being sent an important message."

"You are so dense, Stevie Two Crow, but I love you anyway."

"Huh?"

"Steve, Tommy was just telling us he wants a dog."

18

Two days later, after the usual conversation between a youngster and the adults in his life about responsibility for the dog's care, we came home from the Porcupine County Animal Shelter with a scrawny yellow Labrador mix someone had abandoned on the baseball diamond with a water bowl, a name tag that said "Hogan," and a paper sign around his neck that read "Free to a good home." Hogan, who the vet said was about three years old and weighed a rib-revealing sixty-five pounds, had the graceful, alert conformation of a Lab, and from a distance he could be mistaken for a purebred. But the vet said his deep-set teeth, broad chest, narrow waist, slim tail, basketball head, and steam-shovel chops suggested pit bull somewhere in his ancestry and probably not far back, either.

I had owned a couple of pitties as a boy, and I knew that the breed's reputation for viciousness was largely a myth fostered by unscrupulous personal injury lawyers, lazy cops, and a gullible and often cynical press that knew headlines such as "PIT BULL ATTACKS CHILD" sell newspapers. Cops, I knew, will often identify any rogue dog as a pit bull, even if it may have so little of that breed in it that it bears no resemblance to the real thing, for "pit bull" is easier to spell on a report sheet than "Viszla." Pitties were originally bred to fight other dogs, not people, and their noisy combativeness is almost always directed at fellow members of their species. It's true that drug dealers and other such lowlifes train pit bulls as attack dogs, but just about any breed can be cruelly goaded into such aggressiveness. Pitties' natural instinct is to cherish people, and when treated with kindness, they make great family dogs. I'd rather have a pit bull than a cocker spaniel, the breed that any vet will tell you bites people more often than any other.

From the first, Hogan was friendly enough with Ginny and me, but Tommy was clearly his main man. At home, boy and dog immediately became inseparable. Hogan lay under the desk while Tommy worked, under the table while Tommy ate, and by his bed while Tommy slept. Out on the beach, they played for hours, chasing each other up and down in great explosions of sand. Despite his Labrador genes, Hogan showed absolutely no interest in swimming and just gazed at Tommy in puzzlement when he threw a stick for the dog to fetch. Instead, Hogan displayed the pit bull's propensity for dashing about in happy abandon, butt tucked underneath, eyes rolling, ears flying. Everywhere and all the time he insisted on being petted, a task Tommy enjoyed, and he would sharply lever his massive muzzle up under our hands if we neglected his loving. "Grubbing," Tommy called it. Hogan was "the Grubber." He had both the Lab's sweet, clumsy nature and the pittie's unbridled, tail-wagging exuberance—a singular and sometimes dangerous combination for delicate objects on the coffee table, especially since he quickly filled out, soon reaching a solid eighty-five pounds of muscle and bone. When asked if he wanted to go for a walk or to be fed, Hogan would suddenly burst into an excited little dance Ginny called "the pit bull two-step," his claws drumming an Irish dancer's *rat-tat-tat* on the wooden floor. Tommy, I was coming to learn, was his own boy, and Hogan in turn was his own dog.

Ginny was pleased by the turn of events. "Tommy's an orphan," she said, "and Hogan's an orphan, and because of that they take care of each other in ways we can't even begin to imagine."

"Does it need to be as deep as that?" I asked. "Maybe they're just a boy and his dog."

"You could be right, Steve. But I don't think so. You always simplify things that can't be simplified and complicate things that don't need to be complicated."

I didn't argue.

19

"I've got bad news, Steve," Alex said without preamble on the phone from his office in Wakefield. "Arthur Kling seems to have taken a powder."

"Hmm?"

"About a week ago, my source in Chicago said, a neighbor saw him pack his car with camping gear and drive away. His boss at the Fidelity office in the Loop says he didn't put in for time off and just left."

"Anyone report him missing?"

"The boss. After two days, he got worried and called the Chicago police. That was about the same time my guy started looking for him."

"The neighbor or anybody else have any ideas where he might have gone?"

"Not a clue. He didn't tell anyone in his apartment complex where he was going, and when the cops got in, they found nothing that would suggest he wasn't coming back. It looked quite normal. He left clothes, possessions, fresh food in the fridge, all the sort of stuff anybody would come home to."

"What did the boss say about his behavior?"

"He said Kling's a good investment analyst, but shy and nervous, and in the last few weeks his mind seemed to be elsewhere. He's not the kind who makes friends in the office, and he didn't tell anybody what was going on in his life, so far as the boss knows."

"So he didn't know anything about Kling's hobbies?"

"Nothing, except that Kling seemed to be an outdoors type, a hiker. On casual Fridays he'd wear stuff from L.L.Bean, Lands' End, Cabela's, those stores. And a couple of times he left a phone number where he could be reached on weekends."

"What was it?"

"The Evergreen Lodge." That was a small lakefront mom-and-pop motel on M-64 close to the Wolverine Mountain Wilderness State Park in the western reaches of the county. A gentle elderly couple, the Lemppainens, owned and operated it.

"Check it out already?"

"Did I roll off the turnip wagon yesterday?" Alex said in irritation.

"Who knows?"

"He's not there."

"The Lemppainens have anything to say?" I asked.

"Not much. Kling was quiet, polite, kept to himself, was gone most of the time. Paid cash, though he reserved the rooms with a credit card. The Lemppainens didn't save the number and don't remember the bank."

"Damn. No other paper trail?"

"No. I got Garner to subpoena his Visa and MasterCard billings. Lots of mail-order, local Chicago stuff, but no meals, motels, or gas stations north of the Illinois-Wisconsin state line. He thinks he's a smart cookie, but he's not that clever if he left the Lemppainens' number with his boss. That puts him up here."

"And he's been seen by locals," I pointed out. "Slept with, too."

"Hmm. Maybe he wanted to establish his presence up here at a certain time, and hide it at other times. But why?"

I thought for a moment. "Did the Chicago cops find his computer?" Often a hard drive yields clues to the computer owner's plans. People confide things to their computers they'd never trust to a human being.

"No computer in the apartment," Alex said.

"Could've been a laptop," I said. "Maybe he took it along."

"But where would he go?"

"He's up here in the U.P. now," I said. "I'm almost certain of it."

"Why?"

"You know that returning to the scene of the crime is the most common thing perps do. It's their way of hoarding their own crap, of staying connected to the stuff that's important to them."

"Crap as in—oh, never mind."

"If we can find his car," I continued, "we'll likely find his computer, and I think it might tell us everything we need to know."

"Why are you so sure about that computer?" Alex asked. "Why are you so sure he even has one?"

"A talk I had with Phil Wilson the other day." I had dropped by the Ace Hardware and engaged its co-owner in conversation about geocaching. After a bit of isn't-it-a-nice-day to-and-froing, I asked Phil if he knew of any other geocaching fans in Porcupine County.

"Some," he had said tersely without looking at me. He rarely even glanced at the people he spoke to.

"Who are they?" I asked, pulling a chair into Phil's small office. This was going to take a while, and the pickings turned out to be slim.

He didn't know their names, he said. Most geocachers identify themselves on the Internet with pseudonyms. That's because they want to keep the focus on the sport, not on the participants. Besides, they also give themselves email addresses on Yahoo or Hotmail under invented names so that their personal addresses don't get choked by spam. So much for subpoenaing the membership lists of geocaching Web sites.

Phil said he had met a few fellow geocachers on the trails, and they were friendly enough, but they identified themselves only by their geocaching names. (Phil's was "Trailboss.") He did know of one other local geocacher by his real name—Willie Kemp, a young garage mechanic, husband of a checker in the supermarket, and the father of a little girl. I knew Willie, and while I wouldn't dismiss him entirely as a potential suspect—I learned not to do that years ago—I knew him well enough to doubt that he'd get involved in such a crime as we were investigating. And Phil himself was simple and guileless.

"If these guys who have been strewing bodies over the landscape have their own private Web site," I told Alex, "we'll find clues to it and its members on a computer. Maybe this Kling brought his laptop up here."

"*If* he has a laptop," Alex said.

"True."

"What now?"

"We go hunting for Kling. There's a BOL out for a red BMW, isn't there?" What other jurisdictions call All Points Bulletins, or APBs, we in the Upper Peninsula call Be on the Lookouts, or BOLs.

"First thing I did," Alex said.

"I'll go check with Sharon, that convenience-store clerk Kling got it on with at the dance in Coppermass. Possibly he's contacted her, although from what she said I doubt they'd ever hook up again."

"Do that."

I hung up, grabbed my cap, and walked out to the Explorer.

Twenty minutes later, I rolled up to the convenience store near Lone Pine, parked, and strode inside. The store's owner, an irascible old ex-miner named Mort Johnson, stood behind the counter. Sharon was nowhere in sight.

"Sharon?"

"She don't work here no more."

"Since when?"

"Since yesterday. She didn't come in for her eight-to-five shift and she didn't come in today neither. She won't never work here again."

"She give any notice?"

"None. Just disappeared. Goddammit, my arthritis is killing me. I can't cover for airhead bimbo employees no more."

"What do you know about her?"

"She said she came up here from La Crosse and had tended bar down there."

"You check that out? References?"

"Not really." Lazy bastard. I wondered if she invited Mort into the sack from time to time to keep her job.

"She ever say anything about herself?"

"Once when we were in— Once she said her parents were dead and she had no family."

"No photos of her?"

"No." Johnson looked at the floor, at the wall, everywhere but at me. I knew he was lying. Probably he had photographed or taped himself in bed with her. Without a warrant, though, I was helpless to search the place.

Suddenly a chill ran through my veins. Maybe Arthur Kling had returned to Porcupine County intending to make Sharon Shoemaker his newest geocache.

20

No sooner had I called Alex to ask him to add Sharon to the BOL than I suddenly recalled another election task to perform that very evening: to go up against Eli in a town meeting debate. Nobody in the county could remember the last time there had been such a to-and-fro among the candidates for sheriff. There usually isn't, because in recent decades most offices haven't been contested. But because he had nothing to lose, Eli had suggested going head-to-head, and Jenny Tompkins, the village clerk, had been enchanted with the idea. Not me.

I don't think Eli had ever had formal debate training, but I knew I faced a formidable adversary on the podium. For all his advanced age and often pickled condition, the sheriff was quick on his mental toes, and in front of a crowd exuded friendliness and confidence. As for me, I'm the kind of slow-thinking fellow who comes up with the perfect devastating retort hours after the best time to deliver it.

I feared taking a beating, especially since the ground rules Jenny had laid down said: "No personal attacks. Stick to the issues." Exactly what constituted a personal attack I wasn't sure, but I didn't think pointing out Eli's latter-day failings would please the good people of Porcupine County. Most of them thought of him fondly, and many were unaware of his recent peccadilloes. I would have to tread carefully. Politics in a small Upper Michigan town are pursued with considerably more civility than those on the state and national stages. That's because candidates and voters run into each other every day in the hardware store, at the supermarket, and in church. One just doesn't foul one's own nest with casual invective.

I dressed in my best uniform, because I knew Eli would be resplendent in gold braid and all the shiny emblems of membership in various organizations in the county and state he had joined purely for political reasons, never bothering to attend a meeting. He looks the part much more than I do, and if I hadn't known about his faults, I'd have been impressed, too.

Some three hundred people sat wall to wall in folding chairs in the American Legion Hall, hoping for blood, for this was as close to a dogfight as Porcupine County ever got. As the challenger I strode onto the raised stage first, to a chorus of cheers and clapping from—I hoped—at least half the audience. Few boos, and what there were got shushed by indignation. Porkies are much too polite for overt contempt of that kind. When Eli climbed onstage, his decorations twinkling in the lights, at least as many clapped and cheered. We shook hands, then everyone settled down.

Horace Wright, as the county's foremost (and only) political reporter, had been tapped as moderator. He sat at a small table, back to the audience, as Eli and I stood at lecterns a dozen feet apart. Horace opened the proceedings with all the relish of an announcer at a boxing match.

"In this corner," he boomed over the mike, "weighing about two hundred and ten pounds . . ."

The audience chuckled.

". . . stands Deputy Stephen Two Crow Martinez, candidate for sheriff of Porcupine County. At the other lectern is Sheriff Elias Anthony Garrow, candidate for reelection to the same office. Everyone knows them both. I'm just stating this for the record."

I drew myself up to my full six feet two—Horace had exaggerated my weight by only about ten pounds—and nodded bashfully at the audience. Eli beamed grandly. He did have a dazzling smile.

"Let me just state the qualifications of each candidate," Horace said, fingering a couple of index cards. "First, Deputy Martinez. Forty-four years old. Born in Pine Ridge, South Dakota, and raised in Troy, New York. A graduate of Cornell University and the criminal justice school at City University of New York. A veteran of three years in the military police of the United States Army, including service in Kuwait and Iraq during Desert Storm, rising to the rank of first lieutenant. A deputy sheriff in Porcupine County for almost a dozen years. A member of the Porcupine County Rod and Gun Club and the Porcupine County Historical Society." He turned over the card, looking for more memberships. There weren't any. I've never been much of a joiner.

"And now Sheriff Garrow. Seventy-four years old. Born in Porcupine City and raised in Bruce Crossing. Attended Michigan Tech. Two years in the United States Army, rising to the rank of sergeant. A Vietnam veteran. Forty-seven years of service in Upper Michigan law enforcement, including twenty-four years as sheriff of Porcupine County. Married for forty-seven years. Seven children, nineteen grandchildren. A member of St. Matthew's Episcopal Church in Porcupine City, the American Legion, the Veterans of Foreign Wars, the Michigan Sheriffs Association . . ." Listing all of Eli's mostly specious memberships took seemingly a full minute.

"Here's how we're going to do this," Horace said when he finally came up for air. "I'll ask one question of each candidate, who will have two minutes to answer the question. The other candidate will have one minute to rebut. Then I'll throw the floor open to questions from the audience. Same rules—two minutes to answer, one to rebut. That okay with you both?"

Eli and I nodded.

"Now then. We all know that in the last few years, state and federal funds for rural law enforcement have been drastically cut. How do you think the Porcupine County Sheriff's Department should deal with this? Deputy Martinez, you first."

I took a deep breath. This was the biggest question on everybody's mind, and Gil and I had gone over my answer carefully. Whatever I said, I was to propose *no new taxes.*

"In the last year, the department has had to let two vacancies for deputies go unfilled and spread the work of the rest around as much as it can to cover the gaps," I said. "Everyone knows that. We had no choice."

I looked over at Eli. He nodded. This had happened on his watch, but it wasn't his fault.

"So we've had five deputies cover the eight-to-four and four-to-midnight watches, two on each watch," I said. "We pulled the single deputy off the midnight-to-eight watch during the week, because nothing much ever happens after midnight, except on weekends, of course. There's always a dispatcher, who also works as jailer, on each of the three watches. Two of us are always on call if we're needed. But with two deputies short, there's little coverage for vacations or sickness. We have to put in a lot of overtime. Until we get more money, I don't see this pattern as changing. But we're managing."

I nodded to Horace, yielding the floor.

"Eli?" Horace said.

"The deputy is right," he said, jabbing his finger toward me and then toward the audience, "but there's a solution. It's to be more aggressive in seeking grant money for personnel. I promise that if I'm reelected, we'll find enough money to field a full complement of deputies, and that we'll always have two deputies out on patrol twenty-four hours a day, seven days a week. The safety of Porcupine County is our number one priority. I promise you that."

Much of the audience clapped. They didn't know that thanks to draconian federal belt-tightening, grant money for police personnel had all but dried up all over the state of Michigan. I should have mentioned that in my answer, but I'm not a debater. I should have pointed out that Sheriff Eli Garrow had had plenty of time to write grants but hadn't been in the office for weeks to do so, but I'm not a debater. I think of all this stuff too late, for I'm not a debater. And so Eli took the first round on points.

"Thank you," Horace said. "Now, Sheriff, here is my question for you. What do you think is the most important task of the sheriff of Porcupine County?"

I was appalled. That was practically a gift, the kind of question that could be answered easily with ringing campaign slogans. But Horace was smarter than that.

Eli rose to the bait. "Why, to make Porcupine Countians feel safe!" he declared. "To have law enforcement on the job twenty-four seven. And the best way to do that is to have a sheriff who's been in the county all his life, who's raised a family here, who goes to church here, who's one of us!" He beamed a triumphal smile out over the audience, a good part of which broke into applause.

"Deputy Martinez, your rebuttal?" I could have sworn Horace winked at me as he fed me the ball like a quarterback at the line of scrimmage. And I didn't drop it.

I looked directly at Eli and said, "The most important task of a sheriff is to be on the job twenty-four seven, to be in his office every day doing administrative work so that his undersheriff and his deputies can be out there attending to the safety of all residents of Porcupine County. For reasons you will have to ask him about, the current sheriff has not been seen in his office for almost five months. The undersheriff has been doing the job instead, and so have the deputies. This is not an accusation of anything. This is a simple statement of fact."

The entire audience gasped. Chairs skidded back, and both

my cheering section and Eli's roared. The sheriff blanched. Horace pounded his table with the gavel until everyone had settled down. Round two to me.

"All right then," Horace said. "Now we will entertain questions from the audience."

A sea of hands shot up. Horace pointed to a small, gray-haired woman in the front row. "Peggy Toivonen," he said, "what's your question?"

Most of the audience winced. Peggy Toivonen was an irascible octogenarian who lived alone in a little house on Norwich Road, and like so many of her age, she thought the world revolved around her, and she looked at local, national, and world issues entirely in their capacity to affect her personally. And she didn't disappoint our expectations. Peggy levered herself to her feet with her cane and demanded, "When's the county going to fix my driveway? The highway plows carved it up last winter and nobody's come out to fix it!"

"Now, Peggy," said Horace, "that's a matter for the road department, not the sheriff."

"Let me answer!" Eli bellowed. "Mrs. Toivonen, I'll make sure it gets fixed. You go home and get a good night's sleep. I'll take care of everything."

Horace looked hopefully at me for the rebuttal.

"Horace is right," I said. "Road repairs are properly the job of the road department. I can't imagine the sheriff having anything to do with that. We've got crime to fight."

"Hey—" Eli tried to cut in.

"Sorry, Sheriff," Horace said. "You had your two minutes. Other questions?" Hands shot up. Horace chose one. "Will Brenner, what's on your mind?" I darted a glance at Horace. Brenner, a retired Bergland contractor, was a Garrow cousin, a hostile. But Horace knew what he was doing.

"This question is for Deputy Martinez. Can you give me a rundown of the changes in crime rates in Porcupine County over the last ten years?" I could see the setup coming, but I was ready for it.

"Yes. Burglaries are down seven percent, petty larceny eight percent, general misdemeanors nine percent," I said, enumerating a dozen classifications. I'd anticipated the question and had looked up the figures that morning. "There were just four murders, same as in the previous ten years. Things have gotten quieter."

"And that all happened on my watch!" Eli interrupted with perfect timing. Cheers broke out.

Horace went to work with his gavel. "You're out of order, Eli!"

"I'm not finished, Sheriff," I said. "The crime rates are down across the board in Porcupine County because the population fell almost ten percent in those ten years. There are just fewer of us to commit offenses. Actually, when the drop in population is factored in, the rate of offenses is about the same as it was a decade ago. People have pretty much stayed the same."

Horace turned to the sheriff. "Eli?"

"No answer," Eli said, quietly fuming. Round three to the deputy.

Hands shot up again, and Horace chose one. "What's yours, Emily Hahn?" he asked.

"This is for Sheriff Garrow," said the middle-aged housewife from Green. "We know that three bodies have been found in Porcupine County in the last few weeks. All we have heard is that the sheriff's department thinks they died outside the county and were just dumped there. What's going on?"

That the question had been addressed to Eli and not me suggested that Emily, and probably many other voters, didn't get it: Eli was sheriff in name only. He wouldn't know what was going on, not if he didn't come into the office for briefings. And his answer proved his ignorance, although I wasn't sure Emily understood.

"If I'm reelected, Emily," Eli said with a broad smile, "people won't be dumping bodies in our wonderful county. You can count on that."

"That's not an answer!" shouted someone in the audience.

"They're dumping 'em *now* and you're the sheriff!" shouted another. Not all of the audience bought Eli's smoke screens. Horace pounded his gavel.

When the room settled down, Horace turned to me and said, "Care to rebut, Deputy?"

"I'm sorry, everyone," I said, and I echoed my words to Horace a few days before. His story was scheduled to appear the following morning. "I cannot comment on an ongoing investigation. I can tell you, however, that the investigation has reached a sensitive phase. I can assure you all that when we are finished we will give you all the facts."

That was a slick evasion, though all of it was true, and it surprised me that I had the wit to come up with that meaningless "sensitive phase." Maybe I had been hanging around Eli Garrow too much. Maybe I was turning into a politician. Round four to me, though.

The questions resumed. "Where do you stand on abortion?" Father Jim Sweet wanted to know. Even at the lowly county level, candidates all around the United States these days are always asked where they stand on hot cultural issues. For many voters, a candidate's character is more important than his actions, and they measure that character by how close the candidate's publicly announced beliefs on the issues of the day are to their own, no matter how irrelevant they may be to the office he is seeking.

"I am sworn to uphold the law," I said, "and uphold the law I will." The priest sat back down, clearly annoyed at the rope-a-dope answer.

"I'm against abortion," Eli said in rebuttal, "but the law's the law. I can't do anything until the law's changed. I'll do everything I can to change the law."

Several members of the audience snickered. How a lowly county sheriff in an obscure corner of the Upper Midwest was going to present an argument to the United States Supreme Court to overturn *Roe v. Wade* beggared the imagination.

"How about ho-mo-sex-u-al marriage?" someone in the crowd shouted. Michigan had outlawed that in the state in the last election but many Michiganders wanted an amendment to the United States Constitution as well.

"You're out of order!" said Horace, banging his gavel. He pointed at another man in the back. "What's *your* question?"

"How about it, then, Eli? How about homosexual marriage?"

"An abomination," Eli said. "It'll never happen while I'm sheriff." He fulminated on, warning against the dangers to the American family of unwitting incest, unbridled public sodomy, and the rest of the bogeymen the subject tends to bring up in people who feel strongly about the issue.

"Deputy?" Horace prompted.

"Edna?" I called. Edna Juntunen was the longtime county clerk and the issuer of marriage licenses. I had spotted her while walking into the hall.

"Yes, Steve?" She stood up in the middle of the audience, an upright little woman everyone respected, for she never acted as if she thought her job was a right, although she certainly considered it a duty.

"Edna, how many gay or lesbian couples have come to you in the last ten years asking for marriage licenses?"

"None. No sirree. Not one."

"I have to congratulate the sheriff," I said. "It all happened on his watch."

The place rang with laughter and Eli looked poleaxed.

The appointed ending hour having arrived, Horace gaveled the meeting to a close as the audience stirred restlessly, people squabbling among themselves. As we left the stage, Horace beamed at me, as if I'd been the winner by a TKO.

At the door, Edna patted my hand. "You done good, Steve."

"I hope so."

"I know so," she said. "You showed up that old blowhard for what he is. A lot of people had their eyes opened tonight."

I went home feeling pretty good about the events of the day, so good I forgot all about Sharon Shoemaker until the next morning.

21

Stewing at my desk the next day, baffled and frustrated by the three corpses and worried about the fate of Sharon Shoemaker, I had an idea. To get a feel for the sport, I'd go geocaching and hide a treasure in the woods myself. Maybe that'd give me some insight into our perps' modus operandi—how they chose their sites, for instance. It was time to get aggressive instead of just reacting to events. The smart lawman tries to head the bad guys off at the pass, not chase them through it.

Besides, I didn't know what else to do.

And so on my day off the following Saturday, I stopped by Ginny's to pick up a rucksack and raid her refrigerator for a bit of lunch before starting off into the woods.

"And where are we going?" Ginny said, her eyes widening as I constructed a towering sandwich out of salami, lettuce, tomatoes, mustard, and slices from a loaf of Russian black bread she had scored the previous day in Rhinelander. "That looks good."

"We?"

"The editorial we, I mean. I have things to do at the Historical Society this afternoon."

"Bummer. You'd have fun."

At that, the front door opened and Tommy marched in, Hogan lolloping by his side and bouncing off my legs.

"Why don't you take him along?" Ginny said.

"Well . . ."

"Take me along where?"

What the hell. I could use the company. "The woods," I said. "I'm going to try this geocaching thing."

"Cool," Tommy said. "Now I can see if my new GPS works."

"Oh, it does, I'm sure," I said. Ginny had bought Tommy an inexpensive used GPS, a simple hiker's model, during a previous shopping foray to Rhinelander. With it, the delighted lad had taken so many waypoint fixes along the beach that the unit ran out of room to store them and he had to purge the memory for new ones. Now he could go into the woods and fix some fresh new waypoints.

"Can Hogan go, too?"

"I don't see how I can prevent that from happening," I said as the dog companionably leaned his bulk against my leg and licked my hand.

"Double cool. What are you going to cache?"

"Uh . . . I hadn't thought about that yet."

Tommy clearly had. "Ginny, can I have a bowl?" he said. "One of those things with a plastic lid?"

From a kitchen cabinet, she fished out a squarish Tupperware cake container with a lid, ten inches long by eight inches wide and three inches deep. "Will this do?"

"Yes!" Tommy said. "It'll be great."

"What are we going to put in it?" I asked.

"Toys," he said. "A notebook and a couple of pencils."

He rummaged in a kitchen drawer and came up with a couple of spools, a rubber bathtub duckie, an STP key ring, a folding corkscrew from a Paris hotel, a couple of Heineken coasters, a two-year-old road map of Michigan, a blank CD, two dime-store earrings, a tiny screwdriver, a comb, a Schoolhouse Rock children's book, two Hot Stuff balloons, a bag of ore pellets from a mine in Ishpeming, three refrigerator magnets, a roll of Velcro tape, and, finally, a spiral notepad and two golf pencils.

With a felt-tip pen, he wrote on a note card:

> THIS IS A GEOCACHE.
>
> *The name of the cache is TallBear's Cache.*
>
> *If you do not play, please put the box back where you found it. Thank you.*
>
> *If you play, take something but leave something. Write down in the notebook your name and the date. Write down what you took and what you left. Then put the box back. Then go to TallBear's Cache on www.cache-it.com and write that you found it.*
>
> *Thank you. TallBear.*

"Is that your caching nickname?" I said.

"Yup." Tommy taped the card to the underside of the container lid and sealed the box. "There," he said. "Once we've hidden it, we'll take down the GPS waypoint coordinates and then put them on the Web site."

"You sure seem to know what you're doing," I said.

"I read up on it on the Internet," he replied.

Ginny smiled proudly. This boy did not lead a life of cultural isolation, as did so many youngsters on Indian reservations. His connections extended into the now and the future as well as the past. Tommy was a thoroughly modern American kid.

"All right. Let's go. Bring Hogan's leash."

We drove east to Porcupine City and south on U.S. 45 to Bruce Crossing, then headed west on M-28. Half an hour after leaving Ginny's home, we stopped at the entry to a snowmobile trail that led deep into the Ottawa National Forest. In the summers, the path was used by hikers and four-wheeler all-terrain vehicles, and at any time of the year it carved an easily visible trail through the woods and brush.

As Tommy clipped Hogan's leash to his collar, I reached into the glove box and fished my .357 Combat Magnum out of its leather holster. Checking the cartridges, I slipped the revolver into my fanny pack. We set off northward on the snowmobile/ATV trail, Tommy checking our progress on a hiker's topographical map with his handheld GPS as we strode in tandem atop the flat and level dirt track that plunged into the brush ahead. I carried my GPS, too, but I let Tommy do the trailblazing. The boy quickly picked up the trick of finding our spot on Earth by comparing the GPS readout with the latitude and longitude ticks on the edges of the map. I grasped one end of Hogan's leash, but the dog trotted ahead alongside Tommy, as if they were joined at the hip. From time to time, just to be companionable, he clumsily bumped against Tommy, throwing the boy off his stride, but Tommy didn't mind and rumpled Hogan's ears whenever that happened.

"Heads-up, Tommy!" I said just before the lad, his head down as he watched the numbers change on his GPS, crashed into a sapling that had fallen over the track. "Gotta watch where you're going, too!"

He grinned, amused and embarrassed at the same time. Smart, and can laugh at himself, too.

After a while, we hove alongside a clump of aspen I knew well. "Tommy, can you see what's in there?"

"Yeah. What's that?" Through the aspen, we could see a rusty metal standard, ten feet high, atop which was bolted a splintered wooden V that once had been painted white, one arm of the V broken off halfway.

"An old railroad whistle post," I said. "This trail was a logging railroad a hundred years ago, and the engineers blew their locomotive whistles as they passed by the post so that people down the tracks would know a train was coming. Somehow, when the railroad was abandoned long ago and the tracks and signs were torn up, the salvagers missed the post. And everybody who walks along this trail never sees it, because you've got to be looking for it to see it. Only a few people know about it, and now you're one of them."

For a moment, Tommy didn't answer. He was, I knew, contemplating the small gift I had bestowed upon him: I had entrusted him with special knowledge. Then he turned to me, smiled, reached out a hand, and touched my sleeve. It was his silent way of saying "Thanks." For Indians, gestures are as important as words and sometimes say more.

Hogan looked up at us both and wagged his tail.

"Let's press on," I said.

Forty-five minutes after setting out, we reached a clearing where the trail dipped as it forded the west branch of the Porcupine River, really a narrow but deep creek this far upstream. A steep rapids had carved its way between two low ridges, part of the Trap Hills, and the water gurgled as it pirouetted, corkscrewed, and stair-stepped over basalt boulders and sandstone slabs.

"This looks like a good place to hide the cache," I said. "A GPS antenna would have a pretty clear view of the sky. But where's a good spot? What about here?" I pointed under a low overhang a dozen feet from the water.

"Too low," Tommy said. That surprised me.

"How do you know?" I asked.

"Look at the mark up there on the ridge. The water gets up to there in the spring when the creek floods."

He was right. Tommy Standing Bear had been born to the forest. Someone had taught him woodcraft, maybe his father, maybe the uncle who was waiting to take him in.

"So where's a better spot?" I asked.

"Let's look around."

"Under that downed tree?" I said. Just like the cache near Watersmeet.

"Too easy," Tommy said. "That'd be the first place anybody would look. Got to make it harder."

"You've been studying up on this, haven't you?"

"Yup."

Hiding something in plain sight is an art. The trick is to find a spot the normal eye would quickly pass over at first, but one that, upon finally being found, turns out to be the most logical and obvious hiding place yet causes the finder to marvel at the cleverness of the hider. And Tommy found it.

It was a twenty-by-ten-foot level stretch of broken shale, flat gray rock that had been part of the original streambed millions of years ago. The shale had been shattered by weathering into irregular pieces ranging from the size of a pie plate to a manhole cover. Deep potholes pocked the gaps between the pieces. The shale stood well above the high-water mark.

"This looks about right," said Tommy, who fell to his knees and pulled the Tupperware container from his rucksack. He placed it into a pothole of sufficient depth and dragged a nearby slab of shale over it, strewing a few more pieces around.

"It's perfect, Tommy. Nobody's going to find it unless they're looking hard for it, and it'll take 'em a while. There's no trampled grass or packed down dirt to give away the spot."

"Yeah!" The lad's smile was the broadest I'd seen yet on his handsome little face.

"All right, let's measure a waypoint."

Tommy stood atop the cache with his GPS and called out the coordinates showing on the device's screen as I wrote them on a notepad. He walked a hundred feet south, stopped, then returned to the original spot, again calling out the coordinates he read from the GPS. He repeated the procedure, walking a hundred feet west, then north, then south. We looked at the four coordinates I had recorded. All of them showed numbers identical to the second decimal place, but varying slightly over the third. A possible twenty-foot error, quite accurate for a hiker's GPS.

With pencil and paper, Tommy averaged the coordinates. Finally, he levered up the slab, pulled the container out, and wrote the final coordinates on the note card taped to the inside of the lid. Then he replaced container and slab and smoothed his handiwork.

"Easy to get to," I said, "but not so easy to find."

"Not so easy to find," Tommy said agreeably.

"Okay, let's start back."

We had not gone a hundred yards when Tommy again plucked at my sleeve.

"Steve!" he said in a harsh whisper. It was the first time he had called me by my first name. "Look!"

Four adult gray wolves gazed down at us from scarcely a hundred feet away at the top of a high ridge. They were beautiful specimens, their coats thick and healthy, their almond-shaped yellow eyes fixed on ours. They made no sound. We made no sound. They did not move. We did not move. Humans and animals held each other's stares for long seconds. Hogan, who had neither seen nor smelled the wolves, sat unconcernedly on his haunches, gazing into the creek below. Then slowly I reached into my fanny pack and pulled out the .357.

Most Porkies never bother to carry weapons into the woods unless they're actively hunting, and I don't either, but this trip was different, for we had Hogan with us. Gray wolves have returned to the Upper Peninsula and have established so many new packs that the federal government has removed them from the endangered species list so that their numbers can be controlled by hunting. Wolves will attack any dogs they encounter, for they consider their fellow canines competitors for food and territory. The .357 was simple insurance that any such meeting would not end unhappily.

Pointing the .357 downward, I said in a low whisper, "Let's

go, Tommy. Keep your eye on the wolves and don't run. Walk slowly."

We moved away down the track. The wolves trotted silently along the ridge, watching and following us as we passed below. One of the animals split away and ran farther down the outcropping ahead of us, as if to set up an ambush.

Then the wind shifted and Hogan caught their scent. First his hackles rose all along his back, then he emitted a low growl, followed by a growing snarl full of rocks and nails, and finally a heavy bark, like the backfire of a dump truck. The wolves answered with vicious snarls, baring yellow teeth. Hogan strained at his leash and I had to set my feet against his powerful pull. He was ready to rumble.

Some of his ancestors had been bred for fighting, and he was all muscle and sinew, with powerful jaws. Possibly he could acquit himself well against a lone wolf—but not a pack of them. Two or more operating in tandem would make short work of the biggest and strongest domestic dog.

And that is why I had brought the .357. Not to save Tommy and me, for wolves rarely attack human beings, but to protect Hogan.

"Stand back, Tommy," I said. "Cover your ears."

Into soft ground a few feet away I fired two rapid shots, the heavy cough of the Magnum shattering the silence and reverberating throughout the woods. The wolves quickly turned tail and fled, the curtains of the forest swiftly closing behind them as if they had never been there.

Hogan, I noticed, alerted at the shots but did not spook, as most dogs would have. He had almost certainly spent his puppyhood in a household with guns, probably a hunter's. There was so much we didn't know about him. But what we did know was encouraging.

Quickly I ejected the two spent cartridges from the revolver's cylinder and replaced them with fresh loads. We wouldn't need the weapon again that day, I thought, but better to be safe than sorry.

I looked at Tommy. He stood calmly, no fear on his face, no relief at having survived what many non-Indians would have considered a potentially dangerous encounter with powerful wild beasts. Instead, he gazed at me with that unreadable expression I had grown used to in his presence.

"Think I did the right thing?" I said.

He didn't hesitate. "Yeah. No point killing them. They did what they're supposed to do. They checked us out and then they left."

I was silently impressed. This boy knew how to live with his fellow creatures. He had been taught well. He was a native of the forest, at one with his environment, an existence I was often painfully conscious of not sharing.

"Let's head back now, Tommy," I said. "We've done what we set out to do."

We trudged back to my Jeep, the Magnum in my right hand and pointing downward, ready if the wolves backtracked and attacked—which I doubted they would. That species may be fearless, but it is not stupid. From time to time, Hogan stopped, looked back, and growled a soft warning. But the wolves did not reappear.

22

On the Sunday two days before the primary election, I went hunting—hunting for speeders. I didn't have to look far, either. Like ducks to a gunner in a blind, they flew to me in the sheriff's Explorer, parked on a dirt road screened from the highway by high bushes, my radar tracking them as they sped by. The speeders, mostly from Minneapolis, Milwaukee, and Chicago and used to driving thirty miles an hour over the limit on the interstates around those cities, ignored the fifty-five-miles-per-hour limit on the broad but still two-lane M-64 and tromped their accelerators. I ignored the drivers doing sixty-five and seventy as not worth the trouble and concentrated on those zooming along at eighty and eighty-five, where the fines were in three figures and would help Porcupine County's lean coffers the most. After nailing one driver, I drove back, and almost before I had parked, the radar chirped as another sped past at better than eighty. If duck hunting were like this, I thought, I'd be up to the tops of my hip boots in mallards before the day was out.

I cut slack for none of the drivers, either. If they gave me lip, I asked politely if they were looking for a citation for failure to cooperate with a police officer. There's no such offense. The real one is obstruction of an officer in the performance of his duties, but pissing and moaning is just bad manners. Only the lawyers among them knew that, and up here in the wild North they were fortunately few and far between. If the offenders were polite and contrite, I'd sometimes knock five miles per hour off the citation, especially if they were residents of Porcupine County.

Two were a couple of local teenagers seeing how fast their old but freshly tuned pickup could go, and I not only wrote them up for every mile per hour they had gone over the limit, but I also laid upon them my well-practiced Dutch-uncle speech, which I had polished with the hides of hundreds, maybe thousands, of young men and women over the years. It had mostly to do with endangering not only their own lives but also those of innocents, and I drove home the point by showing them several grisly eight-by-ten color photographs of accident victims I carried in the Explorer's glove compartment, winding up my little talk by saying, "See, you wouldn't want to be decapitated or disemboweled like them, would you now?" Sometimes they staggered off to the bushes and lost their lunches, but most of the time they just sat in their seats, pale and shaking. Rarely did I ever have to stop them again.

I had just cited the fourteenth offender of the morning when the radio crackled. "Steve, car fire at Page Falls," Joe Koski said. "Silverton's on the way." That meant the single wheezing pumper that constituted the entire equipage of the Silverton Volunteer Fire Department had already trundled out of its tumbledown garage and departed for the scene, and I quickly swung the Explorer onto M-64 and accelerated west at ninety, siren keening and strobes flashing. Drivers ahead of me hit their brakes and pulled off onto the verge, guilty expressions on their faces as I sped by.

Within ten minutes, I pulled up at the dirt road that deadends at the falls a few miles west of southbound M-64 and six miles south of Silverton. The latest "TO PAGE FALLS" highway sign was gone, as I expected. They never last more than a few days before being uprooted and carried away by a furious Porky. Page Falls, a breathtakingly beautiful glade on the Agate River flowing northward through the Wolverine Mountain Wilderness State

Park and eventually Lake Superior, is a place Porkies cherish as their very own secret.

For approximately three hundred yards through an opening in the forest canopy, the Agate winds and tumbles down three layers of prehistoric shale, dropping nineteen feet to a broad trout pool full of fat brookies we mostly leave alone, for fear strange anglers that follow us might discover the gorgeous glen. Spray from the falls wreathes the place in mist, and through it the setting sun on a summer's evening intensifies and saturates the colors of the forest, turning Page Falls into what we consider the nearest thing to heaven on Earth.

It is true that Porcupine County's shaky economy depends heavily on tourism—campers and hikers in the summer and skiers and snowmobilers in the winter—and we are eager to share our natural beauties with these visitors. But there are some special places we never tell outsiders about, and Page Falls is one of them. It is such a beautiful wonder of nature and so ecologically delicate that the unspoken and long-standing rule is never to congregate there in large numbers for fear of damaging its glories. We Porkies visit the falls alone or in twos, limiting the numbers of our visits to one or two a year, and we rarely encounter others there.

I had lived in Porcupine County for almost ten years before Ginny vouchsafed the secret to me after making me swear on my parents' graves that I would never reveal its location to anyone except a true Porky. The state highway department, however, brooks no such homegrown sentimentality, and it regularly erects a new sign directing M-64 traffic to the falls. The road guys, most of whom live outside the county, complain bitterly that law enforcement in Porcupine County deliberately refuses to hunt down the sign thieves. It's true that we don't try very hard, but we just tell the highway boys we're doing our best.

It takes a good ten minutes to bounce over the rocky two miles from M-64 to the falls, and the odor of burning automobile, an amalgam of charred metal, melted plastic, and smoldering rubber, grew stronger the farther I drove. By the time I pulled up in the Make-out Meadow, as we called the narrow verge of grass and gravel between the dirt road and the river just below the falls where Porky teenagers occasionally parked to neck and pet, the Silverton firefighters had struck the blaze. Heavy, sooty black smoke had given way to billows of white vapor, itself dwindling under the onslaught of water from the pumper, asthmatically inhaling its supply from a hose dropped into the river.

The hulk of the automobile stood squarely in the center of the single-lane track off the verge, its passenger side parallel to the river. It clearly had not been parked before the fire started.

Peggy Strauch, the Pine Yard Inn's owner and captain of the fire volunteers, stepped over to me, streaks of soot around her eyes giving her the look of a cute raccoon. "Looks like it was set, Steve," she said. "Much too hot to have been an engine fire. I'm sure we'll find accelerant."

"Like what?"

"Gasoline, probably."

"Think it's an insurance scam?" People who can't make the installments on expensive automobile loans sometimes destroy the vehicles, by fire as well as other means, so that the insurance covers the payments.

"No."

I looked at Peggy. Sweet as she is, she's one of those people who are naturally stingy with their words. She's perfectly forthcoming, but you have to ask questions to get answers. She won't volunteer them.

"All right. Why?"

"There's a body in the driver's seat."

"Jeez. Couldn't you have let me know that first?"

"You didn't ask."

"Well, damn. What make of car?"

"Beemer."

Immediately I strode over to the still smoldering car. Enough paint remained near the sills to show that it had once been cherry red, and the distinctive BMW grille had not burned away.

"Plates?" I asked.

With a gloved hand, Peggy wiped soot and ash off the front license tag, careful not to burn herself. The car was still hot.

REBEMER.

"I know this car," I said. "Belongs to a guy we've been looking for."

"Maybe he's the cinder behind the wheel," Peggy said neutrally. I wasn't surprised by her studied nonchalance. She had seen more than her share of ugly death as an emergency medical technician in the Minneapolis Fire Department before moving to the Upper Peninsula. EMTs, like cops, hide their emotions behind a veneer of cynicism to help them get through the night.

"Let's take a look." I peered into the window of the driver's side, holding my breath against the smell of burnt flesh.

Indeed it was a cinder. The body behind the melted steering wheel had nearly been incinerated. Fire had shrunk it to almost half its size. It leaned to the left, against the driver's doorjamb and the left windowsill. The eyeless head, now not much bigger than a softball, faced out from the car at a forty-five-degree angle. I took a closer look at the face. Lips and nose had been burned away, but enough probably remained of the teeth for dental identification. It was impossible to identify the sex of the corpse.

Stepping to the other side of the car, I played my Maglite on the corpse. Much of the back of the head had been reduced to coals, but a large scooped-out indentation suggested that a projectile, probably a rifle-caliber bullet, had carried away some of the occiput before the fire. On a line with the angled position of the head, one of the charred headrest supports had been broken—maybe by the same bullet that possibly had killed the driver.

I straightened up. "I don't know who this is yet," I told Peggy, "but I think we're looking at murder."

Back at the Explorer, I radioed Joe Koski.

"Joe? Steve. I'm at the car fire. It's a Beemer. And there's a corpse behind the wheel. Please call the staties at Wakefield and raise Sergeant Kolehmainen. We need him. Looks like homicide."

"Yeah. Just a sec."

I waited.

Barely sixty seconds later, Joe radioed back. "Alex's on his way."

"Thanks. Now would you send Chad out here? We need a block at the junction of M-64 and the road to Page Falls." No use letting gapers near the crime scene to gum up the works and slow us down.

Forty minutes later, Alex arrived in his Ford Police Interceptor, escorted by a state police Suburban carrying two other troopers.

"What's doing?"

I told him.

"Hmm."

Two hours passed as Alex and his comrades meticulously did their thing, I watching closely as the troopers carefully combed the area in a hundred-yard radius.

"I think you're right," Alex said presently, holding up a shapeless lump of copper with a pair of tweezers. "This is likely the bullet that killed the vic before the perp torched the car. Found it in what's left of the backseat. Too bad it's melted. That'll prevent us from matching it to a weapon. But maybe the forensics guys can find traces of copper from the bullet in the body. At least that'll be a start."

"Male or female?" I asked Alex, fearing the answer.

"Male. Enough pelvis remains to tell us that."

I breathed a sigh of relief. Not Sharon Shoemaker, then.

"Arthur Kling?"

"Most likely. A stiff behind the wheel is usually the owner of the car. The teeth'll clinch it, but here's a pretty good preliminary ID."

Alex held up the charred, partly melted remains of a Rolex. "Found this on the floor between the driver's seat and the window. Look on the back."

"A.K. 8-17-95" said the engraving.

"Fits. Kling was wearing a Rolex at Jerry and Adela's party."

We looked at the watch in silence. Then I spoke for both of us. "Um. Then who? And why?"

"Hell if I have any idea," Alex said. "We're back at square one."

"See where the car is," I said. "The driver never parked it on the verge. If you ask me, he had just driven in. The driver's-side window's rolled down. That suggests to me that someone stepped out of the woods to the left and a little in front and hailed the driver, who stopped the car and rolled down the window to answer him. And when the perp came close enough, he put a bullet through Kling's—the victim's, 'scuse me—head from that oblique angle as the driver was looking toward him."

Alex nodded. "Makes sense."

"What's more," I said, "either the shooter was local or a local was with him. He, or they, must have told the vic—if he indeed is Kling, he's an outsider—about Page Falls and invited him here for a meeting or something. Maybe to cache another body."

Alex looked at me. "No sign of a cache."

"Maybe Kling, if that's him, was meant to be the cache and something went wrong."

"I'm not able to connect the fire with that," Alex said. "Nobody was out here. The killer could have done the job with plenty of time and privacy if this guy was meant to be a cache."

"I think you're right. Maybe there had been a falling out elsewhere and this was where the shooter wanted to end it. That would work for someone who stepped out of the trees as the car arrived and fired quickly."

"But why Page Falls?" Alex said. "There have got to be thousands of other secluded spots in Porcupine County that are better suited to bumping off people."

"Let me think out loud some more. Maybe the killer and the vic agreed that Page Falls was going to be the next site of a cached corpse, and the vic arrived thinking the killer would already have a corpse ready for caching, but the killer really intended to get rid of him instead."

"I don't know," Alex said. "It would take a real Porky to know about Page Falls, but would a real Porky use this place for a cache and risk outsiders finding out about it? I doubt that."

"Yeah."

"Maybe the killer's car made one of the tire tracks we've casted," Alex said. "But judging from what we've got, there were at least two dozen cars in here in the last week since it rained and softened the dirt enough to capture a tire tread. I'm not sure that's going to lead anywhere."

We looked at the car for a long time, shaking our heads, but we could come up with nothing else. As dusk fell and the state police Suburban crept away with the body and the tow truck with the charred hulk, Alex and I stripped off our latex gloves.

"This can't be good for you," Alex said.

"Why?"

"Too close to the election. Once Eli gets wind of this, he's going to blame it all on you."

"Oof. The October Surprise, but this one has come in August."

"Huh?"

"The last-minute event that throws an election up for grabs."

"Oh, yeah."

My radio crackled. "Steve? Joe."

"What's up?"

"The word's out, and you-know-who's making hay."

"See?" Alex said with a grim smile. "Already."

23 "I suggested to Gil that he relieve you for a day," Garner Armstrong said on the phone that night. He sounded worried, and Garner, a man of unshakable equanimity, never sounds worried, even when everyone around him is frantically losing his mind and running around in little circles.

"Why?"

The prosecutor sighed. "Steve, the sheriff is calling everybody he knows and telling them this homicide proves that you and I and Alex and everybody else don't know what we're doing. Eli is poisoning the wells. You've got to go campaign all day tomorrow. There's just one day left before the primary."

"All right."

"Steve?"

"Yes?"

"Wear your best uniform."

"But I won't be on duty." I've always avoided wearing a deputy's browns when I'm not working. It's less intimidating.

"Doesn't matter. You know Eli will be turned out in all his glory."

"All right."

And so on the day before the election, I arrived in my Jeep at Merle's Café in downtown Porcupine City for ham and eggs and as many hands as I could shake.

"Never rains but it pours," said the proprietor, Merle Lahtinen, heartily grasping my paw and holding it against her ample chest a little too long for propriety. She must be pushing eighty, but she still flirts shamelessly with her customers. The food at Merle's is okay, just okay—it used to be unbeatable, especially her meat pasties, but time and age had dulled her skills at the grill. Still Porkies flock to Merle's just to bask in her mildly libidinous Auntie Mame charm.

For a couple of minutes, I chased hard egg yolks around the plate with a corner of soggy toast, thinking about Merle's words, a veiled but still crystal-clear reference to the events at Page Falls the day before. Then I wiped my mouth, laid a five-dollar bill on the table, breathed in a deep sigh, and started politicking.

"Boys," I said to a table of four burly loggers, "tomorrow's election day, and I hope I can count on your votes."

"Yeah, Steve," chorused three of the loggers.

"I ain't registered," said the fourth. The other three turned and glared at him. He shrank into his seat, at least as much as a logger with yard-wide shoulders could shrink. This was a major transgression in Porcupine County, where civic duty is a given. After the quartet left Merle's, his mates would abuse him thoroughly.

"Why?" one of them said, jumping the gun.

"Didn't want to have to do jury duty."

"Dummy! They pick people for juries from driver license lists, not the voter rolls!"

"Oh." The logger's hangdog expression deepened.

Then followed one of those disapproving silences as uncomfortable as they are brief.

"Next election, then?" I said lightly.

The unregistered logger nodded quickly under the gimlet gaze of his companions.

I worked table after table, shaking as many hands as I could, glad there were no babies to kiss but receiving swift hugs from women young and old. Some of those embraces surprised me, for by nature most folks keep policemen at arm's length. What's more, I am not a member of the loose clan of whites that makes up more than 90 percent of the Upper Peninsula's population. And even though I've lived in Porcupine County for going on a dozen years, I'm from elsewhere and I'm still, in many eyes, an outsider.

Maybe, I mused, it takes running for office to get accepted as a true Porky. With the next thought, I rejected that notion. From time to time, someone, often a summer person from a big city, decides Porcupine County is where he has always wanted to live and moves in, soon deciding to volunteer for something, to become a closer part of the community. If that person is willing to start at the bottom and humbly learn while expending lots of sweat, native Porkies will encourage the labor and sooner or later accept it as a ticket to anointing the newcomer as one of their own.

The arrogant and overeager, however, will meet a brick wall. More than once, someone who was a high-powered professional in the city, perhaps an attorney or accountant, has moved in and quickly let it be known to the rubes that they are doing everything wrong and should adopt more modern methods. Some of them even ran for office and invariably were beaten badly at the polls.

From a place like Merle's, word travels fast. In the half hour since I arrived, customers had jammed all the booths and stools, and dozens packed the foyer up front. They had come not to eat, but to see the candidate at the eleventh hour. "Speech! Speech!" they cried.

There was nothing I could do except make one. At Merle's nod of consent, I stood atop a chair.

"Friends," I began. "That is, if you *are* friends . . ."

"We are!" the crowd chorused.

I had not really prepared a stump speech, but one had been forming in the back of my mind, thanks to all those appearances at church suppers and the like. And to my own surprise, I delivered it, without too many hems and haws.

"Tomorrow we go to the polls," I said, "and I hope you'll all do the right thing: Vote."

"For you!" shouted a highway engineer from the back of the room.

"Yeah!" echoed most of the crowd.

"As you all know, we've got a tough case on our hands right now," I said. "The investigation is still going on. But I am sure we'll get to the bottom of it, as we did at the Venture Mine."

Chortles and knee slaps greeted the joke. There were also thoughtful nods at the reference to the celebrated case of the year before in which the sheriff's department, the state police, and the tribal police joined to break up a murderous drug-growing ring that had been operating under our noses for a couple of years. I had been the tactical commander of the effort, and near the end of it, Garner Armstrong asked me to put my hat in the ring for sheriff.

"And don't forget the Paul Passoja case." With Ginny's help a couple of years before, I had caught the killer of Porcupine County's most powerful business leader and shadow politician.

"Yay!"

I blushed. I was not used to heralding my own accomplishments. My adoptive father had taught me never to boast, and in any case, Indians are not given to self-congratulation. But if I was going to be a successful politician, I had to learn to let my light shine from under the bushel.

"What's more," I said, "my fellow Porcupine County deputies and I have been going to the office every day and putting in a full day of work. It may take us some time to break the case everybody knows we're working on, but I promise you that sooner or later, we'll do it. Staying home out of spite isn't going to do the job."

The assembled Porkies knew exactly what—and who—I was talking about. "Yeah!" some shouted. "Vote Eli out!" others called.

Now that his name had been mentioned, I could afford to be magnanimous.

"Eli Garrow was a great sheriff," I said, "and he's still a great guy. We should respect him and what he has done for the county. More than once he has put his life on the line, and for a long time he has helped to keep the county a law-abiding one. But time and age take their toll. We all get old and less effective, and someday I will, too. But right now, Eli has, and so it's time for him to pass his star on to someone else. He's done it proud and I hope to do it just as proud. Thank you."

Amid the cheers, I stood down and strode out of Merle's under a shower of backslaps. Then I drove to Frank's, parked the Jeep, and stood by the entrance to the supermarket as shoppers trickled in and out, shaking their hands, even hugging some of the ladies. I'd swear I was getting almost as good as Eli at that kind of thing.

Soon a large knot of onlookers formed. I climbed atop a bench under the store canopy and began, "Tomorrow we all go to the polls, and I hope you'll do the right thing. . . ."

And that was my whole day, with stops in Silverton, Bergland, Matchwood, Coppermass, and Bruce Crossing, meeting and greeting outside gas stations, taverns, cafés, and wherever I could find more than three people together. Maybe I was only kidding myself, but I thought the reception in the southern reaches of Porcupine County was warmer than it had been earlier in the campaign. Only a few catcalls broke the benignity. And, as luck had it, I did not run into Eli or his far-flung kinsmen. Later I discovered they were essentially following in my tracks, stopping where I had stumped and trying to quench enthusiasm for me.

That night I stayed at Ginny's after putting away the better part of her signature pot roast and wild rice at dinner, Tommy matching me forkful for forkful. In the presence of superior cuisine, Indians have always displayed excellent appetites, and we were not about to insult the traditions of our ancestors, let alone the talents of our hostess.

"This was a good day," I said as Ginny and I snuggled under the coverlet of her huge oaken bed upstairs, Tommy having fallen asleep in his room at the other end of the house.

"And it's not over yet," she said with a giggle. "Come here."

24

I woke up on primary day fretting, as usual, about those cached bodies. They were not ordinary victims of crime. Except for the hooker's homicide—which might not even have been committed in Michigan—the offenses against them had been done after their demise, not before. Victims of violent crime have histories and personalities, and good cops painstakingly try to learn them for clues to the perps, because crimes are often committed by people who know their victims. But these corpses had no past, no selves, that we could discover. They were just nameless shells their former occupants weren't using anymore. They would lead us nowhere. All we had to go on was Arthur Kling.

In a black mood, I rolled out of bed, knowing that Eli would work the hustings all day, buttonholing incoming voters at just the legal distance outside the polling places while election judges watched him with narrowed eyes. I chose to do my job instead. I'd done my best the day before, I figured, and anything more would only be wasteful. Besides, campaigning on primary day was, I thought, an act of desperation. I wanted to seem cool and confident. Of course I was anything but.

One way or the other, this was going to be a life change. Running for office means putting yourself out on the line in the most public way, where people can poke and prod you like a side of beef and tell you whether you make the grade or not. If you do—

if you win—you are forever a public figure and a piece of you belongs to other people. If you lose, you can look forward to a lifetime of pitying handshakes and snickering whispers. I do not understand how candidates who lose an election can find the strength to run again, but then I am not a professional politician and hope never to be one.

For much of the morning, I inventoried my bare desk, desultorily shoving reports from one side to the other, lining up pencils, dusting the bulb in the gooseneck lamp, and stewing. Stewing about the election and stewing about Sharon Shoemaker, that burned-out BMW and its grisly contents, and those three plastic-wrapped corpses. Finally, I thumped the desk and stood up.

"Go out on road patrol?" I finally asked Gil, who that morning had assigned me to paperwork, a task I didn't object to.

"In a pig's eye," he said severely. "What if you pinch somebody on his way to the polls? You stay right here."

"Yes sir."

Idle minutes passed.

To kill time, I opened the growing case folder I'd jocularly labeled "Cache of Corpses." The small calling card Arthur Kling had given Sharon Shoemaker tumbled out. Might as well start there. I called the number scrawled on the back.

"Hong Sing Cleaners," the voice said, in a thick Cantonese accent.

I identified myself. "Do you know an Arthur Kling?"

"Shirts long time ready. Pick up today?"

"Is that a yes?"

"Yes."

"How long have they been ready?"

"Many, many days. Pick up today?"

"I'll send someone. Thank you." I'd tip off the Chicago police. Maybe there'd be a clue in those shirts. Perhaps a bloodstain ordinary washing couldn't get out. Perhaps a clue in the label on the collar. But we—I, mostly—had been reduced to shots in the dark.

I looked on the other side of the card. ANDREW MONAGHAN. BEAR STEARNS AND COMPANY. Another arrow worth shooting into the night. People picked up calling cards for all sorts of reasons. Kling might have met Monaghan at some investment function and pocketed the proffered card automatically, like a piece of lint, and probably had. But calling the number wouldn't hurt. I dialed.

"Bear Stearns." The female voice was haughty and impatient in that inimitable New Yorkish I-don't-want-to-be-bothered-with-you-but-I-have-to-because-it's-my-job fashion. "Mr. Monaghan's office."

"This is Deputy Sheriff Stephen Martinez, Porcupine County, Michigan," I said, mustering the sternest police-officer tone I could. "May I speak to Mr. Monaghan, please?"

"About what, may I ask?" she said icily. "Mr. Monaghan is very busy."

"Police business."

You had to give the woman credit for tenacity. You could almost hear her spike heels dig into the carpet. "I am his personal administrative assistant," she said, turning up the haughtiness. "You can tell me whatever you need to say to Mr. Monaghan."

She tried to cover the receiver, but I could hear the tag end of her whisper to someone else in the office. ". . . Michigan cop," she breathed.

"What is the nature of the police business?" she asked, still starchy.

"It's a homicide investigation. Please put Mr. Monaghan on."

She couldn't stifle a small gasp. "Just a moment, please."

An electronic click. Then a male voice. "Monaghan here. What's this all about?"

"Good morning, Mr. Monaghan," I said, then identified myself as a deputy sheriff in Porcupine County, Michigan. "I'm calling about an unexplained death here." I waited for Monaghan's reaction.

It was swift. "I've never been to Upper Michigan in my life," he said. "What's going on there?"

My eyebrows rose. I hadn't said Porcupine County was in Upper Michigan. Either Monaghan was dissembling, or he had a remarkable knowledge about the state.

"I have a calling card here with your name and number on it. It had been in the possession of the deceased."

"Who?"

"His name is Arthur Kling. He lived in Chicago. He was an investment counselor. Worked for Fidelity."

A short silence. "Don't know him, I'm afraid. I give out business cards every day to lots of people. Might have met him at a meeting somewhere." Monaghan's voice was even and smooth— too even and smooth, I thought. Maybe he'd practiced this response. But his statement was perfectly logical, maybe even true, and I had no reason to challenge it.

"Well, thanks anyway, Mr. Monaghan. I'll give you my number so that you can call if you remember anything." I did so.

"Okay. Anything else?" That old Manhattan impatience.

"Nope."

"Good-bye then." Click.

I took a deep breath. Monaghan had not asked how Kling had died, let alone when or where. Ninety-nine people out of a hundred would have. That's just normal human concern and curiosity. There was, I thought, a good deal more to Andrew Monaghan than met the eye.

I riffled through my Rolodex—unlike some of my law enforcement brethren, I still use horse-and-buggy paper databases— and found the number of an NYPD Vice Enforcement detective who'd been a friend at criminal justice school at City University a decade and a half ago. I could have called the NYPD Detective Bureau, but the cops there are extraordinarily busy and likely wouldn't want to waste time helping out a boondocks deputy grasping for straws in a case far from their jurisdiction.

"Dick?" I said. "Steve Martinez."

"God, it's been years. How the hell are ya?" Dick Franciscus's voice was genuinely friendly, and I was grateful. We *had* been good buddies. You never really know the true depth of a friendship until years later, when a need arises.

I explained in some detail, finishing up with my phone call to Bear Stearns.

"Now that's a strange one, all right," Dick said. "You want me to check out this Monaghan?"

"I'd be in your debt," I said. "Whatever you can find out might help."

"Gimme half an hour."

I went back to my game of file-folder hockey.

"Bearing up okay?" asked Joe Koski from his counter.

"Yeah, but I'll be glad when the day's over." It would be a long day. The polls in Porcupine County close at eight in the evening, and while Porcupine City's voting machines are automated and the results tabulated immediately, every other precinct in the county uses paper ballots that must be stuffed into locked boxes and driven to the courthouse for hand scanning. It would not be until well past midnight that we had the results.

My phone rang.

"It's Dick," the voice said.

"Tell me."

"Be careful. Be *damn* careful."

"Why?"

"Monaghan's connected."

"Connected? The mob?"

"Not the mob. Politically."

"How?"

"Uncle's the mayor's right-hand man."

"Yeah?"

"Gotta take it easy here, ya see?" Dick said. "Tread on the wrong toes and I'll be back walking a beat in the projects."

I sighed. "Anything else?"

"Yale grad, twenty-four years old, not married, typical young professional about town, travels a lot, nothing unusual. He's pretty much clean."

"Pretty much?"

"Half a dozen unpaid parking tickets, everybody has those, and a juvenile arrest on suspicion of killing and mutilating a dog. He was fifteen. Not the dog, the boy."

"What was the outcome?"

"Doesn't say."

"How'd you find that out? Aren't juvenile arrest records expunged from the computer?"

"They're supposed to be." I could almost hear Dick wink. "But this one wasn't. It happens."

"That could be a useful bit of information."

"Yeah, but don't tell anybody where you got it, okay?"

"Thanks for the facts," I said. "Now what do you really know? The unofficial stuff?"

"You really want to know?"

"You bet."

"Poster child for tougher inheritance taxes. He's a trust-fund parasite. Great-grandpa got filthy rich by owning Irish sweatshops in the garment district at the end of the nineteenth century, exploiting his own people. Grandpa and papa never worked a day but lived off the family fortune, and the kid got his job through pull and doesn't seem to do much on his own."

"Ah. We have some of those out here, too." The wealthy— among them the idle rich—from Chicago, Minneapolis, and

Milwaukee have been buying up choice Lake Superior beachfront property in Porcupine County, sometimes for sprawling summer homes, sometimes for long-term investments. All too often, these people contribute little to the county, choosing to import labor from northern Wisconsin to build and maintain their houses, and alienating the locals with their arrogance and overweening sense of entitlement.

"There's more. Couple of vice dicks who grabbed him up in a hooker sweep—of course Uncle pulled strings and got the record expunged—say he's a piece of work. Arrogant puppy. Didn't seem to give a shit when he was pinched and all he cared about was the cuffs didn't dirty his shirt. Pushed the hookers around some. Propositioned a female vice cop right in the station. Laughed all the time."

"That's a lot for a couple of vice detectives to turn up in one prostitution sweep."

"I didn't say there was only one. There have been three arrests, all swept under the rug on orders from above. Mr. Monaghan likes to buy his jollies."

"Well, this is an education. Thanks."

"Call me if you need more," Dick said. "I'll do what I can. This one sounds interesting."

A few more pleasantries and we hung up.

I leaned back in my swivel chair and gazed up at the ceiling. The North Country Trail victim was a prostitute. Andrew Monaghan consorted with prostitutes. Was there a connection? Maybe. But a little pasteboard card wasn't much of one. The whole thing could be a coincidence. Coincidences can be important, though.

More time passed, and in the late afternoon my fingers began drumming on the desk. Gil heard the soft noise.

"Deputy!" he called from his office. When he is irritated with me, which thankfully is not often, he calls me by my rank, not by my name.

"Undersheriff?" I do the same thing.

Gil harrumphed. "Think you can deliver this summons to this guy in Bergland without getting into trouble?"

"Of course!" I was glad for the chance to get out of the office and into the fresh air. Gil handed me the papers and turned back to his office.

"Be good," he said as I left. That was about as close to humor as he ever got.

Half an hour later, I handed the summons to a concrete contractor who was being sued by the county for shoddy work. The expression on his face suggested dismay not only at having been handed the papers, but also by a candidate he hadn't voted for that morning. I didn't ask.

I was driving back to Porcupine City when Joe Koski called on the radio.

"Deer-car accident on M-64 five and a half miles south of M-28," he said. "Driver called. New Caddy."

"On my way," I replied.

25 In the Upper Peninsula, suicidal deer throw themselves into the paths of oncoming cars with alarming regularity. The beasts always come off second best, the drivers of the old beaters that hit them not bothering to report the accidents and often scooping up the carcasses to butcher for the freezer. Sometimes they just drive off, leaving injured deer suffering by the roadside, and it's the deputies' sad task to euthanize the animals.

But deer are big and can smash good-sized dents into automobile grilles and fenders. Owners of newer cars who want to collect the insurance do report the accidents, and several times a week a Porcupine County deputy is called out to view the damage, do the paperwork, and call the road commission to send a truck to dispose of the carcass.

The Cadillac in question—almost brand-new—was parked on the verge of the highway, a few feet north of the sign that said "WELCOME TO GOGEBIC COUNTY." A bloody brown heap, a large doe, lay in the middle of the road squarely atop the double yellow line a good twenty feet from Porcupine County. The Caddy had Minnesota plates, and its owner, a middle-aged woman in smartly fitted blue slacks and matching jacket with a simple strand of pearls around her neck, stared in dismay at the crumpled left fender, smeared with deer dung. *Urban culture meets rural in a nexus of violence,* I thought absently as I parked the

Explorer behind the Cadillac, my blues-and-reds flashing to warn oncoming traffic.

"You okay?" I said. "Nobody hurt?"

"Nobody but my new car," the woman said. "I know all about deer on the road, but I never thought it'd happen to me."

"It does."

"I saw the first deer and managed to avoid it," she said, "but I never saw the second."

"Par for the course," I said, shaking my head in sympathy. "Is the car drivable?"

"I think so."

"I'll write a report," I said, "and give you a copy, and then you can send it to your insurance company."

"I've got a five-hundred-dollar deductible," she said in a forlorn voice.

"I've got good news for you. Deer-car strikes are *comprehensive* claims. The deductible won't apply. If you'd swerved to miss a deer and hit the guardrail, then that would have been a chargeable accident that goes under the collision coverage of your insurance policy, and you'd have to pay the deductible to get the damage fixed. But not if you hit the deer."

"All right." She sighed, but she didn't look as if she felt better.

I didn't tell her that some drivers who accidentally mash a fender against the garage try to avoid paying the deductible by claiming the incident as a deer-car strike, planting deer hair and turds—easily obtainable in the U.P.—over the crumpled metal and radiator. They rarely get away with it, for the damage to a car caused by a deer is distinctive and almost impossible to fake.

At that moment, a big red Dodge extended-cab pickup from the Gogebic County Sheriff's Department stopped behind the dead doe and flicked on its own flashers to ward off traffic from the other direction. A burly, redheaded deputy sporting a Sir Francis Drake goatee alighted and strode up.

"Hiya, Dan," I called. Dan Roane was a veteran North Woods lawman who had worked every police job in Gogebic County during a career that spanned more than two decades, and he was now the county's animal control officer. In fact, he was the only certified police animal control officer in the entire Upper Peninsula. Dead deer, stray dogs, feral cats, animal abuse, and wildlife complaints in general were his bailiwick. He wore his uniform trousers bloused inside old-fashioned lace-up boots like a Mountie, justifying his departure from the Gogebic sheriff's rigorous dress code by saying it made sense for an officer who had to chase animals through heavy brush every day. The sheriff didn't argue.

Dan was full of stories about his job, and the ones he liked to tell the most involved successful rescues of distressed animals. Once he and a Department of Natural Resources officer had to get a deer out of a manhole it had fallen into in downtown Bessemer. They sedated the deer with a shot of tranquilizer from a dart gun borrowed from a local veterinarian, then a city crew tenderly hauled it up in a sling and nestled it in Dan's pickup to be taken to the woods, where it revived and was released to high fives all around.

"Looks like this is going to be a border dispute," Dan said with mock gravity. "Car hit the deer in your jurisdiction and it ended up in mine. Who's going to catch the carcass?"

"Rocks, scissors, or paper?" I replied.

The woman stared at us both in consternation.

"Just a little cop humor, ma'am," I said.

"What *will* become of the deer?" I gazed at her with new respect. She cared about the animal. She was sorry her car had killed it.

"Inasmuch as the deer's in Gogebic County," Dan said, "I'll carry it to a sand pit in the woods west of here where it'll become food for eagles, wolves, and coyotes."

"At least it won't go to waste," the lady said.

"Nope. That sand pit's one reason why our eagles are so fat and happy," Dan said. "I've seen as many as twenty of them feeding there."

The paperwork completed, the Minnesotan drove off. A few minutes later, Dan and I had heaved the carcass into his truck bed.

"Come along for a bit?" Dan said. "Want to see our zoo?"

"Why not?" I said. Porcupine County had a similar site for disposal of animal remains, but it was about time for a break, and I enjoyed Dan's company. It turned out to be a serendipitous decision.

I radioed Joe to let him know I'd be out of the jurisdiction briefly, and half an hour later we arrived at the Gogebic County Gravel Pit in Ironwood Township. Right away, the place creeped me out. It looked like an outdoor charnel house, a football-field-sized wound of reddish earth scraped from the hide of the green forest, dried white rib cages, spines, and bones scattered all around by picnicking scavengers. The man-made pit, first scooped out of a prehistoric dune deep in the forest by bulldozers decades ago and kept open with front-end loaders, provided sand and gravel for the highway department. The high walls of the pit also made a perfect backstop for a shooting range, and not only did the county's deputies perform their monthly weapons qualifications there, but local civilian shooters also used it to keep up their skills. Animal carcasses were tossed over a berm to one side, and today half a dozen eagles and a couple of osprey were contesting loudly for possession, their skreeks and squawks reverberating from the trees. The eagles were both young dark brown specimens and fully grown ones with brilliant white heads. Two scruffy coyotes lunged at the birds, trying to drive them away from their dinner, but the eagles held their ground, snapping their beaks and flashing their talons.

A pair of turkey vultures perched on a low pile of foot-thick pulpwood logs at the far edge of the pit, alternately watching the eagles and scratching with beaks and claws at the topmost logs, as if trying to move them to one side.

"That's odd," Dan said. "Something's going on over there."

"Have a look?"

"Yeah."

I followed Dan around the perimeter of the pit and up the shallow sides, our boots scrabbling in the gravel, to the log pile. The logs, all cut to the same ten-foot lengths in proper U.P. lumbermen's fashion, had been laid on top of and parallel to one another in a neat pile. Dan waved his arms at the buzzards. The huge, ugly birds slowly flapped out of range, grumbling loudly, and alighted on the ground, watching us with their piercing eyes.

Dan peered into the pile.

"Hey, look at this," he said.

I followed his gaze. Dew glinted on cloudy plastic two layers of logs into the pile.

"Jeez," I said. "Not again."

"Yeah?"

"I think I know what's in there. We'll need to take off some of the logs."

Dan took one end of a log and I the other, and with a mighty *whoof* we tried to muscle it up enough to roll down its neighbors to the ground. It wouldn't budge.

"Just a sec," Dan said. He walked over to his truck and returned with a homemade "rabies stick," a hollow steel pole five feet long through which was threaded a plastic-clad steel cable ending in a noose. With it, Dan controlled obstreperous biting animals. With only a small grunt, he used the pole to lever the log up over its cousins, and it thumped to the sand. Three more logs and our quarry lay open to daylight.

It was an oblong plastic package nearly identical to the one we had found at the Poor Farm. But its yellow-green contents were male, youthful, and unmarked except for the missing head and hands.

"Another one," Dan said unnecessarily. I strode to my Explorer and picked up the mike.

Two hours later, Alex and his assistants finished the job and sent the corpse to Marquette.

"A cadaver for sure," he said. "The lab'll back us up."

"That's five," I said. "Two cadavers, a burial, and two homicides. How many more are we going to find? And how many of them are going to be homicides?"

"I don't know," said Alex. "But I have this awful feeling that the homicides aren't over."

Alex got into his cruiser and I into my Explorer.

"Bearing up okay?" Dan called back from his truck just before we all pulled out.

"What?"

"The election. Hope you win."

"It's going to be close."

The polls were still open, and the word about the fresh corpse was already out, thanks to a couple of riflemen who had driven to the pit for a little target practice. *I could lose this thing,* I thought, as I headed back to the sheriff's department.

26

At six P.M., I signed out and drove to Ginny's for supper. A knot of half a dozen cars and pickups clogged her driveway, including a state police cruiser.

"What are you guys doing here?" I demanded as I opened the door. "I didn't tell anybody I was coming!"

"Now, now," Garner Armstrong said from behind an enormous Old Fashioned. "It's election night and we're your crew and we'll see you through." He laughed at his own rhyme.

"Hear, hear," Alex chortled.

Joe Koski stood smiling in a corner as Tommy handed him a plate of crackers and cheese. Even Gil was there, looking about as relaxed as a man with a fist for a face could, patting Hogan on the head, rumpling his floppy ears. The dog's tail thumped the floor in greeting.

"Evening," Horace Wright said. "Stopped in for a bit, then I have to go to Eli's, of course, and then the courthouse. But I'll have some of Mrs. Fitzgerald's leg of lamb, if I may."

"Typical newsie," Alex hooted. "Freeloader!"

"Sergeant!" Horace said with mock severity. "That's no way to talk about the Fourth Estate!"

The banter rolled back and forth all during dinner. Although a certain imposing case of cached corpses and allied homicides squatted like a great gray toad in the back of everyone's mind, nobody mentioned it, as if to do so might hex the outcome of the election. As the hour for the closing of the polls approached, eyes glanced nervously at the clock and the conversation grew strained. Another thing I hate about election night is waiting for the shoe to drop, like the blade of a guillotine.

At five minutes past eight, the phone rang and everyone jumped, the chatter instantly cut off. Ginny answered.

"It's the county clerk's office. The polls have closed and Edna's about to call the results for Porcupine City," she said. "We'll have them in a couple of minutes."

Dead silence fell around the dinner table. Minutes ticked away on the tall walnut grandfather clock in Ginny's hallway. Not even Alex could break the hush with a wisecrack.

The phone rang again. Ginny picked it up.

"Martinez, one thousand two hundred twenty-eight votes," Ginny said. "Garrow, seven hundred forty-three."

"Mr. Martinez's ahead by four hundred eighty-five," Tommy, the human calculator, said almost instantly.

"Not too bad," said Alex, who earlier had predicted that I'd need to be ahead of Eli by well over five hundred votes in Porcupine City to stay a boat-length ahead of the sheriff while the ballots trickled in from the rest of the county. But Alex didn't look confident.

"Let's have another piece of that coconut cream pie," said Garner calmly. He's a man with a sound sense of proportion about life. We tucked in and Ginny served the coffee.

Just before nine, the phone rang again, and we all jumped. "The ballots have arrived from Rockland and Silverton," Ginny said. Those are the two towns closest to Porcupine City in the northern reaches of the county, where I was strongest.

At 9:14, their ballots had been scanned and the results reported via Ma Bell. "Martinez, one hundred ninety-eight," Ginny said. "Garrow, one hundred sixty-six."

No surprise there, and I was grateful that my lead had been padded by thirty-two votes. I'd need them all.

For as the results slowly trickled in from the rest of the county, that opening 517-vote lead began to shrink, and it steadily shriveled as the hours ticked away toward midnight.

"Bergland," Ginny said. "Martinez, two hundred two. Garrow, two hundred eighty-three."

That brought an uneasy stirring around the dinner table. We'd hoped to break almost even there.

"Matchwood. Martinez, nine. Garrow, eighty-two."

Unsurprising, for that was the heart of Eli's power base.

It wasn't until half past eleven that the results arrived from Lone Pine, Ewen, Trout Creek, Paulding, and Bruce Crossing, whittling my lead to 181 votes. Just two more towns to hear from— Coppermass and Greenland, in the eastern portion of the county, both of which we thought would favor Eli, but not by much.

At almost midnight, as we began to nod, those two towns were heard from. When the grandfather clock struck 12:18, we all jumped as the phone rang. The mistress of the house answered, as she had all evening. A slow smile spread over her face.

"Final results," Ginny said. "Martinez, two thousand two. Garrow, one thousand eight hundred ninety-four."

I had never dreamed a sobersided county prosecutor could whoop so loudly. Garner enfolded me in his arms two seconds before Ginny planted a wet kiss on my lips. Alex hoisted a Molson's in my direction, and Gil gravely shook my hand, maybe the first time he had ever done so. A happy grin spread over Tommy's face. Hogan added a flurry of barks to the excitement.

But it had been close.

"A hundred eight votes," Garner said. "Eli won't demand a recount. If it had been less than a hundred, I'm sure he would have."

Edna Juntunen, we all knew, is so meticulous in the counting of votes that her results have never been challenged.

The phone rang again.

"It's for you," Ginny said, handing me the receiver. "It's Eli."

"Hi" was all I could think of to say.

"My congratulations, Deputy Martinez," the sheriff said, in a tightly controlled voice. He did not want to appear bitter.

"Thank you. You ran a fine campaign," I said, not meaning it at all.

"It's not over."

"Hmm?"

"You'll be surprised."

Eli hung up. Silence fell around the table as everyone took in my grim expression.

"'It's not over,' he said. What's he mean by that?"

Shrugs all around. "Sore loser," Alex said dismissively. Nobody wanted my victory spoiled. But a more pressing matter took hold of my thoughts.

27 Two days after the primary, we held another war council, as an increasingly frustrated Garner Armstrong was calling our conferences about those damned corpses, at the Porcupine County Courthouse. Alex reported the crime lab's findings on the Gogebic Gravel Pit corpse. A cadaver, sure enough. I reported my phone calls to Andrew Monaghan and Dick Franciscus.

"Monaghan sounds like a slim possibility," said the prosecutor. "But awfully slim. We'll need a lot more than a vague circumstantial feeling that he's involved with these corpses to go after him. And I think Detective Franciscus is right—one has to be careful with the politically connected. Not only Franciscus, but his sergeant, his lieutenant, his captain, his watch commander—hell, his *commissioner*—wouldn't want to get their balls in a vise with a powerful mayoral assistant in New York City. If we do anything, we'd better have a lot of ammunition."

"I've got an idea," I said. "How about a subpoena for his credit card records for the last year or so? We can keep that quiet."

"What good would that do?" Alex said. "If he was in this thing with Kling, he'd likely have been careful not to leave a paper trail, too."

"Maybe not," I said. "Even brilliant crooks get careless. Anyway, it won't hurt."

"All right," Garner said. "I'll get the subpoena and you get those records."

It took forty-eight hours and some shin-kicking of both the legal and quasilegal type—I had to threaten an officious young lawyer at one credit card company with a contempt charge—but the fax in the squad room finally began to spit out the records from Visa, MasterCard, Discover, and American Express. After a couple of hours, I gathered up all the sheets and examined them.

The American Express card was a platinum one. The young men who carried them thought they'd impress waiters and auto rental clerks as well as their girlfriends, but the merchants who took the cards knew their holders were suckers enough to pay four hundred dollars a year just for the prestige of flashing one and maxing it out to a ridiculous sum. Andrew Monaghan had an indiscriminating ego, and maybe that could be a weak point.

Immediately, a few patterns emerged from the lists of charges. In New York, Monaghan used the Amex card almost exclusively to pay for restaurant meals and retail purchases. He wanted other New Yorkers to think he was rich. But when he went out of state, he used the Visa, MasterCard, and Discover almost exclusively—and his forays took him to Minnesota and Detroit, though not the Upper Peninsula. If he had ever been in Upper Michigan in the last year, his credit trail didn't show that at all.

But I noticed something. Seven times in the past year, he had flown to Minneapolis, then upstate to Duluth, often staying overnight in the small city at the western edge of Lake Superior. Ten days or two weeks later, he had turned in a rental car in Detroit and flown back to New York, sometimes overnighting in the Motor City. That, I thought, was a lot of vacation time even for someone who very likely was a dilettante at his job. He alternated among the three credit cards to pay his air fare and car rentals. One set of sheets might not show much of a repetitive pattern, but taken together, all three did. There were no charges for meals or lodging other than at Duluth the day he arrived and Detroit the night before he left—no charges *at all,* meaning he did not use the credit cards at all for periods of seven to nine days. He was paying cash. And why?

And where did Monaghan go in that rental car between Duluth and Detroit? The shortest distance between those cities was along U.S. 2 to the Straits of Mackinac—straight through the entire length of Upper Michigan—then south on Interstate 75 to Detroit, a total of 699 miles. The route via Chicago added up to 760 miles, plus clotted bumper-to-bumper traffic around the south end of Lake Michigan. The Chicago route easily would have taken two hours longer to drive, maybe three. I was now certain, although I couldn't prove it, that Andrew Monaghan had spent a good deal of time in Upper Michigan that spring and summer, and that he had been lying when he said he had never been in these parts.

As for those airline tickets, he was probably buying round-trips and tossing away the return portion. Another subpoena of ticket records would prove that, if we needed the additional evidence.

Not so smart a guy. It's what a paper trail doesn't say as well as what it says that can convict a perp. Of course, what I had was still circumstantial in the extreme, but I was now certain Andrew Monaghan was our guy—or, rather, one of our guys. Or people, I could hear the scrupulous Camilo saying.

I picked up the phone and dialed Dick Franciscus's number.

"Dick? Steve Martinez."

"Argh."

"Argh?"

"You're calling about Monaghan again, aren't you?"

"Yup."

"What now?"

I told him.

"Hmm. You're getting somewhere, but I can't grab him up on just that."

"I'm not asking you to. What I'm asking is can you get me a photo of him, a clear head-and-shoulders shot?"

"Who am I, fucking Ansel Adams?"

"I was thinking Weegee."

"Weegee? Shit-kicker deputies don't know about Weegee."

"This one does." Arthur "Weegee" Fellig was a famous Manhattan crime photographer in the 1930s and 1940s who specialized in crooks, thugs, and other lowlifes, some of them society matrons. His dark and malevolent stuff hangs in art museums today.

"Smart guy," Dick said, but his tone was admiring, not disdainful.

"If you could get a photo from the driver's license people, I'd appreciate it. I could do it myself, but it'll be faster if the request comes from a New York detective."

"All right. But I don't remember liking you that much back at CUNY."

"You didn't care for my cooking, as I recall."

Dick laughed. "Now *that* I remember."

"It's improved since."

"It couldn't have gotten any worse."

Two hours later, I had a fax photograph of Andrew Monaghan. Driver's license photos normally make the subjects look either stupid or dyspeptic. I decided Monaghan's made him look cruel and unscrupulous. He had slicked-back dark hair and those saturnine eyebrows that made the urbane television newsman Edwin Newman look like the devil's consigliere. Driver's license photos are usually several years old and don't account for weight changes and facial hair, but Monaghan had renewed his license just the year before and the photo clearly was of a handsome young man in his midtwenties.

I made several copies and faxed them to the state police and sheriff's departments in the Upper Michigan counties surrounding Porcupine County. Monaghan wasn't wanted, I said in the accompanying notes, but he was a "person of interest" in the recent case involving three corpses discovered in Porcupine and Gogebic Counties, and I'd appreciate it if fellow officers would discreetly ask restaurateurs and motel keepers if they recognized the face, and if they did, to let me know.

28 A week later, we finally caught another break. A motel owner in Bessemer at the west end of Gogebic County called the state police when a guest, who had paid cash for two weeks in advance, did not show up at the end of the rental period to collect his belongings. In fact, the motel keeper said, he had not seen the guest since he checked in. A team of troopers, led by Sergeant Alex Kolehmainen, arrived and examined the room and the clothing and luggage it contained. There were no names, no identifying marks of any kind except laundry tags on the shirts. The address the guest had given was false, and the MasterCard number he had proffered to hold the reservation was bogus. So were the numbers on the Illinois license plate he had given the motel keeper. So many of them, including clerks at big chain motels, let alone the mom-and-pop ones, never check out those things until it's too late. It's understandable. There are so many tasks to get done around a motel and so few hours in the day.

But the two items the troopers found behind the ironing board in the closet were real enough. One was a nearly brand-new Bushmaster AR-15 rifle, a heavily modified version—with a powerful long-range scope—of the military M16. The other was a Toshiba laptop computer. If the rifle and laptop weren't stolen, their serial numbers could lead to the person who had left them there. That might not be absolutely necessary, for the motel keeper made a definite identification of the Illinois driver's license photograph the troopers showed him. The photo was of Arthur Kling. And the Chicago laundryman, shown a fax of the tags on the shirts from Kling's luggage, identified them as belonging to our man.

"The laptop's passworded," Alex said, "but we've got a pretty good hacker here at the post. Come on down and we'll wait for you before we open it. Bring your case files, too."

Less than an hour later, I pulled up at the red-brick state police post in Wakefield, parked, and strode into the squad room. Alex, a young trooper named Willie Hanson, and a tall and attractive woman were awaiting. Alex performed the introductions, carefully stating that I was the lead investigator in the case, the first corpse having turned up in my jurisdiction.

Sergeant Susan Hemb was a criminal psychological profiler for the state police who had driven in from Lansing that morning. Tall and trim, blond and attractive, she gave me a polite handshake and smile. She wore a smart black-and-white business outfit and heels, like a lawyer or businesswoman. Only the shield at her belt revealed that she was in law enforcement. I pegged her age at close to forty. If she was a sergeant she had to have been with the staties at least a decade.

"Sergeant," I said.

"Sue."

"Steve."

"Right."

I relaxed. She wasn't going to be severe and officious and overbearing toward a lowly deputy sheriff. And maybe she could help.

"May I have the case files?" she said without preamble. No wonder she was a chum of Alex's. Wasted no time, like him. Absolutely no nonsense. They must have had quite a thing together once. I pushed the alarming picture out of my mind and handed over the folders.

"If it's all right with you," she said, "I'll read these and do my job while you guys do yours. I'll listen in."

"Okay," Alex told Willie Hanson, a young trooper sitting at a long low folding table, the Toshiba open before him. "Let's break in."

Willie, who had minored in computer science at Michigan Tech, answered with a flurry of clicks of the keys.

"Piece of cake," he said. "Passworded only on the Windows level."

"What's there?"

"The usual stuff. Internet Explorer, Outlook Express, bunch of financial software—this thing probably belonged to somebody in the investment business."

"We already knew that," Alex said. "What else?"

"Something called MapSource—one word, capital M, capital S."

"That's GPS tracking software," I said. "I use it myself."

"The MapSource data folder is encrypted," the young trooper said. "So are a couple of Word folders. It might take a little work to find the passwords to open those folders."

Alex and I huddled around the coffeepot at one corner of the squad room.

"What do you make of this rifle?" Alex said, handing me the AR-15 the troopers had found in the motel.

"I don't know," I said. "It's a specialized varmint rig, isn't it?"

That particular Bushmaster model, with a heavy twelve-power scope and a folding bipod to support the muzzle, shot a .223-caliber high-velocity bullet over long distances, three or four hundred yards. Gunners would lie patiently on rises at the edges of meadows and wait for woodchucks and other small animals considered vermin to amble into view. Varmint shooting wasn't a kind of hunting I particularly cared for. Woodchucks do dig holes in meadows that might break the legs of horses and cows, but those who hunt varmints hunt mostly for the joy of killing, not to put meat on the table. Killing for its own sake is not a pastime I approve of, but it is legal, and I generally keep my mouth shut when I see a varmint hunter on property that is not his to protect. Varmint hunters almost never are Indians, whose cultural taboo against the unnecessary slaughter of animals is so deeply ingrained that even the most modern of them shun the practice.

"From what we've been able to find out about Kling," Alex said, "he wasn't a hunter of any kind. At least his neighbors didn't seem to think so. So what was he doing with this rifle?"

"Maybe it wasn't intended for varmints of the furry kind," I said.

"If somebody wanted to do Arthur Kling in," Alex said, "maybe Arthur Kling wanted to do somebody in."

"And got done in first."

"Looks like it. This rifle's brand-new. I'm not sure it's ever been fired. Barrel's clean, action's immaculate."

"I'm in!" Willie called.

Alex and I crowded behind him in front of the laptop screen. Sue looked up from her desk.

"What do you see?" I asked.

"Let me call this up. It's the GPS program."

A few taps of the keys and a click of the mouse brought up a topographical map of the western Upper Peninsula of Michigan.

"Looky this," Alex said. Seven tiny red flags speckled the map. Five of them lay inside the boundaries of Porcupine County, two in Gogebic County.

"Put your cursor on this one," I said, pointing to a flag that looked as if it had been pasted on the map at a point five miles northeast of Watersmeet.

The young trooper did so.

"Now click on it."

Right next to the flag a small box suddenly appeared, with the legend WILDHAWK in tiny letters inside it.

On the left side of the screen lay a large box headed WAY-POINTS. Inside the box appeared seven names: ROEBUCK, FISHER, WEASEL, WILDHAWK, EAGLE, MARTEN, and FOX.

"Click on WILDHAWK," I said.

The trooper did so. Another box opened. In it lay the legend N 46 19.107 W 89 09.740.

"Sue, let me see the file a minute," I said. She handed it to me, and I riffled through the contents until I found the page I wanted. I checked the numbers on the computer screen against those we'd decoded from the bar code tag on the Poor Farm corpse. They matched down to the last decimal place.

"Bingo," I said. "That WILDHAWK waypoint's where we found the corpse near Watersmeet."

"What's a waypoint?" Sue said.

"It's the name GPS users give a spot on the Earth whose coordinates have been marked with a receiver. Those flags show waypoints."

"Look at MARTEN," Alex said. "Bet that's right on the North Country Trail where you found the third stiff."

"Not to mention FOX," I said. "That's the Poor Farm cache."

"And ROEBUCK. The Gogebic County sand pit."

"What about FISHER, WEASEL, and EAGLE?" asked Sue. She had been paying careful attention to us while studying the case file. I admire people who can multitask.

"What do we think those are?" Alex asked rhetorically.

"More corpses?" Willie interjected.

"Have you ever bet on a sure thing, son?"

Willie sat silent for several beats. Then he spoke.

"Seven cached bodies, one of them a homicide, plus a car

homicide and a missing person? Are we dealing with a serial killer?"

"Possibly," Sue said. She was a little more than half through the thick file we had assembled. "Maybe. Probably. I don't know. We won't know till those other three corpses are found, and maybe not even then. Right now, I'd say we've got a weirdo of some kind. Got to keep plowing through this stuff."

"Weirdo?" I said. "Is that what you shrinks call them?"

"Among other things," she said. "And I'm not a shrink, I'm a psychologist." Her tone was amused.

"Or serial weirdos," Alex said.

"Indeed," Sue said. "That's why I'm here. We're usually called in for serial homicides."

"Before we go look for those other three bodies," I said, "let's figure out what we're going to do when we find them. I don't think we should scoop 'em up right away."

"Why not?" asked the young trooper, who didn't yet know all the details.

"We don't want to tip off the perps that we've got this laptop," Alex said. "We don't know who they are yet. For now, we're going to treat those caches as bait for the cachers."

"Right," I said. "Let's clue in Andy."

Andy Messner was Gogebic County's longtime sheriff. He knew all about the corpses at Watersmeet and the sand pit and was letting Dan and Camilo handle those headaches. In fifteen minutes, Andy arrived from his headquarters at Bessemer, four miles west of Wakefield on U.S. 2, and quickly we told him all the details. In outraged disbelief, he shook his massive, bejowled head, wattles flapping—he looks like a Shar-Pei, although he's as tenacious as a fox terrier—and said only one word: an appalled "God." People just did not do that kind of thing in *his* jurisdiction.

Half an hour later, deputies and troopers had been dispatched with GPSs and coordinates to locate the three undiscovered corpses and instructions to leave them untouched exactly where they were as they were, but to photograph them as much as possible in situ.

"What else we got on that 'puter?" Alex asked Willie, who had further explored the contents of the laptop while Alex, Andy, and I had worked on the manpower.

"Quite a bit. The encryption code was kid stuff. There was just one password for everything."

"Talk to us."

"Okay, first we got an Excel expense spreadsheet with motels and meals and gas and stuff. Started four months ago and ended ten days ago. Dates and places, they're all there."

"Can you print everything out?" I asked.

"Sure," Willie said, hooking a cable to the laptop. In a moment, the office laser printer began coughing out evidence.

"Now we got this Word file, and I think you'll find it *very* interesting."

"What is it?"

"It's kind of a diary."

"Print it, too."

Alex collected the printouts, and he, Sue, and I sat down to examine them.

"MAY 1. FOX placed by PLUMBER at coordinates N 46 50.889 W 89 15.940. Clue: Bar code."

Under that, "MAY 18. Found by FIREMAN. Comment: 'Great cache, easy to locate, hard to find. Took two hours of searching.'"

Then, "MAY 18. Found by BROKER. Comment: Took him three tries." And so on later in the summer, by ACTUARY, MEDIC, and CLERK.

The FOX paragraphs were followed by six neat entries for the other caches, again listing when they had been found and by whom. Their cachings spanned the early summer, the last one having been cached on July 10. Not all caches had been found by all participants in the scheme. Only two caches, FISHER and WEASEL, were followed by all six names plus the one who had done the caching. FISHER, judging from its map coordinates, was located close to the powerhouse just below Victoria Dam, an impoundment on the Porcupine River in the high Trap Hills twelve miles south of Porcupine City. A mile-long concrete flume carried the river down from the dam to the powerhouse, which provided considerable megawattage to the Upper Peninsula power grid. The pool below the powerhouse was a favorite Porky fishing spot, and I'd caught bass and bluegill there. Scattered around the area were lots of copses and rocky outcrops perfect for stashing a large cache.

We found the laptop's coordinates for the cache called WEASEL spang in the middle of a Gogebic County campground at Little Girl's Point on Lake Superior. Interstate tourists rarely visited that remote but beautiful shore, popular with locals as a site for weekend partying as well as camping.

And EAGLE? Quick work with a topographical map placed that cache squarely on Fourteen Mile Point, an outcropping of beach fourteen miles northeast of Porcupine City along the lakeshore. A ruined old lighthouse stood there.

Andy threw up his hands in frustration. "This is too damn complicated for my poor simple brain," he said. "Waypoints, caches, code names, dates, corpses, all that shit. Put it up on the blackboard, will ya?"

The blackboard covered nearly an entire wall of the Wakefield post's squad room. In ten minutes, Alex and the young trooper had posted almost all we knew about the case.

"Look at that," I said. "All six of the cachers who were looking found WILDHAWK. Why would Kling come back to the site if he'd already been there, stashed the corpse there?"

"Beats me," Alex said.

"Maybe he was BROKER, the guy who placed the cache? Checking up on it?"

SITE OF CACHE	NAME OF CACHE	MAP COORDINATES
POOR FARM	FOX	N 46 50.889 W 89 15.940

Placed May 1 by PLUMBER. Found by FIREMAN May 18, BROKER May 18, ACTUARY May 20, MEDIC June 10, CLERK June 13.

Discovered June 20 by local youths. Sent to MSP Crime Lab Marquette for analysis. Fully embalmed medical cadaver, good condition, slight decomposition, head and hands missing.

| WATERSMEET | WILDHAWK | N 46 19.107 W 89 09.740 |

Placed May 18 by BROKER. Found by ACTUARY May 22, MEDIC May 28, CLERK June 3, BARTENDER June 14, FIREMAN June 15, PLUMBER June 18.

Discovered June 25 by PCSD deputy and LVDTP officer. Sent to MSP Crime Lab Marquette for analysis. Funerary embalming only, head and hands missing, decomposition begun. Suspect (Arthur Kling) observed on-site July 3 by LVDTP auxiliary.

"Wait a minute," Willie said. "How come PLUMBER knew what to put on that bar code on FOX if he didn't know where BROKER was going to cache WILDHAWK? PLUMBER didn't even know BROKER personally, did he? They knew of each other only on the Internet." We mulled that one a while in silence. Then it came to me.

"Maybe, instead of posting the location of WILDHAWK on the Internet," I said, "BROKER affixed that bar code to FOX when he found it, thus making it a multicache."

"Multicache?" Willie and Andy asked simultaneously.

I explained how a clue at a multicache sent the seeker to another cache.

"That's a possibility," Alex said. "Let's look at the rest."

N. COUNTRY TRAIL   MARTEN   N 46 40.340 W 89 27.036

Placed July 2 by ACTUARY. Found by MEDIC July 5, CLERK July 9, FIRE-MAN July 10, BROKER July 17.

Discovered by hikers July 20. Sent to MSP Crime Lab Marquette for analysis. Stabbed to death. Head and hands missing. Well decomposed, weak attempt at embalming.

GOGEBIC GRAVEL PIT   ROEBUCK   N 46 33.865 W 90 05.298

Placed June 17 by BARTENDER. Found by CLERK June 26, BROKER July 14, PLUMBER July 21, MEDIC July 24.

Discovered Aug. 3 by GCSD and PCSD deputies. Sent to Marquette. Fully embalmed medical cadaver, good condition, head and hands missing.

LITTLE GIRL'S POINT   WEASEL   N 46 36.384 W 90 19.449

Placed May 22 by MEDIC. Found by ACTUARY May 30, CLERK June 7, BROKER June 11, PLUMBER June 15, FIREMAN June 19, BARTENDER June 22.
Not yet located.

VICTORIA POWERHOUSE   FISHER   N 46 41.847 W 89 12.508

Placed June 5 by CLERK. Found by BROKER June 10, PLUMBER June 12, BARTENDER June 14, FIREMAN June 27, MEDIC July 7, ACTUARY July 22.
Not yet located.

FOURTEEN MILE POINT   EAGLE   N 46 59.501 W 89 07.003

Placed July 10 by FIREMAN. Found by PLUMBER July 25.
Not yet located.

I stepped to the blackboard. "We're forgetting a couple of things," I said, quickly scrawling them in:

PAGE FALLS

Car fire and homicide August 2. Victim: Arthur Kling. Shot to death.

UNDETERMINED LOCATION

Missing person of interest: Sharon Shoemaker. Last seen July 28. Possible homicide victim?

We stared at the blackboard for a while, taking it all in, trying to establish patterns and trying to perceive questions that needed to be answered.

"How'd they stay in touch with each other?" Alex suddenly said.

"Easy," Willie said. "Email. This stuff suggests they may all have used the same Yahoo email address, each of them adding a few lines to a single stored message without ever actually sending it out over the Internet. That's a common dodge with criminals who worry about leaving an electronic trail for Internet snoopers to pick up."

"Can we find out who owns that email address?" Alex asked, not very hopefully.

"Naw. We could subpoena the records, but the guy who set up the address would never have used his real name when he registered, probably from a stolen computer or a public one in a hotel lobby. Take it from me, this stuff is untraceable."

"But *who* are these people?" Alex said. "Surely they didn't use their jobs for their code names? That would be too easy."

"Maybe *former* jobs," Sue said. We all looked at her in surprise. She held up another page from the file. "Arthur Kling started his career as a stockbroker."

"And Sharon Shoemaker used to be a bartender," I said. "But I don't think she's that one. That's probably a coincidence. She didn't strike me as having a geocacher's kind of intelligence. Much too simple a person. But I have no idea where she is, and I hope she's not one of those three caches we haven't found yet."

"What about Andrew Monaghan?" Alex said. "If he's in the financial business, too, he might've been an actuary once."

"It'll take me a few minutes to find out," I said. "Alex, your phone?"

"Be my guest."

I called Dick Franciscus at Manhattan Vice. He answered immediately, unsurprised that I was calling. I explained briefly why I was on the line, telling Dick that Monaghan may have had the code name ACTUARY.

"A bit ahead of you," he said. "I knew you'd call again. I've done a little more digging. Monaghan did begin his career after Yale with Penn Mutual Life as an intern in the actuarial department. He moved to Bear Stearns after three years."

I whistled.

"What now?" Dick said.

"Nothing for the moment. We've got to put together a strategy."

"At your service. This is more interesting than hookers and druggies."

That reminded me. "The slashed-up body we found at the site on the North Country Trail called MARTEN, which the laptop credited to ACTUARY, almost certainly was a prostitute. She had needle tracks and the semen of four different men. Hmm. You missing any hookers?"

"Around here they come and go and nobody takes any notice. Once in a while, somebody, usually a relative or friend, reports a disappearance. I can check. But don't expect anything. This'll be true anywhere."

"Thanks. It's a long shot, but maybe we can identify her by DNA and tie her to somebody."

I turned to Alex, Willie, and Andy. "We seem to be getting somewhere, don't we?" I said.

"Why would the perps use such obvious names as former jobs?" Willie said. "They're such easy clues."

"Maybe they weren't so obvious to them," Andy said. "In-joke, maybe. Those names are easy to remember, at any rate."

"Or they thought they were putting one over on us."

"That happens once in a blue moon," Alex said. "But it's not going to happen in this case."

I snapped my fingers.

"PLUMBER," I said. "Phil Wilson! He's a geocacher and he used to be a plumber."

"Phil Wilson?" Alex, Andy, and Willie said almost simultaneously. "Oh, no, not Phil."

"Tell me about him," Sue said. I told her all about the Phil I knew. Quiet, shy, lonely, kept to himself, Vietnam vet, apparent post-traumatic stress disorder. A respected citizen, however, a native-born Porky, a successful businessman in a place where simple survival is the greatest mark of success. The last person on Earth you'd think would get involved in a scheme like this.

"I don't know," I said, grasping for straws. "Maybe some people like to lead secret lives. Maybe it's a way of getting a little excitement into their lives."

"Yeah, but *Phil*?" Alex said.

"It's hard to say right now," Sue said, closing the case file and placing it on the table directly in front of her, gazing at it as if it were a crystal ball. "But in Mr. Wilson, we could be looking at a kind of depression. Often reclusive people with low self-esteem become obsessed with Internet chat groups. They give them a sense of belonging, for the need of human beings for community is powerful.

"Chat groups also give many lonely people a sense of participating in something unique. They feel helpless and hopeless and are easily enticed into irrational acts by people with magnetic personalities. Lonely women who really ought to know better hook up with men they meet in chat rooms who just want quick sex and sometimes the woman's bank account. Once in a while, she gets murdered.

"At the other extreme, in Japan, hundreds of young people suffering from clinical depression have died in suicide pacts put together on the Web. That almost happened here. Just last year, a charismatic drifter in Oregon was charged with trying to talk almost three dozen lonely and depressed housewives from all over the country and Canada into coming to Klamath Falls on Valentine's Day and having sex with him, then hanging themselves naked from a beam in his house afterward. And remember Jim Jones and all those people he talked into drinking cyanide-laced Kool-Aid?"

Alex, Andy, Willie, and I stared at one another.

"Something analogous to that could be happening here with these geocaching enthusiasts," Sue added. "I agree that you ought to talk to Mr. Wilson. And to Mr. Monaghan. He could be another Jim Jones. Or Charlie Manson. Or Ted Bundy."

"How's that?" I said.

"That report from Detective Franciscus in New York. The vice cops' description of Monaghan suggests he's glib, charming, emotionless, deceitful, affects an air of boredom, has a sense of grandiose self-worth, and is probably a pathological liar. The childhood arrest for cruelty to animals is a classic early marker. And the car fire after the killing of Kling might be pyromania, not just intent to get rid of the evidence. Those are all classic traits of a sociopath."

"Motive?" I asked.

"Power," Sue said. "Not sex or money or revenge, but lording it over his followers, enticing them into committing an act that society considers one of the most forbidden of taboos. In enticing people to cache human bodies, he may have beaten down whatever weak objections they may have had about respect for the dead by arguing that no living person was being injured by their game."

"Could some of them be necrophiliacs?" I asked.

Sue took a deep breath. "Death and sex go together like apple and pie," she said. "That's why after a funeral, everybody goes home and makes babies. And it's well known that sex can be made more exciting by games that simulate danger and pain, games that come close to death.

"But in this case, I don't think the cachers want to have sex with a dead body. You know Erich Fromm, the psychoanalyst and philosopher? He argued that attraction to human corpses isn't necessarily sexual, that it's just an attraction to that which is dead, therefore totally under the person's control. Dead people are not people—just objects, things that can be dealt with. That includes being hidden under logs in the forest."

"In other words," Willie said, "they're all sick fucks."

"Not a term I'd use," Sue said with feigned primness, "but it'll do for now."

29 Phil Wilson was sick but in no way a fuck, I felt certain as I entered his hardware store the next morning. At my hello he looked up from stocking shelves with Black & Decker power tools, the favorite weapons of weekend woodworkers. "Need a word with you," I said. "Somewhere we can talk in private?"

"My office." He stood and walked toward it.

Although he did not look me in the eye, his gait was calm and unperturbed, his voice even, his hands steady. Either he was a very good actor, I thought, or he didn't have a damned thing to do with the case.

"Do ya for?" he said, gazing at the wall as he settled into a scarred but still valuable antique oak swivel chair behind a small table camouflaged with piles and piles of invoices. Phil had been offered as much as a thousand dollars for it on the spot by antique dealers who dropped in to buy a screwdriver and discovered a treasure. Up to then, I thought Phil had liked it too much to let it go, and that he was not an avaricious man. Now I was beginning to think he just didn't care.

I took a plastic lawn chair from a pile beside the door, pulled it into the office, closed the door, and faced Phil. Maybe a frontal assault would jolt him into dropping his guard, if his calmness indeed were a guard he had put up against me.

"Phil," I said, "we have information that suggests you are involved with those embalmed corpses we've found around the county in the last couple of months."

I wasn't prepared for his answer.

"Knew you'd find out sooner or later," he said, looking me in the eye for the first time, maintaining his composure. "I tried to tell the others we couldn't get away with it for long."

I stared at him. Phil *Wilson?* It had been my idea that he might be involved in this appalling game, but I still couldn't believe the truth. For a few moments, he returned my silent gaze.

"Phil, I think you'd better come down to the department and make a statement," I said. "This is pretty serious and it could take a while."

"Can I bring my lawyer?"

"That's your right. Tell him to meet us there."

"I'll call him now."

He did so while I stood sentinel outside his office, watching him through the glass door, mindful of lawyer-client confidentiality. The conversation was short. Phil rose from his chair and nodded.

"Ready?"

"Yup. Let's go."

He shrugged into his jacket and stood facing me, hands slightly forward, as if anticipating being cuffed.

"Am I under arrest?" he asked.

"Not at this moment. You're cooperating in our investigation. But I'd like you to ride with me." I wasn't letting him out of my sight until we'd gotten to the bottom of this matter.

"All right," he said unconcernedly, his expression morose. If he had been anyone else, it would have appeared that the situation at last was beginning to sink in, chipping at his armor. But Phil was beyond caring what happened to him.

At the sheriff's department, Grady Craig was waiting for us. Following his heart to the U.P.—like those increasing numbers of summer outsiders from the cities who fall in love with Porcupine County and move here—the skinny, bearded lawyer had retired early, in his fifties, from his job as a veteran assistant state's attorney in Peoria, Illinois, and had set up a general legal practice in Porcupine City. It wasn't often that a criminal case broke up the daily and not very busy country grind of wills, probates, land deeds, and other civil matters. I liked him. I thought he was a reasonable fellow. Maybe that was because he usually saw things my way, but he also knew how to do his best for his clients without needlessly pissing off the other side. That was the mark of a good advocate.

"Conference with my client?" Grady said.

I let them have the interrogation room to themselves while I called Alex and filled him in. Their chat lasted less than a minute. That told me Phil probably had already informed Grady of his involvement and they had discussed the best course to follow.

I sat across the small table from Phil and Grady.

"Steve, before you turn on the recorder," Grady said, "I'd like to say that my client has agreed to speak freely in exchange for immunity from prosecution. He had planned to come forward, anyway."

"I can't promise immunity. You know that. I'll have to talk to the prosecutor first and see what he says. I can't say what the charges will be. I think he'll give Phil every consideration, though, if he agrees to be open and frank with us."

"That's all right," Grady said. He knew the ropes and was just going through the motions. "Phil has agreed to talk no matter what."

I looked at Phil. He nodded.

"Go ahead," Grady said. "Turn on the recorder."

I delivered the usual warnings and Phil gave the usual response that he had been instructed and was speaking of his own free will.

"Shall I begin at the beginning?" he asked emotionlessly, his eyes on the desk in front of him.

"Please do."

And he did, the flood of words suggesting that he was at last beginning to emerge from the lonely darkness that had so long enveloped him.

A little more than a year before, Phil said woodenly, he had been cruising an Internet chat room devoted to geocaching when the discussion suddenly turned jokingly to extreme forms of the sport. Most of the talk was absurd, such as suggesting hiding a handgun somewhere on the grounds of a high-security prison or caching a tin full of cookies at the top of Mount Everest. LOL. :-). Et cetera.

Then someone suggested digging up a grave and caching the contents in another cemetery.

"Everybody said 'Yuck,'" Phil said in a monotone. "Then somebody said, 'This is going too far. We really shouldn't be talking this way.' He was right. Geocachers know the rules of the sport have to be obeyed or somebody's going to ruin it for everybody.

"It was at that point I got a private instant message from a geocacher in the room who had been calling himself MONEYBAGS. He'd been cruising the chat rooms for a couple of weeks."

I kept my expression neutral.

"He said, 'Hey, that gives me an idea. You can't beat dead bodies as a cache, can you? How about getting together a few guys for a private group caching game, each of us to hide one in the woods somewhere for the others to find?'"

For a brief moment, animation entered Phil's voice, and he reached across the table, touching my sleeve. I did not pull back.

"I've got to tell you, Steve, that blew my mind. The idea's not only awful, but it goes against everything in the rules of geocaching. But when MONEYBAGS invited me to a private chat room to talk about it, I couldn't resist. He was so smooth and persuasive. 'Nobody's ever done this before,' he said. 'We'll be pioneers. We'll be the only geocachers on Earth who've ever used bodies as caches. That'll set us apart from everybody else.' The great thing about it, he said, was that nobody would get hurt, because nobody would ever know. He said what we'd do is use medical cadavers, bodies that nobody would miss. Cadavers are easy to get, he said. He'd help us with that. And the bribes wouldn't need to be very big. Piece of cake.

"There were eight of us in that room, and everybody but one said okay. He said, 'Not for me, sorry,' and clicked off. MONEYBAGS then said that to protect ourselves we all should use new names for this particular round of caching, and suggested we take them from old jobs we'd once done. He said he would call himself ACTUARY. I used to be a plumber, so I became PLUMBER. The others were BROKER, CLERK, FIREMAN, MEDIC, and BARTENDER."

Now I had no doubt that Phil was telling the truth.

"Okay. Go on."

"Part of the deal was we would never meet each other. We would know absolutely nothing about each other—only our code names. We didn't know what the others did for a living, or even where they lived, let alone what their real names were. That would protect the rest of us if one got caught. MONEYBAGS—ACTUARY, actually—said part of the fun would be in not getting caught, and if anyone was, it'd be his own fault."

The conspirators then decided they'd all cache their treasures in the same general region, to make traveling simpler and finding the caches easier. "I suggested the western Upper Peninsula because there are so many good places to cache things," Phil said.

"And I volunteered to do the first cache, while BROKER agreed to be the coordinator of information. He set up an untraceable email address on Yahoo for us all to use."

Phil took a deep breath and shuddered.

"Where did you find your cadaver?" I said.

"ACTUARY gave me a cell number to call in Duluth. The guy said he had a body whose head and hands had been harvested and was waiting for orders for more parts, but he could let me have it for fifteen hundred bucks, that he could easily doctor the records. The guy met me with a van down by the docks with the package, already wrapped in clear plastic. I put it in my truck and brought it back that night."

"Where'd you get the fifteen hundred?" I asked. That was a considerable sum in Porcupine County for even a successful small businessman to spend on a whimsy, even if it had turned into an obsession.

"Savings bond I'd had since high school. It was a graduation present."

"Oh," I said. "So you didn't have the head and hands removed to prevent identification?"

"No. That was just a convenient extra. I told the others about it right away, and they all agreed they'd make sure their caches didn't have hands or heads, too. It would be more protection for everybody."

"Where and when did you place that first cache?"

"May first, at the Poor Farm."

"Why the Poor Farm?"

"Nobody would ever think of going to that room in the house. Nobody had been there in maybe years. You see, the idea was that once everybody had located a cache, the guy who put it there would carry it away and bury it deep in the woods somewhere where it never would be found. And so we'd be safe."

"Did you give the cache a code name?" I asked.

"Yes. FOX. We decided to use the names of forest animals. It seemed to be appropriate to the Upper Peninsula."

Again that matched the information we had found on Kling's computer.

"Did everybody find FOX?"

"I don't think so. FIREMAN and BARTENDER said they hadn't found it yet. But I don't know. It's been a couple of weeks since our email drop was updated."

"Email drop?"

"We all use the same Yahoo email address, adding to the single message there and not sending it out."

"Yeah, I understand that."

"How'd you know?"

Phil was cooperating. Everything he had told me corresponded exactly to what we had learned from Arthur Kling's laptop. I decided to cooperate, too, to tell him some of what I knew so that he would be encouraged to keep on talking.

"We found a laptop, and we think BROKER was using it. It had the locations of all the caches on it as well as all the participants in the game. Did you find all the locations yourself?" That was a trick question, for I already knew the answer. Phil didn't disappoint me.

"No. I didn't find MARTEN. I hadn't looked for it yet when the word got out that you guys had found a corpse on the North Country Trail. I knew from the email site that ACTUARY had put one in that area. That's when I started to get scared. I knew you guys would find me sooner or later. ACTUARY said you were dumb but I know you're not."

"Wish you'd done that earlier, Phil," I said. "Would've saved us a lot of trouble."

"Yes, I'm sorry," he said, genuine contrition in his voice. He looked up. "Did you find BROKER, the guy with the laptop?"

"Yes."

"Where's he now? Is he under arrest?"

I stared at Phil's guileless face. He had not made the connection to the homicide in the burned Beemer. Yes, he was being honest. No reason for him not to be.

"Phil, he's dead. Murdered. He was that guy in the car fire at Page Falls."

Both Phil and Grady gasped audibly.

"Yes, Phil, this is a homicide investigation now," I said.

He buried his hands in his face and said in a quavering voice, "I was afraid this whole thing would go too far, that somebody would fuck up. I'm so stupid. Stupid, stupid, *stupid!* We all fucked up the day we decided to do this thing."

We all three sat silent for a while. Then I said, "Hang on a moment. I'll be right back."

At my desk, I called the prosecutor and told him what I had learned. "Garner, I don't want to move on Phil right away, if that's okay with you. To detain him right now would take him out of circulation on the Internet, and that might tip off the other perps that we've cottoned on to their game and might ensure we'll never be able to catch them. Can you postpone your interview with Phil for a day or two?"

"Sure," Garner replied. He is one prosecutor who knows the value of patience in a criminal investigation.

Back in the interrogation room, I said, "Phil, I'll probably want to talk to you some more. I'm not going to charge you now. I'm going to let you walk out of here a free man. What I want you to do is go about your business as if nothing has happened, and to say absolutely nothing to anybody about this. Can you do that?"

He nodded dumbly.

"If you feel you have to talk to somebody, go see Grady. Or come to me."

I glanced at the lawyer. He nodded. He understood perfectly well.

On the way out, I gripped Phil's shoulder. "I'm sorry," I said. "Soldier to soldier."

He began to weep.

30 I called Alex at Wakefield and quickly filled him in. He did the same for me.

"FISHER and WEASEL are gone," he said. "There's no WEASEL, as far as the Gogebic deputies could find, at Little Girl's Point. They did find a scooped-out spot in the sand that looked as if it had been disturbed recently. It was under a downed pine, four feet thick, just below a bluff right at the tree line of the beach. Anything put there would've been well out of sight from the beach and the woods. They found a quarter and a dime at the bottom of the depression."

"That's good enough for me," I said. "We can chalk off WEASEL."

"And right at the coordinates the laptop gave for FISHER, just below the Victoria powerhouse, we found a broken cairn of rocks that was big enough to easily have covered a human cache. The rocks had been scattered very recently. The earth was disturbed and it was raw."

"That should pretty well clinch it," I said. "Phil said when everybody found a cache it'd be removed and disposed of. That leaves just one we haven't found: EAGLE, at Fourteen Mile Point."

"Correction. Chad just called. He found it. Right inside the open wall of the old lighthouse at exactly the waypoint he was looking for. Another clean cadaver in heavy plastic, the usual M.O., no head or hands."

We sat silent for a moment. "Now what?" Alex said.

"Let's backtrack a bit and add things up. If Phil didn't know Kling had been killed, that probably means most of the others don't know, either."

"Except the guy who killed him."

"Right."

"So that leaves five geocachers we haven't found. Remind me," Alex said. "How many of the other caches haven't been found by everybody yet, according to that laptop?"

"WEASEL and FISHER seem to have been the only ones everybody found. That leaves five."

"Stakeout time for the remaining five caches," Alex said. "Stake 'em out till somebody shows up."

"That's a lot of guys for five stakeouts," I protested. "Two twelve-hour shifts each. That's ten guys.

"Look, it's already out that four corpses have been found by the cops," I added. "Maybe the five surviving cachers all know the story. They've already all located WEASEL and FISHER. Maybe they know we've found FOX, WILDHAWK, MARTEN, and ROEBUCK. If they do, that would leave only one cache that really needs staking out: EAGLE, at Fourteen Mile Point."

"But you're assuming that all the cachers read the newspapers. Maybe they don't. And I don't think the case has become a national story yet. If any of the cachers live outside the Midwest, maybe it hasn't been in their papers. I've checked the Internet, and it's still only a regional story."

I could hear Alex riffling the pages of the printouts from the laptop.

"You may be right," he said. "And I guess you've got a point about our manpower shortage. Yeah, we ought to stake out one cache right now, the one at Fourteen Mile Point."

"That's gonna take some pretty hard camping."

"That's what Chad said."

"He already figured on a stakeout?" I said.

"Yup. He's learning."

"What say we give him the first couple of days?"

"That's cruel."

"He's younger than either you or me. He'll hold up better."

"Speak for yourself, old man."

I chuckled. "I'll give him a call right now and get him going out there. The sooner we have that covered, the better. I have a feeling we're going to make our big pinch there."

"Something else you ought to know," Alex said.

"Yes?"

"Eli's not giving up. This morning he announced in a full-page ad in *The Globe* that he's starting a write-in campaign for November."

"Oh, damn. That's what he meant when he said it wasn't over."

Alex and I both knew the implications. A lame duck who won't stay lame can complicate life for a sheriff's department. I'd have to keep campaigning for three more months, for I couldn't afford to relax. It's true that write-in campaigns rarely if ever win an election anywhere, but this was not the usual anywhere, nor was it a run-of-the-mill election. The citizens of Porcupine County are veteran ticket-splitters and quite capable of write-in voting en masse. Moreover, Eli was still determined, powerful, and dangerous, perfectly capable of running the kind of intense campaign that turned things to his advantage.

And I wondered where he'd gotten the money for that ad. *The Ironwood Globe* was a daily with a circulation of several thousand, not a weekly seen by a thousand or so. Full-page ads are costly. Someone must be supporting him. But who and why? I had no idea about the first, but I entertained some suspicions about the second. Some people in the far North, even at the beginning of the twenty-first century, don't care for the idea of a nonwhite person in a position of authority over them. And, I thought, perhaps Eli was in somebody's pocket, although Porcupine County is so poor that the fruits of official corruption would be so thin and starved that they were hardly worth the bother.

I sighed and called Chad. He was all ready to go and only needed the order.

At the sheriff's department the next morning, I made up an excuse to drive to Matchwood and pay a call on my erstwhile and still titular boss.

He was not friendly. As I dismounted from the Explorer, his glowering face appeared inside the screen door, and as I walked up the flagstone path to his modest frame house set into a clearing just off a dirt road fronting onto Highway M-28, he opened the door and stepped out onto the porch, bristling so fiercely that I looked carefully to make sure he was not holding a weapon. He wasn't.

"Martinez, you have some nerve coming here," he said, his sun-ruddied cheeks quivering with anger.

"Yeah, Sheriff, but I have to talk to you. Departmental business."

He glared, and we stood awkwardly on the porch for a moment, eyeing each other like roosters at a cockfight. Then he said, "You'd better come in," and he held the door open.

"Sit anywhere," he said, sweeping his arm around the small living room. It was modestly furnished with a clean but threadbare sofa and easy chair, a battered walnut coffee table, crazed yellow china lamps that probably had come from St. Vincent de Paul's, and a brand-new fake Oriental rug of Wal-Mart quality. One wall almost sagged with the weight of scores of family photographs in cheap metal frames. Chintz curtains dressed the windows, and an aged golden retriever lying on the rug thumped his tail in lazy greeting. This was not the house of a politician on the take, not that I had ever thought Eli might be. He was the kind of pol who did questionable favors for people because either they were relatives or he just liked them.

Dorothy came in from the kitchen, followed by the aroma of baking bread. Ever polite and welcoming even in the most awkward social situations, she said, "Coffee, Steve?"

"He won't be here that—" Eli started to say before his wife's iron stare cut him short. Dorothy takes no crap from her husband. She will not allow her hospitality to be compromised.

"Yes, please. Black with one lump, please," I said.

When Dorothy returned to the kitchen, Eli heaved a deep sigh and said resignedly, "All right, Martinez, what's on your mind?"

"A lot of things."

"What's the first?"

"Why are you still running for sheriff, Eli? I beat you fair and square in the primary. You haven't got much chance as a write-in."

"Maybe not," Eli said, his gaze drilling through me, "but it's still a chance."

"The talk is you spent all your money in the primary. Where's the dough coming from for those full-pagers in *The Globe*?"

"None of your business."

"It's the people's business. You and I both know that." Election laws everywhere require full disclosure of political donations over a nominal sum.

"Yeah, I'll file the info when it's required." Eli's tone was only slightly conciliatory.

"But that doesn't explain why you're doing this. You're risking all your assets as well as your reputation on this . . . this . . . this wild-goose chase." I wanted to say "Thermopylae," where in 480 B.C. Leonidas, the hopelessly outnumbered Spartan king,

made his last stand against the Persian army, but I didn't think
Eli, hardly an educated man, would recognize the classical allu-
sion.

"You don't have to know."

"Maybe not, but, goddammit, I want to. I care. I care about
this county and I care about who I work for."

"Used to work for," Eli said dismissively.

"Still do."

Eli grunted.

Dorothy swept in with a tray, a carafe of coffee, three cups,
cream and sugar, and sat down in an armchair next to Eli's. I
looked at her.

"Anything we say she can hear," Eli said. "From all over the
house. She might as well be here. I don't keep stuff from her any-
ways."

It struck me that he might have wanted a witness to anything
that ensued, whatever it might be.

"No problem," I said. "Thanks for the coffee, Dorothy."

She nodded. I had always been on first-name terms with her,
and there was no reason to change.

I looked at Eli. "We were talking about why you were still
running."

"No Garrow has ever backed down from a fight. We've always
been in it to the last."

"Why?"

"We care. Like you, we care. We care about the county and we
care about the job. And we care about history."

"History as in?"

"History as in how it'll remember me." Eli's voice quavered
slightly, and his ruddy cheeks colored even more deeply. I had
never heard that from him before, not even at the cop funerals
where he often spoke, and he is not an unsentimental man. But
for the first time that morning, Eli looked old, as if he had finally

realized that he was no longer the vigorous lawman he had been in his prime. The color suddenly faded from his face, leaving it gray and almost sunken.

I made a decision. "I'm going to tell you something, Sheriff."

"What?"

"What's been going on with all those bodies. You have a right to know."

"All right." He sat up straight and fixed his gaze on me, awaiting his deputy's report. He almost looked like the old Eli again.

I filled him in, leaving nothing out, making sure he understood the fine points of geocaching and outlining Sergeant Sue Hemb's hypotheses. He listened attentively, nodding in all the right places and shaking his head in all the right places, too.

"It's hard to believe that anybody could be talked into doing something this weird, joining a game to plant bodies in the woods for somebody else to find," Eli said. "That isn't a game, it's . . . it's evil. It's a *perversion*."

"Yes," I said. "But I think Sergeant Hemb is right. In an Internet chat room, psychologically susceptible people can be manipulated into doing things they'd never even think about out in the light of day. Think how easy it'd be for a psychopath to mesmerize a bunch of mentally ill people into playing around with the illegal transport of human remains."

"God." Eli's eyebrows shot up disbelievingly. "I don't know anybody who'd bite."

"But you do." When I told him about Phil Wilson, his eyebrows rose even higher, and he said *"Phil?"*

"That's what we said, too."

"I'll be damned. But . . . I see what you mean." Eli knew Phil well, too.

"And so we're keeping a lid on the case," I finished.

For a few moments, we sat silently as Eli digested my story.

"That stiff at Fourteen Mile Point," he finally said. "That wasn't humped in by any stranger. Those old logging trails were grown over long ago. It had to have been carried there by boat and by somebody who knew the place." The only other ways to reach the lighthouse there are to hike the fourteen rugged miles of lakeshore from Porcupine City, or, in the winter, to go by snow-mobile.

"The other geocachers had to have come in by boat, too," I said. "And if any of them don't yet know we've found some of their caches, they'll come in from the lake as well."

"Should be easy to stake out," Eli said. "Haul the camping gear in with the department's Whaler, hide the boat up the first creek east of the lighthouse, pitch a tent inside the tree line, and keep an eye on the beach. If it takes more than a few days before we make a bust, we could borrow a couple of old Indians from the tribal police, give them the tent and a wanigan of grub for the duration."

Eli, once again the veteran cop, had anticipated exactly what Alex and I had done.

"Yes," I said. "Chad's gone out already."

"Anything more?" said Eli, his tone still commanding.

"No, that's it," I said. "You know everything."

"I'll let you know if I think of anything else."

"Yes, sir," I said, keeping my tone deferential.

Eli stood up. "Thanks for coming," he said. He did not hold out his hand.

I put on my ball cap and turned to leave.

"Steve, I'm not going to quit," he said. "I'm going to run. And I'm going to beat you." Leonidas, defiant as ever, facing the hordes of Xerxes. Leonidas was a stubborn old son of a bitch, too.

"It'll be a contest," I said noncommittally, and stepped out the door.

As I started the Explorer, it finally struck me: Eli had called me "Steve." Not "Martinez." Not "Deputy."

"What's in a name?" Shakespeare's Juliet asked. She didn't know the half of it. "Everything"—that's the real answer.

32

True to his word, Eli campaigned hard. But, for a change, he campaigned cleanly. From the day of our meeting at his house, his ads and his words focused on his record and his proposals, not on innuendo about the perceived shortcomings of his opponent. In fact, he barely mentioned me at all, and he said absolutely nothing about the case that had so frustrated four police forces for weeks. Yes, he was cranky and contrary and stubborn and self-involved, but under all that old man's blather, his essential decency was emerging again. You can't despise a man for caring.

Voters talked about the change. The political junkies took it as a shrewd new tack taken by a candidate for whom negative campaigning hadn't worked. The broad Garrow fan base treated it as something they'd known about all along. The Steve Martinez brain trust worried about it. "I've never heard of a write-in winning any office in Porcupine County," Garner Armstrong declared, "but there's going to be a first time, and this could be it."

I changed my own campaigning in the same way, avoiding the subject of Eli's absence from office and never mentioning the issue of age. Instead—at Garner's insistence—I uneasily focused on my education, experience, and accomplishments. I didn't want to rub my master's degree under people's hides in a region where high school and maybe a year or two at a community college was as much formal education as most people had. Nor did I want to talk about having been an army officer to people whose sons and daughters had been enlistees. All that sounded too elitist.

I had less trouble telling people about tracking down the murderer of Paul Passoja, who had been the most powerful citizen of Porcupine County when he was killed in an act of revenge concocted by a female deputy sheriff he had sexually abused when she was a girl. Nor did I hesitate to mention catching a big-city drug lord who had grown world-class narcotic plants deep inside an abandoned copper mine and shipped them to South America. To my surprise, the slightest hint of those cases drew cheers during my campaign stops, temporarily banishing growls of dismay over the vexing case of the corpses strewn around the countryside. Maybe mentioning the earlier victories raised hopes that the new case would also be solved.

I was beginning to have doubts, although we were making progress.

On my day off a few days after I went to see Eli, I got a phone call at home from Dan Roane. "We caught one of the geocachers this morning," he said.

"Tell me."

"It's FIREMAN. His name's Ted Wilt. He's a Wal-Mart superstore manager in Minneapolis, and a summer resident here. He has a cottage on Lake Gogebic. I busted him myself at the sand pit. He drove into the pit and was poking about with his GPS when I rolled up behind his car with a couple of deer carcasses in my truck. Caught him right at the cache site, levering the logs aside. He's scared and he's talking, but he's not telling us much we don't already know. He says he's never met any of the other players except on the Internet."

"Where'd he get his corpse?"

"Duluth," Dan said. "A cell phone connection ACTUARY gave him. Just like the other guy's."

I whistled. This case was getting ever deeper.

"What about Fourteen Mile Point?" I said. "Did he admit caching there?"

"Yes."

"Doesn't surprise me that he's the one. I always thought some of these places had to have been picked by people who knew this country. What's he like?"

"Very cooperative. Quiet, mild-mannered, nerdy, baldish, dumpy, lives alone—poster boy for Sergeant Hemb's theory. He seemed shocked when we told him that homicide was involved, and he wanted to know exactly how. When I told him about the car fire, he said he hadn't heard anything about that because he'd been back in Minneapolis. He also said he'd been there most of the summer and had no idea we'd found any of the caches. He didn't seem to be trying to hide anything. I believe him."

"Maybe that's a good thing he didn't know about the fire or that we'd found the caches," I said. "Maybe our killer doesn't know we know, either. Dan, can you keep this guy on ice for a day or two?"

"I'll charge him with the dead-body felony and get the judge to set the bond high enough to keep him in jail until Monday. I'll tip the press then."

"Good."

A moment of silence while a radio crackled in the background, then Dan said, "Shit. Got another deer-car call. That's the third one today."

"The eagles love you, don't they? You're their best buddy."

"Ha. Later, Steve."

Almost as soon as I hung up, the phone rang. It was Ginny.

"Could you stop by?" she said. "I need a favor."

"Sure. What is it?"

"Tell you when you get here."

I hung up and walked out to the Jeep, whistling. Two geocachers down—actually, three down, if we included the dead Arthur Kling—and four to go. At Ginny's, I'd wheedle a little lunch out of her in return for that favor, whatever it was. I pulled into her driveway still in a good mood, thinking that at last the assembled law enforcement community of the western Upper Peninsula was getting closer to a resolution of the vexing Case of the Cached Corpses. Of course we were, but unknown to me another rock was about to be thrown into the machinery of my life.

A black Rollaboard stood just inside Ginny's front door as I walked in. Small as it was, it held at least a couple of changes of clothes. Ginny knew how to travel light and still make the most of what she took along.

"Going somewhere, Ginny?" I called.

"Yes," she replied from upstairs. "Thanks for coming by. I have to go to New York today. Would you take Tommy for a few days?"

"Sure, but what's happening in New York?"

She swept downstairs in a smart gray executive suit I'd seen her in only once before, when her lawyers visited her to discuss foundation matters. Neutral hose and heels and a faint spray of Vol de Nuit completed the ensemble. When she wanted to, she could dress in the trappings of power and wealth. She knew exactly how to present herself.

"Sit down."

I groaned inwardly. Whenever she told me to sit down, I knew heavy news was about to be laid upon me. "All right."

"Steve, Malcolm called me last night."

"Malcolm Benson?" He was the gold digger who had very nearly persuaded the wealthy young widow Virginia Fitzgerald to marry him so that he could plunder her fortune to support the

Baptist international refugee agency he ran. He had been married five times, Ginny discovered just in the nick of time, soaking every one of his wives for most of their assets before they threw him out of the house and consulted a divorce lawyer. Ginny's heart had been slashed and bruised, and it had taken her a long time to learn to trust a man again.

"Yes. He's dying of cancer at Memorial Sloan-Kettering. He wants to see me before he goes."

I took a deep breath. "Is he really?" I said skeptically. "Or is this another scam he's running?"

Ginny's green eyes flashed, as they did every time I called her judgment into question. Whenever this happened, I was usually wrong, but not always.

"I've had my lawyers check out the situation," she said. "They said it's true, that he hasn't long to live."

I nodded. Ginny's Detroit law firm, though small, was one of that city's shrewdest and most powerful. It handled the foundation through which she secretly supported much of Porcupine County. It was very, very competent.

"Why is he reaching out to you after all these years and after what he tried to do to you?"

"He wants to apologize, to make peace with those he has wronged," she said. Not "He says he wants to . . . ," the words a cop would have used. Cops are careful. Cops expect the worst and are surprised at the best.

"Born again, huh?" Cops are cynical. Deathbed and death row conversions are as common as baptisms, but the newly saved are still guilty as hell. Salvation doesn't always change their behavior toward others, either. They were born sinners and they will die sinners. "Being sorry doesn't change history," I said.

Ginny glared. I winced. I shouldn't have said that. I should have gathered her into my arms and whispered words of support and assent. But I couldn't help it. A cop is a cop. Cops can be dumb. Even smart ones.

"I'm sorry. Flying out of Houghton? Want me to drive you to the airport?" I said quickly in a futile attempt to cover my tactlessness. She'd take a little commuter jet to Detroit, then a Northwest 737 to LaGuardia.

"Thank you, but no," she said coldly. "I'll drive myself. Thank you for taking Tommy. He's packing upstairs."

She did let me carry her Rollaboard out, and she coolly held up her cheek to be pecked before getting into her minivan.

"When will you be back?" I asked.

"Don't know," she said. "A few days. Maybe a week."

She drove away, her face still set in granite.

Tommy appeared on the doorstep, gazing at me sadly. He had heard everything. I could have sworn he shook his head slightly, as if to say, "You've blown it."

I took a deep breath. "Let's go."

He whistled, and Hogan bounded out the door. Suitcase, backpack, dog gear, and dog in the backseat, we drove to my cabin a few miles west down the lakeshore. When we arrived, I said, "Tommy, I've got some errands to run in town. Can you keep yourself busy?"

"Sure," he said. "I'd like to take Hogan and put a little geocache in the woods. Can I?"

"Where?"

"Just off Town Line Road near the old Finn cemetery," he said. That was just a quarter of a mile up a lightly traveled asphalt road through the woods. The place was fairly close to civilization. Plenty of houses kept watch along the road. And Tommy knew how to handle himself in the woods.

"Okay," I said. "Be back by six and we'll have a steak for dinner, okay?"

"Sure thing! Thanks!"

I was in the doghouse, but there was hope if Ginny had entrusted me with Tommy. I wouldn't let her down, either, I thought as I got back into my Jeep and drove to Porcupine City.

33 Tommy hadn't returned from his mission when I arrived at my cabin shortly after four. I wasn't worried. The kid was twelve, knew his way around the woods, and carried a GPS. Hogan was with him, but that wasn't worrisome either, for wolves hadn't yet been seen so close to civilization. So far they'd stuck to the most remote wilderness in the county, many miles south and west of the Finnish cemetery.

Five o'clock arrived. Tommy is a lad with seemingly inexhaustible curiosity, the kind who, like a cop, carries plastic Baggies in his backpack—not for evidence, but for specimens. When I was growing up, we collected interesting bugs, plants, and garter snakes in screw-top jars for later examination, sometimes forgetting our stashes until our mothers' screams announced their discovery of strange creatures slithering down the stairs into the living room. The invention of the zip-top Baggie has brought considerable modern convenience to the young backyard explorer, and when the backyard is as big as Porcupine County, those Baggies pile up in the kids' bedrooms. Sometimes Ginny has to remind Tommy to either feed his menagerie or let it loose—outside, of course.

Five-thirty. Tommy must be loading down his backpack with lots of weird critters. I hoped none of them were the biting kind.

Five forty-five. Looks like the lad planned to use all the allowed hours of his freedom. I'd done the same as a kid, walking into the house at almost the last minute while Mother glanced suspiciously at the clock. Dad's concept of time was a lot looser. So long as I got in before dark, he didn't mind. He understood the need of boys for adventure. "Don't upset your mother," was all he'd ever say, and if she heard that, she was always upset— with him, not with me.

Six o'clock and no Tommy. I stood up from reading Google News on my laptop and looked out the kitchen window onto the driveway, hoping to see his small figure trudging toward the cabin. I sighed. Ginny hadn't ever complained that Tommy abused the privileges of the clock. Maybe, having come to crash with me for a few days away from his foster mother, he was seeing how far he could stretch the envelope. Or maybe he'd just lost track of time, would suddenly glance at his watch, shout guiltily, and hotfoot it for my cabin at flank speed.

Six-fifteen. The first stirrings of irritation. Another glance out the window. A lecture about time and reliability awaited that young man unless he had a good excuse.

Six-thirty. Maybe Hogan had had a run-in with a skunk or maybe Tommy had twisted an ankle and was hobbling slowly home.

Seven. An hour late. Where could that boy be? Now I was beginning to get worried.

At seven-thirty, I threw on my denim jacket—mid-September brings cool evenings and chilly nights—and took my Jeep south on Town Line Road, stopping at every house to inquire if they'd seen a small boy, brown-skinned like me, with a dog. Three housewives had, and Mrs. Peters, the widow who lived almost across from the Finnish cemetery, said she'd had a brief chat with Tommy at about three in the afternoon before he crossed the graveyard with his dog and disappeared into the forest on a deer trail. "Nice kid," she said. "Ginny must be delighted with him."

"*I* am not," I said. "Not right now."

I walked to the deer trail and shouted, "Tommy! Tommy!"

No reply. I didn't really expect one.

After five minutes on the trail, I decided to turn back. In places the thick leaves blanketing the trail had been disturbed, and a couple of twigs had been stepped on and broken. I may be an Indian, but I'm not a tracker, and I had no idea whether the sign had been left by Tommy, a deer, or something else. And dusk was beginning to fall. It'd be dark a bit after nine, in less than an hour. Nightfall comes late in this part of the Upper Peninsula. Porcupine County lies farther west than Chicago, but we're on Eastern time, not Central as Chicagoans are.

It was time to raise the hue and cry.

I walked back to the Jeep and keyed the new eight-hundred-megahertz handheld radio the department had issued to all deputies for their personal vehicles.

"Twelve-year-old boy missing in the woods," I told Joe Koski, who was working the night shift this week. "We need a search team out at the Finnish cemetery on Town Line Road. He was last seen there about three this afternoon."

"Who's the boy?"

"Tommy Standing Bear. Ginny Fitzgerald's foster son. He's staying with me while she's out of town."

"Good Lord."

I don't mean to imply that Porcupine County's search-and-rescue squad, made up of law enforcement, firefighters, and civilian volunteers, wouldn't give its all to hunt a complete stranger lost in the woods. We're professionals at what we do, and if we sometimes seem a little reticent about showing our feelings, that doesn't mean we don't care. Cool detachment means we can think straight and consider every angle carefully without the baggage of emotion nudging us down a dangerous path. But when one of ours in the law enforcement community is killed, hurt, or just missing, we unconsciously try a little harder. Family is family.

And though he had no official connection to Deputy Stephen Two Crow Martinez, Tommy Standing Bear was linked to me through my liaison with Virginia Fitzgerald. He was one of ours. He was one of *mine*.

Within the hour, every deputy in the county, on duty and off, the better part of the Porcupine City Volunteer Fire Department, Doc Miller from the hospital, several emergency medical technicians from local ambulance companies, and half a dozen loggers—all of them experienced woodsmen—had gathered at the Finnish cemetery. There Gil was setting up a command post.

"You stand down, Steve," Gil immediately barked when I arrived. "That's the rule." He was right. An emotionally involved officer might take unreasonable chances and endanger himself and others, and therefore must be removed from the case. This is standard operating procedure in law enforcement departments everywhere.

"But who's going to fly the plane?" I asked. An air search for someone lost in the woods is also SOP.

"Yeah, you'll have to," Gil said. "But not tonight. New moon. Overcast. No starlight."

"Yeah. If Tommy doesn't turn up tonight, I'll launch at daybreak. There'll be low clouds but high enough for a low-level search."

"Tell me what you know about Tommy."

I told him, not forgetting to include Tommy's Ojibwe education in the woods, and wound up with Mrs. Peters's conversation with the boy before he disappeared into the forest.

"Think he went to the old Hawthorn Hill Farm?" Gil said.

"Possibly. He said he was going into the woods here, and there's a trail to the farm that branches south a hundred yards or so into the trees."

The Hawthorn Hill Farm, or rather what remains of it, is an abandoned, overgrown ruin, with mostly crumbling stone foundations but with a few almost fallen sheds still leaning askew, just south of the Finnish cemetery. During the nineteen twenties, one of the county's lumber magnates, a man who adored the Upper Peninsula—unlike so many of the plutocrats who raped the land and abandoned it to the tax man—decided to do something with the countryside his loggers had denuded instead of walking away. He started Hawthorn Hill as a model farm, first laboriously destumping a hundred acres, and then stocking it with the best bulls, cows, and pigs he could find in the United States. He had flyers distributed far and wide, including northern Europe and Finland, and he advertised in major city papers, touting Hawthorn Hill as a showplace for the land of opportunity for immigrant farmers. Unfortunately, the meager provender they were able to produce in the harsh climate couldn't compete with the animals and crops of more temperate Ohio and Indiana, Illinois and the Plains to the south. The immigrants had to scratch out a living in other ways.

Hawthorn Hill today is mostly older second-growth pulpwood, much of it aspen, and some of the most god-awful brambles to be found in the North. Few people go there except firewood gatherers from the immediate vicinity, and now and then a hopeful fellow with a few marijuana plants. And it was exactly the kind of place an adventurous kid like Tommy might explore, looking for early-twentieth-century farm artifacts abandoned in odd corners.

"How was Tommy dressed?" Gil said.

"A blue light warm-up jacket with a Cubs emblem, jeans, Nikes."

"Not enough for a cold night." The temperature often drops below forty degrees after midnight in September this far north.

"No. But I think he'll have the sense to hole up somewhere, break off boughs, cover himself to stay warm. And he has the big dog."

"That's good to know," Gil said. "But the subject could be

injured and need immediate medical aid and we'll have to send a few search teams into the woods now."

"The subject . . . immediate medical aid." Gil was thinking like the professional he is, and I was grateful for that.

"Why don't you go home?" Gil said, as gently as he ever does. "You'll need your rest for the flight tomorrow if the subject doesn't turn up tonight."

I looked at my watch. Ten-thirty. Fifteen searchers dressed in hunter's orange for visibility and carrying powerful flashlights, a couple of them with night-vision scopes mounted on military helmets, stood ready for orders.

"In a minute," I said.

"All right."

Gil turned to the group. "Gonna sound the alarm," he said.

As we covered our ears, he reached into his cruiser and flicked a switch. For several seconds, the *ooh-ah-ee-ah-ee* of the vehicle's powerful siren knifed into the screen of trees.

"Tommy!" everyone called.

Not a whisper of a reply, nor did anyone expect one.

But the searchers had to start somewhere. At least there had been no howling from wolves in response.

Men began moving up the trail, the beams from their big flashlights bobbing and weaving on the thick foliage as they stepped over roots. At intervals, pairs of searchers would split off the trail, calling Tommy's name as they headed southwest, following not only the path to Hawthorn Hill, but also the low ridges and valleys of the creeks that ran northward into Lake Superior. Only five miles separated Town Line Road from the vast moonscape of copper tailings from the Lone Pine Mine to the west, but the trails and ridges ran south for nearly ten miles to the L.P. Walsh Road. That was fifty square miles, which does not sound like a lot but is almost all thick forest interspersed with a few small clearings. It is full of deer and bear and coyotes and maybe—I hoped not—wolves. Over the decades, scores of people, many of them drunken hunters, have vanished into that country and never turned up again, not even as scattered bones. I did not think the searchers would locate Tommy in the dark. I hoped he and Hogan had gone safely to ground somewhere for the night.

"I'll be by in the morning," I told Gil just as the clouds opened and a steady rain began to fall. He nodded silently and turned back to his cruiser, listening to the steady hum of the searchers as they reported on their progress and complained about the wet.

Back at my cabin, I took a deep breath. Time to call Ginny and break the news that her foster son was missing in the woods on a dark and rainy night.

There was no answer. Her cell phone was switched off. She had not told me where she was staying in Manhattan. It was too late in the day to call her lawyers in Detroit and see if they knew.

I slept badly, frequently waking to feelings of overwhelming guilt. I should have had the sense not to allow a minor given into my care to enter the woods alone, even in the middle of the day, no matter how good a woodsman he might be, no matter if he's an Indian who grew up with the Indian skills I do not have, no matter how doughty a companion animal was with him, no matter if boys of all ages in Porcupine County have gone into the woods since time immemorial. Tommy Standing Bear was only twelve years old.

Each time I awoke, I tried Ginny again. No answer.

34

After scarcely five hours of sleep, I returned to the command post at the cemetery an hour before first light, my head logy, running on guilt and adrenaline. Taking just a splash of coffee from the big urn Mrs. Peters seemingly had kept filled all night—a pilot who may be aloft four or five hours without a place to relieve himself cannot afford more than a few sips of diuretic—I stepped over to Gil's cruiser, where the undersheriff slept across the backseat. I nudged him, and he instantly snapped awake ready for action, the product of years as a soldier. Other searchers stirred in their cars.

"Brought back the guys at two A.M.," Gil said. "We didn't find a thing. They'll be ready to go at daybreak. Mrs. Peters is bringing over some breakfast."

I could smell the bacon frying across the road. I wondered where she kept the rations to feed two dozen men, one of whom, I noticed, was Chad Garrow, who with Fred Kohut, a retired tribal policeman, had been pulled from the stakeout at Fourteen Mile Point to join in the search. Fred had gone home to the reservation to attend to an ailing wife, but big Chad could eat as much as two ordinary men himself. Part of me was unhappy that the stakeout had been left unmanned, but a more important issue flooded my heart: Tommy was missing.

"Andy Messner's sending up his search-and-rescue crew from Bessemer by ten A.M. if we don't find Tommy by then," Gil said.

"Alex asked if we needed the troopers from the Wakefield post. I told him not just yet."

I knew the drill. In an area of this size, if the subject of a search was not found within a few hours of daylight reconnaissance, a line of men twenty feet apart would begin traversing the forest from the cemetery in a broad skirmish line, examining every tree, hollow, downed branch, rock, and bush along the way. They would be looking for a body or bodies.

"Okay. I'll be in the air as soon as I can see the end of the runway."

"Take Joe with you."

The dispatcher, who had also spent most of the night sleeping in his pickup, nodded. Two pairs of eyes are much better than one in an air search, especially if one pair was Joe's. He'd flown shotgun with me several times during hunts out on the lake for lost boaters and sweeps of the woods for lost hikers, and on every occasion he spotted our target before I did. So much for the keen eagle vision of an Indian.

"Can't beat a Finn's eyes," Joe often said. His grandfather had emigrated from Helsinki to the Upper Peninsula in the early twentieth century along with many thousands of farmers and woodsmen seeking a new life in a bountiful land. I wonder if he bought clear-cut land from Hawthorn Hill's founder and destumped it. But Einar Koski, I know, died a miner in an accident at Lone Pine, the Upper Peninsula's last copper mine.

After I had preflighted the Skylane and we had strapped ourselves in it, I started the engine, throttling back to low RPMs and holding the plane on the ramp to warm up. It had been a chilly night, the temperature dropping to thirty-eight degrees. I hoped Tommy had been able to stay warm. In ten minutes, the Skylane's oil temperature needle had climbed over two hundred degrees into the green arc, just as the eastern sky began to bloom a reddish gray with the approaching sun, illuminating the trees at the south end of the runway. I released the brakes and taxied down to the south threshold for a takeoff northward into the soft but increasing breeze off Lake Superior.

A few minutes later, we arrived over the Finnish cemetery, where the few members of the search party left at the command post waved as we flew by at seventy knots scarcely two hundred feet above the ground. The rain clouds had cleared out and daylight had just started to outline the wet hills and trees below, but I wanted Tommy to hear the airplane as early as possible so that he would know we were looking for him. I set course for the south over Hawthorn Hill, aiming to fly a pattern of parallel north-south tracks, each one a couple of hundred yards farther west, so that Joe and I could scour every square foot of ground below. As the sun rose and the details of the ground below emerged into high relief, I could see the dark shapes of the searchers fanning out along the ridges and valleys.

For twenty minutes, we flew between M-64 and the southern boundary of L.P. Walsh Road, working our way west. Suddenly, Joe slapped my shoulder and pointed ahead and slightly to the right. A growing tendril of smoke from a smudge fire crept upward from a small clearing. As we reached the clearing, I throttled back to just above minimum controllable speed, lowered two notches of flaps, and put the Skylane into a tightly banked circle above the clearing.

"It's him!" Joe shouted through the intercom as, at the same instant, we saw a small figure wrapped in an olive drab blanket emerge from the tree line into the tall grass, waving both arms, followed by a big yellow dog.

I am not a religious man, but silently, tears brimming in my eyes, I thanked God, the Great Spirit, all the angels of the heavens, and all the manitous of the forest for Tommy's deliverance.

Joe keyed the mike. "We've got him!" he called, passing the coordinates of the clearing on his handheld GPS to the searchers below.

"This is Chad," came the first reply. "We're just half a mile east and are proceeding directly to the spot."

"Write a message to Tommy," I told Joe. "Tell him to stay where he is and the rescuers will arrive in a few minutes. Put it in this backpack and tie this banner to it."

The banner was the four-foot-long orange streamer reading "REMOVE BEFORE FLIGHT" that plugged the airplane's pitot tube against mud dauber wasps on the ground. It would make the backpack more visible to Tommy. A small plastic canteen of water and a few granola bars gave the backpack some heft. Joe opened his window and latched it up under the high wing.

This early in the morning, there was little breeze, so I didn't have to allow for the wind. Still in the tight circle, I increased the bank slightly, to place the right wing almost on Tommy's head in my field of view, and shouted, "Drop it!"

Joe tossed out the backpack and streamer. The package hurtled down, and in three seconds, it bounced off a hillock not ten yards from the boy and the dog, who both scampered for it at top speed—an exultant sight for me, for it meant Tommy wasn't hurt. Hogan reached the backpack first and carried it to Tommy in his mouth—the first time I had ever seen the dog retrieve anything, half Lab or not.

Tommy pulled out the note, read it, and waved to us as he and Hogan sat on the hillock to eat their impromptu breakfast. Joe and I kept circling until three searchers emerged into the clearing and made their way to Tommy.

"He's fine," Chad radioed. "But hungry."

"Yee-haa!" shouted another voice I couldn't recognize over the slight static.

"Who's that?" I said.

"Garner. I'm at the command post. Everybody's celebrating."

"Yep," I said, the lump still in my throat. "Heading back to the airport now."

In less than half an hour, the Skylane was back in its hangar and Joe and I had returned to the cemetery. Grinning searchers still trickled back from the woods, slapping one another on the back. Garner gave me a high-five as I got out of my Jeep. To my surprise, Eli was there, having driven up from his home during the air search, and he nodded to me.

"Well done," he said in his old genial but authoritative voice, as if the last few months had never happened. Whether he was actually back in command could have been debated, but he wasn't forcing the issue. It didn't matter. As undersheriff, Gil had tactical command over the search operation. Even in old times, Eli wouldn't have second-guessed Gil or tried to override his orders. But everyone at the cemetery noted Eli's presence. It meant things were changing, maybe for the good.

"Tommy back yet?" I asked Gil, whose preternaturally sour expression hadn't softened a smidgen. He knew that I was at fault for letting Tommy go into the woods by himself, but he wasn't going to say a word. He knew that I blamed myself, and that I faced much worse than he could lay upon me when Ginny found out what had happened.

"Just heard from Deputy Garrow," Gil said, ever the professional. "They're still about an hour south. The going is tough."

I nodded.

"That's a smart boy," Gil said. "Deputy Garrow reported the boy stated that he found himself in thick woods when the batteries in his GPS ran out. He tried to backtrack, but couldn't find the right trail. When night began to fall, he remembered a hunting camp he had passed on the way in. He forced a window open and found a couple of cots and army blankets inside. He built a small fire in the woodstove, and he and the dog stayed warm all night."

"What's his condition?"

"Excellent. Good color, plenty of energy, just a little hungry, Deputy Garrow said. He had a couple of candy bars for supper. He's walking home with the team. Wouldn't let them carry him."

"Good," Eli cut in. "Did he say why he went so deep into the woods?"

"He said he spotted a red fox and followed it down a trail and lost track of both time and location," Gil said, professional deference to a superior in his voice. Eli had returned, sure enough.

"I believe that," Eli said, and I agreed. Many times I had seen Tommy on the beach and in Ginny's backyard, rapt in thought and oblivious to the world as he contemplated the newest natural wonder he had found. He was smart, but he was, after all, only twelve.

We heard Chad and Tommy chatting and laughing before we saw them stride out of the forest. Tommy had the presence of mind to put on a somber face when he saw me standing with Gil, and he walked directly to us, unbidden.

"We'll talk about this later, Tommy," I said. "But I'm very glad to see you again."

"Yes sir, Mr. Martinez," he said, gazing at the ground.

"Steve's okay," I reminded him for the thousandth time.

I wanted to hug the lad but felt awkward. I stuck out my hand instead, and Tommy quickly took it.

Gil studied the tops of the trees intently. Eli beamed avuncularly, as if he had been in charge all along and we had all loyally done his bidding. But he still did not behave as if he were the boss and we his underlings, although that had just been silently established by Gil's deference.

"Be sure to thank everyone who went out looking for you, okay?" I added.

Tommy strode around and shook everyone's hands, including

Eli's, accepting their hair-tousles and congratulations. Doc Miller, who could accurately assess a kid's health with one glance, listened to Tommy's chest, took his temperature, peered into his eyes, and patted him on the back. Mrs. Peters, who was cleaning up after the enormous breakfast she had served—she would accept no payment for doing her part in the search—grasped the blushing boy to her enormous bosom. There is no greater satisfaction for wilderness law enforcement and its civilian friends than the successful rescue of a lost child, and everybody grinned widely, our laughter heartfelt.

35

"Tommy, it's not my place to chew you out for last night," I said quietly when we had returned to my cabin. "That belongs to your foster mother. But maybe we can talk about what happened and maybe we can make sure it doesn't happen again. Does that make sense to you?"

"Yes, it does," Tommy said, looking directly into my eyes. He was neither defiant nor defensive, just a kid who knew he'd made a mistake and was bravely ready to take his medicine.

"What do you think is the most important lesson you learned from last night?" I asked, expecting Tommy to say the obvious—to keep track of the time, especially the remaining daylight.

"Never go into the woods without fresh batteries for the GPS."

"Well . . . yes," I said. "And maybe don't forget how to use a compass. You didn't have one, did you?"

"No, I was using the GPS for a compass." When its batteries died, the device didn't know which way north lay. No hiker or pilot can afford to be without a magnetic compass as a backup.

"I think you're right about the batteries, Tommy, but sometimes the signals from the satellites in orbit can fail, and people who are navigating by GPS can get in deep trouble if they don't have a backup of some kind." Countless pilots of small planes had become so dependent on their handheld or panel-mounted GPSs that a battery or electrical system failure, or the disappearance of the signals, caused them to panic and fly frantically in circles, their hearts pounding, trying to get their bearings from their aviation charts. More than one had run out of fuel not far from an airport that way, sometimes with fatal results. Against such an event, I practiced frequently not only with a compass, but also with the old-fashioned direction-finding radio equipment in the sheriff's aircraft—and I regularly checked my position on a chart, making sure I could recognize where I was from landmarks. GPSs are wonderful tools, but when you let down your guard, they can bite you.

"I didn't think about that," Tommy said forthrightly. "I'm going to get me a compass."

"And maybe a hiker's map or two," I said.

For a few minutes, we sat lost in thought.

"You did do some things very well," I said. "Making that smudge fire was very smart. So was finding a camp and spending the night inside. It got pretty cold. How did you get in?"

"The door was locked with a padlock, but a window was loose, and Hogan and I were able to squeeze inside."

"Were you frightened?"

"Yes, a little, when the wolves came."

"Wolves?" A chill coursed through my stomach.

"Yeah. Two of them took down a deer right by the cabin before dark came. Hogan smelled them and started barking."

"What did they do?"

"They growled and snarled and threw themselves against the door. But it was locked tight. When they'd finished eating, they moved away into the forest."

I stifled a gulp. That was the first time I had heard of wolves ranging so close to the northern part of the county, where the human population was heaviest. While Tommy himself probably had been in no danger of a direct attack from the animals, he very likely would have tried to go to his dog's aid, and in the melee the slashing predators might not have discriminated between boy and dog. Now the full force of my error in letting even an accomplished woodsman like Tommy go into the forest alone struck me. We had been very, very lucky.

For the rest of the afternoon, Tommy and I went about our respective businesses, he catching up with the homework he hadn't done the night before, and I repairing a few rotted boards in the woodshed next to my cabin. At about four, the phone rang. It was Ginny.

"I'm at Houghton airport," she said. "Malcolm died last night. If you tried to reach me, I turned my phone off so I could sit with him without being disturbed."

"I'm very sorry, Ginny," I said, only partly meaning it. Malcolm had hurt her badly, and I resented that.

"It was a hard death. It was prostate cancer. He was in a lot of pain. Nobody should have to endure that. Especially alone. That's why I went to him, despite everything. He needed somebody. He had no one else."

I'll admit it: Ginny is a better human being than I am. She is comfortable with the grace of forgiveness, while I can never seem to let go of a grudge.

"How's everything?" she continued. "How's Tommy? Was he a good boy? Was Hogan a good dog? Were they any problem?"

"Uh, no, not at all," I said. "We did have an exciting time, but I'll tell you about it when you get home."

"What's for supper?"

"Hmm, how about spaghetti?" My meat sauce is justly famous in the Upper Peninsula, at least among those who have sampled it, and there aren't all that many.

"Perfect. I'll be by about six. Bye for now."

She sounded a lot friendlier than she had the morning before, but she was not going to be happy when Tommy and I told her about the events of the last twenty-four hours. An iceberg of dread settled in my entrails. To keep my mind off the impending ordeal, I called Joe Koski.

"Ginny'll be home tonight," I said, "and I'll be able to take over the stakeout at Fourteen Mile Point tomorrow morning."

"Good," Joe said. "No point in Chad going back now. He's due for his rotation back to regular duty anyway. The stakeout will have been unmanned only twenty-four hours—what could happen in such a short time?"

I didn't want to think about that. I called Alex instead.

"News for you," he said. "On a hunch, Sue called a contact in the New Jersey State Police an hour ago and asked about Monaghan. His name turned up in the records of that case about the illegal organ transplant harvesting. For a while, he was a person of interest. He was suspected of money laundering for the harvesting ring. But that lead went nowhere."

"Enough probable cause right there," I said. "I'll call Dick Franciscus."

A few minutes later, after a bit of thought, the New York detective agreed to move on the case.

"It's my neck," Dick said, "but it's my gut, too."

"Come again?"

"The commissioner could chop off my head if you're wrong, but my stomach tells me you're right. I'll take some guys and visit Monaghan in the morning for a little talk."

"Thanks, Dick," I said with feeling, and hung up.

While waiting for Ginny to arrive, I put together my camping kit—a goose-down sleeping bag, an Ensolite ground pad, a canteen, coffee, and a few military-issue dried Meals Ready to Eat that Gil somehow had scrounged from the state police. Chad and Fred had left a cooking kit inside a forest green two-man nylon backpacker's tent pitched inside the tree line, well hidden from both the beach and the human geocache at Fourteen Mile Point. To my gear I added my hiker's GPS and the new novel by one of my favorite crime writers, P. D. James. After all the hugger-mugger of the last day and night, I looked forward to the quiet of the stakeout and two days in the woods with a fellow Indian. With Camilo's assent, Gil had recruited Billy Bones, the retired Lac Vieux Desert tribal cop, to keep me company. I would need two days, anyway, to heal the welts and cuts Ginny's forthcoming eruption most likely would inflict on my hide.

And it was not long in coming. She arrived hungry, and after hugging Tommy fiercely and me warmly—a lot more warmly than I had expected or even thought I deserved—she tucked into the spaghetti while Tommy and I sat mostly silent, stirring now and then to say something trivial. As she slurped away—she is usually a dainty eater, but not where pasta is concerned—I asked if she wanted to talk about New York.

"Some other time, Steve," she said. "It was tough, and revisiting it is going to be tough, too."

"All right. But I'm here whenever you need to unload."

She put her hand on mine. "Thank you," she said. I was forgiven. For a while.

Presently, stifling a belch in ladylike fashion, she pushed her chair back. "I always know," she said, drilling her eyes into both Tommy and me, "when you've got something to tell me. Give."

We gave. She listened, her expression unchanging but her eyes smoldering, as we told our story. Tommy related the events as he had seen them—including the encounter with the wolves, which I'd hoped he would save for a later day—and I told my side. When we were done, Ginny took in a deep breath.

"Go upstairs, Tommy," she said calmly. "I have things to talk about with Steve."

"Uh . . . there isn't an upstairs here," he said. My modest four-room cabin occupies all of one story.

"The bedroom then."

"Yes'm." He shot me a look full of remorse and sympathy.

When he had closed the door, Ginny directed her full gaze upon me.

"What. Were. You. Thinking?" she said slowly and evenly, as if each word were a complete sentence, without raising her voice a notch or changing her iron expression. I hate that. I can deal with frenzied yelling and screaming—a professional lifetime of squelching domestic disputes involving sometimes armed combatants gives a cop that capacity—but calm, measured anger is a lot tougher. She did not cast ugly aspersions on my ancestry, one of the most ordinary forms of a thorough bawling out, but concentrated on the inadequacy of my intelligence and judgment. For the next ten minutes, I quietly absorbed my drubbing, which involved weighty and completely deserved abstractions such as "what if?" and "stupidity" and "irresponsibility" and "idiocy."

I did not try to mitigate my guilt by bringing up Ginny's own words about her childhood next door to the forest. "We country kids *lived* in the woods," she had said over dinner several years before. "I'd go there on expeditions, gathering wildflowers, looking for birds, hunting treasures like old bottle tops and cans. Maybe we'd get lucky and find a hundred-year-old garbage dump in a gully where people threw things they couldn't burn, like broken dishes and patent medicine bottles. There were old foundations and maybe an abandoned shack.

"If I had a friend with me, we'd take a lunch and a jar of Kool-Aid. We'd make little shacks in the woods, perhaps finding a downed tree to make one wall and dragging branches over to make the rest. They were our forts. We were at home in the woods as much as we were in our own houses."

But Ginny, I knew, had changed. She had grown up and become a parent. Parents look at things differently from those who aren't parents.

When Ginny's batteries finally ran down, she sat silently in the deathly calm she had maintained the while, her fiery green eyes lasering holes through my soul. I sat in a puddle of sweat.

"You're right, honey," I said. "I completely screwed up. I am so very sorry." That was all I could think of to say.

"Don't honey me!" she said.

I spread my hands in supplication. She ignored them.

"Tommy," she called. "Let's go home." As they walked out to her van, her arm around him lovingly, I knew she wouldn't lambaste him with what she'd lambasted me. He was only a boy. I was a grown man and should have known better.

36

The next morning, I woke up still feeling bruised and prepared to suffer, at least in spirit, for quite a while. Ginny is not often stirred to anger, but when she is, she holds on to her mad for a long and thoroughly satisfying time until she is certain the object of her fury has truly repented of his sins. I'd been there before.

But now an urgent task awaited me. Thanks to the search for Tommy, Fourteen Mile Point had gone unwatched for nearly twenty-four hours and needed to be staked out quickly again if we ever were to catch the subject of our hunt—a subject who most likely was a psychopath and a killer. I dressed quickly, gulped a quick bachelor's breakfast of toast and coffee, and headed for the marina. Dawn was sunny and already warming, the temperature climbing into the sixties, a balmy day for the middle of September in the Upper Peninsula. But a sharp breeze tousled the still green tall grass along Highway M-64 to the Porcupine City Marina. A cool front was blowing in from the north and would stir up the lake.

On the way to the marina, I radioed the sheriff's department to tell the dispatcher I was on my way to Fourteen Mile Point.

"Billy Bones there yet?" I asked Joe.

"Can't make it till noon," he said. "Has a teacher conference with his granddaughter." Billy, I knew, was the only caregiver for his three grandchildren.

"Damn," I said. "I don't want to leave that stakeout unattended a minute longer than we have to."

"We won't have to," Eli cut in on the radio. My eyebrows rose.

"Back at the shop?" I asked needlessly. Most of me was delighted that Eli had gone back to work, but part of me—the political candidate part—was dismayed all the same. Maybe he was just playing figurehead and still relying on Gil to administer the department, but the voters wouldn't know the difference

"Yeah. I'll go with you in the Whaler. Billy can come out in my boat as soon as he gets here this afternoon. When he arrives at Fourteen Mile, I'll come back in it." Eli often went out for lake trout from the marina in his sixteen-foot runabout.

"Yes sir."

"That way we'll be on the job but you won't be without backup."

"Yes sir."

I had to smile at that "we."

The sheriff's search boat, a workaday eighteen-foot Boston Whaler powered by a 150-horsepower Evinrude, is not the fastest or most comfortable craft on Lake Superior, but it still is a sturdy fiberglass hull that can hold its own in a rough seaway. I threw my gear on its well deck and stowed in a seat locker a waterproof plastic case containing my holstered .357 and the military-issue M-16 light assault rifle we deputies preferred for open country rather than the short-barreled riot shotguns we carried in our cruisers for close-quarters combat. Eli arrived shortly later at the marina, lunch pail in hand and Glock holstered at his waist, warmly but lightly dressed in white uniform shirt and sheriff's Windbreaker because he would be returning to base while the sun was still high. It was not lost on me that a Kevlar vest, which he rarely wore, added a couple of inches to his already considerable bulk. Eli had come back on the job and had dressed the part.

"Great day for police work," he said amiably. "Ready to go?"

"Yup." I waved to Paul Betty, the septuagenarian harbormaster, who during boating season lived in a small shack next to the docks and missed nothing.

"Seen anything go out yesterday?" I called. "Any strangers?"

"Naw," he said. "Just a couple of locals. They came back yesterday evening."

I felt better—the Porcupine City Marina is the largest and best-equipped harbor for a hundred miles along the lakeshore—but there are other ways to launch a boat onto the lake, such as the public access ramps at Silverton and the Wolverine Mountain Wilderness State Park thirteen and fourteen miles west of Porcupine City. There are also rough, rarely used skids—little more than loose wooden boards—on the beaches near summer cabins for scores of miles in both directions. I hoped nobody we were looking for had taken advantage of those.

"Heads-up, guys," the harbormaster called as Eli pulled in the dock lines and I started the outboard. "The lake's running a bit high today. Four-footers."

I waved in acknowledgment and pulled away into the channel. The breeze wasn't a gale, but it wasn't going to be an easy ride northeast over the fourteen miles of shoreline, long stretches of it uninhabited, that gave Fourteen Mile Point its name. The Whaler had an enclosed steering cuddy big enough to shelter two people, and that, I hoped, would keep us mostly dry from spray as the boat pounded its way over the heavy chop through the harbor channel to the open lake. But my knees would take a pounding, for I stood at the wheel, the better to see where I was going, while Eli sat upon a couple of cushions. He could have taken the wheel, being the senior officer, but senior officers are used to their juniors doing the driving, and so I did.

Once out into the lake, I had to throttle back to six miles per hour so that the Whaler could shoulder safely over the quartering swells, its high freeboard keeping the crashing waves out of the cockpit. The spray, however, dampened me thoroughly. I grumbled. We'd have to dry our clothes over a fire as soon as we reached Fourteen Mile Point. The afternoon would be warm, in the midsixties, but by nightfall, the temperature would drop to forty degrees or less. This wasn't going to be a luau in the tropics.

Eli and I exchanged few words, partly because of the roar of the outboard and the thumping of the boat's hull on the waves, but mostly because we were a little uncomfortable in each other's presence. We were still political rivals, after all. We were polite, but hardly chummy.

Still, when I thanked Eli for coming with me, he replied, "No problem, Steve. Thanks for coming out to my house to see me."

Ten minutes into the voyage, the radio under the cockpit coaming crackled.

"Steve? Alex. Dick Franciscus and his squad tried to pick up Monaghan at his condo this morning, but he wasn't there. His secretary said he left on vacation the other day. He's been taking a lot of vacations, she said. Goes to Minneapolis, she said. Be careful. Be damn careful."

"Thanks."

Over the next several minutes, I brought Eli up to speed on the latest developments in the case, and in soundless response, the sheriff drew his Glock and checked the magazine. We both patted our armored vests.

Fourteen Mile Point is easy to spot even from a low boat running two miles offshore. Eli and I had decided to pass the lighthouse to the east as if we were just a couple of fishermen heading to Houghton, then turn the boat inshore around the point, out of sight of the lighthouse. If anyone had arrived there in the last twenty-four hours, we reckoned, they would have come from the east, and maybe we could land unnoticed.

The ruins of the massive light station, built late in the nineteenth century, still tower over the forest, and the station's big fog signal building still squats on the shore. The lighthouse had been manned until it was automated in 1940, and the light was finally extinguished in 1945 when radio-beacon navigation rendered it obsolete. A few years later, the place was sold to a private owner, and in 1984 vandals torched the main structure, burning everything combustible. The fog building escaped the torch, although its two ten-inch whistles, designed to throw an ear-shattering noise miles across the lake to provide a bearing to blinded vessels during fog and storms, will never scream again.

Decades ago, the lighthouse keepers brought in equipment and provisions over a rough dirt track, four miles long, leading to a gravel road that originally was a logging trail. But, as Eli pointed out, it was long grown over and had become impenetrable, and now the only reasonable way to reach Fourteen Mile Point is by boat, by a long, rugged shoreline hike past several streams, or by snowmobile in the winter. The remoteness of the place made it the most challenging of the caches we had found.

Chad and Fred had discovered the cached cadaver, like all the others headless and handless but apparently well embalmed in plastic, tucked between the double walls of the ruined keeper's quarters, right where the waypoint on Arthur Kling's laptop said it would be. The deputies had left it there for the duration of the stakeout. After we'd caught our perps or given up on the attempt, Alex would come in and do his thing, and then we'd move the corpse to Marquette.

Meanwhile, the Whaler chugged slowly past Fourteen Mile Point as I squinted at the beach still more than a mile away through binoculars, searching for signs of human presence. A boat beached while the stakeout was unmanned or a tendril of smoke from a campfire might have betrayed an intruder. Nothing. A bald eagle rose majestically from a tall snag on the low granite outcropping that marked the point and soared out low above the waves, seemingly to greet the boat passing by. A traditional Indian might have said that the eagle was acknowledging the presence of another who shared its existence on Earth. But I knew the bird was ignoring me, that my arrival had nothing to do with its stirring, that it was scanning the waves below hoping a fat fish would rise into the shallows to be snatched with sharp talons.

I checked the GPS, looked up, and immediately spotted directly onshore the sandy bluff we sought. There was no sand beach in front of the lighthouse, only rocky shallows, but a small stream lay under a low bluff half a mile east of the lighthouse, emptying onto a sandy bottom. There, as we had planned during the trip out from Porcupine City, Eli and I could winch the boat over the shallow inlet and hide it in the creek a few yards in behind the grassy dunes, where it couldn't be seen either from the lake or by anybody walking along the beach. Chad and Fred had made camp just inside the tree line, where the tent would also be invisible. It would be my home for the next two days.

"Ready now," I said, yielding the wheel to Eli. I gathered up a sixty-foot nylon line and took up position on the coaming at the port side while Eli swung the Whaler so its stern faced the waves. He opened the throttle to drive the boat into the inlet as far as it could go before grounding on the sand. At just the right moment, Eli killed the motor and yanked its propeller out of the water before it churned into the bottom. I leaped over the side with the nylon line and strode over the sandbar into waist-high water along the creek bank, ready to tie one end to a tree ten yards in so that Eli could operate the bow winch, pulling the boat off the sandy bottom and into the creek.

I was reaching up to secure the line to a stout birch when a woman yelled, "It's a cop!" from just inside the tree line fifty yards to the west. I knew that voice. It belonged to Sharon Shoemaker.

"Where?" a strange male voice called from farther away.

"The guy in front of that boat!"

"Oh, shit." He sounded irritated, not anxious—like a man who had prepared himself for any eventuality, including the unwelcome but not unexpected arrival of the law.

My blood curdled. My revolver and rifle lay zipped inside that waterproof bag at the bottom of the Whaler, thirty feet away.

I motioned to Eli to stay down. They hadn't seen him yet. The sheriff nodded and crouched out of sight in the cuddy, his Glock drawn, but I stood unarmed out in the open, a perfect target for a man with a gun. I am forever getting caught this way, with a lot of open space between me and my weapons. This time, I told myself futilely, it wasn't so much poor judgment as it was the accident of circumstance. In this instance I could hardly be expected to carry a revolver at my waist when wading through deep water up a creek. Could I? Shit.

I tried to play it cool. "Hello!" I shouted. "Didn't expect to find anybody so far from civilization!" But I knew they knew why I was there.

"It's Deputy Martinez!" Sharon called.

The man stepped out from the tree line and raised a rifle. He was tall and handsome, with arrogantly flaring nostrils and a sardonic, contemptuous smile, and outfitted in expensive outdoor clothing he no doubt had paid for with a platinum American Express card at the original Abercrombie & Fitch store on Water Street in Manhattan. I recognized Andrew Monaghan immediately, having seen his photograph.

"Sorry about this, cop," he said calmly. With a swift twist and click he snaked the rifle bolt back, loaded a cartridge into the chamber, and drove it home. Even at that distance, I could see that it was a costly Weatherby Magnum, the kind of rifle wealthy captains of finance buy for guided antelope hunts on game ranches in Texas. I didn't know what caliber the rifle was, but I knew it was capable of blowing a very large hole in me.

"He's armed," I whispered to Eli. "Rifle." I thought I heard a soft click from inside the cuddy. Likely Eli had quietly pulled back the receiver on his Glock, charging the chamber with a cartridge.

"Don't!" the woman called to Monaghan. She emerged from the tree line halfway between Monaghan and me, but well out of his line of fire.

"Haven't seen you for a while, Sharon," I said, trying to keep my voice conversational and my hands down, as if I hadn't noticed that a loaded and cocked rifle was pointed at me.

"Shut up!" Monaghan said. He raised the rifle to his cheek and sighted through the scope as Sharon Shoemaker's jaw dropped in dismay.

"Monaghan, don't shoot!" I called.

He lowered the rifle, his smile slowly disappearing. "How do you know my name?" he demanded.

"I'm the deputy who talked to you on the phone last month," I said. "Remember? We know all about you, Monaghan, my department, a bunch of others, and the state police of Michigan, New York, and New Jersey. The New York Police Department, too. Think, man! I'm a cop. If you kill me, you'll be hunted down. And you know what cops do to people who kill cops. Drop the rifle."

Instead he returned it to his shoulder and took another bead. I took a deep breath.

"We all know you're ACTUARY, that you cached the body of a murdered prostitute on the North Country Trail, and that you killed Arthur Kling and torched his car. We know all about the geocaching game and where you guys planted all those bodies."

"How the hell did you find that out?" he said, looking up from the scope, his expression wreathed in unbelieving fury.

That amounted to a confession, but fat lot of good it would do me if Monaghan made Eli and me his second and third victims—or third and fourth, if he had killed that prostitute. And, I thought absently, Sharon would be his fifth.

"Come on, drop the rifle. You know Michigan and Minnesota don't have the death penalty. You can spend the rest of your life in prison. But if you kill me, I can assure you that a cop will see to it that you die, too. And I guarantee you it'll be a painful, *painful* death."

Whether that was true I didn't really know—nor was I sure Camilo Hernandez was capable of torture—but I couldn't think of anything else to say. Monaghan kept the rifle at his shoulder.

"You're not as dumb as I thought," he said. "Gotta give you that." The cheerless smile returned to his face.

"Why'd you do it?" I said, as much to buy time as anything else, to keep him talking.

"If you have to ask, cop," he said, "you're not as smart as you think." He sighted through the scope, the muzzle steady, pointing directly at my head. At this range it would be impossible to miss.

But Monaghan wasn't as smart as *he* thought, not if he refused to consider the possible consequences to himself. He was so caught up in his own game, so possessed by his own magnetic personality, that he could see no way out except more killing.

Just before he squeezed the trigger I dived to the side, toward the boat, making a large splash in the shallow water of the inlet and spoiling his aim. But just before I reached the Whaler, the bullet caught me in the last rib in my left flank just below the armor that had hiked up my torso as I dived. The round whined out into the lake.

In the movies, the winged lawman holds his side with one hand and with the other resolutely raises his weapon and takes aim, drilling the bad guy squarely between the eyes. In real life it doesn't work that way. Getting shot, even by a bullet that glances off bone, is a powerful insult to the human body. The first shock usually incapacitates the victim, allowing the shooter to take his time with the coup de grâce.

But I had dived into the cold, cold water of Lake Superior,

and within two seconds my head had cleared and, my side screaming with pain, I had splashed around the port side of the boat and
huddled behind the steel mass of the big Mercury outboard, grop-
ing for the gun case in the stern well. Monaghan still hadn't seen
Eli, a good thing because the quarter inch of fiberglass that made
up the walls of the cuddy couldn't have stopped a .22 bullet, let
alone a Weatherby Magnum round.

Eli still crouched out of sight, waiting to make his move.
"You okay, Steve?" he hissed.

"I'm hit," I whispered back from behind the motor, "but stay
down. He'll cut you to pieces."

Monaghan loosed three more shots at me, one striking the
water a foot away and ricocheting way out into the lake, another
splattering against the cast steel of the motor and possibly crack-
ing its case, and the third punching through four layers of fiberglass hull, entering at the bow and exiting at the stern a foot from
my head. That Weatherby was a small-caliber cannon.

While Monaghan reloaded, I reached around the motor and
snaked the rifle case out of the well. Quickly I wrested the M-16
and a couple of loaded thirty-shot magazines out of the case,
drove home one of the magazines, and cocked the action. I had
the advantage in firepower now. Although the M-16's lightweight
5.56-millimeter bullet is nowhere near as heavy as even a small-
bore Weatherby Magnum, the military rifle can fire three-
cartridge bursts of automatic fire as well as accurate single shots.

But Monaghan had the advantage of higher ground as well as
stout pines and birches to hide behind. I had only the small mass
of the Evinrude to protect me, and I could not move away from
the boat without exposing myself. I was losing blood, too, growing weaker by the minute. If Monaghan took his time, another of
his bullets eventually would find me.

Whang! Another Weatherby bullet slammed through the hull
and ricocheted off the lower unit of the Evinrude, the wind of its

passage ruffling the hair on my exposed neck. In blind reaction I stood and fired two bursts at the gap in the trees where I had seen Monaghan last, the rounds ripping flinders of bark from the trunk of a hemlock. Just as I ducked back down, I caught a glimpse of Monaghan aiming his rifle from around a tree a good dozen feet from the spot I had shot up. I ducked to the right of the outboard and the bullet punched a ragged hole through the stern exactly where I had been.

This couldn't go on much longer.

Suddenly Eli's pistol barked from the other side of the boat. I glanced around the stern. A few feet away, resplendent in brass-bedecked white shirt and garrison cap, stood the sheriff, Glock cradled in both hands and aimed at the tree line, coughing every three seconds in carefully timed fire as he waded through the water and strode up the sand in a gunfighter's crouch. Despite his arthritic bulk, he had quickly rolled over the side of the Whaler into the shallow water while Monaghan was reloading.

"Get into the woods, Steve!" Eli yelled. "I'll cover you!" It took every ounce of my remaining strength to stagger out of the water and across the sand, spraying the woods behind the beach with the M-16 as I stumbled up behind a screen of heavy logs atop a low dune, thinking that this must have been what it was like for the Marines hunkering on the beaches of Tarawa, pinned down by deadly Japanese fire.

Eli continued to advance, firing.

"Run!" I yelled, ready to cover Eli. His Glock wasn't very accurate at a fifty-yard range, but his bullets were striking close, forcing Monaghan to whip around from behind a thick white pine and snap off wild shots. Eli's ancient legs responded, breaking into a trot that was little more than a fast shuffle. Ten yards from the hummock that sheltered me, his pistol emptied, and he stopped for a second to dump the magazine and ram home a new one. It was a fatal pause.

The Magnum bullet struck Eli squarely in the center of his Kevlar vest and punched through and through in a spray of blood. The sheriff fell on his back onto the sand, his arms and legs flung out. The armored police vests worn under a roomy uniform shirt will stop a pistol bullet, but a high-velocity rifle load just keeps going. Only heavy tactical vests with steel rifle plates will stop such a slug, and those are normally worn by SWAT teams outside their uniforms.

"Whoooo!" yelled Monaghan in his moment of victory, stepping out from the tree line onto the beach. That was *his* fatal mistake.

Groaning in pain, I rose from behind the hummock, took a quick bead, and pumped two bursts into Monaghan's chest. He staggered, then fell to his knees and collapsed on his face, blood from his tattered lungs pouring from his mouth.

Then I fainted.

I wasn't out long. I came to with a female form leaning over me, her hands binding a rough compress made of my ripped-up shirt around my ruined side.

"Ginny?" I very much wanted to see her lovely face.

"No. It's Sharon."

"Why?"

"Long story, Deputy. And it's not my fault. But nobody's going to believe me. I'm sorry, but I have to go. When I get out of the woods, I'll phone the police and tell them where you are."

"Don't do that. There's no trail out of here anymore. Stay here. I'll put in a good word."

"Sorry, Steve. I'm leaving. But help's coming." With that, Sharon sprinted west down the beach, stumbling over logs and rocks as she ran, once falling to her knees on the unsteady sand.

She was unarmed. She could have taken my M-16, still with a dozen cartridges in its magazine, with her. But she did not. That counted for something. I passed out again.

Presently I awoke to the thrum of outboard motors, rose on one elbow, and peered out onto the lake. Two boats bounced through the surf. Reinforcements. Before he assaulted the beach, Eli must have radioed the sheriff's department and told Joe what was going on at Fourteen Mile Point.

Five minutes later, the boats beached on the flat rocks offshore, and four deputies, including Gil and Chad, leaped over the side and waded through the water.

"The sheriff's down," I called weakly as they approached. "So's the shooter. It's Monaghan. I think he's dead. Sharon Shoemaker was with him and she's gone west on the beach. She's not armed, though. Try to grab her, not shoot her. She likely knows the whole story."

A deputy knelt at Eli's side and searched for a pulse. When he looked up and shook his head, Gil shoved Chad away before he could approach his fallen uncle. "Stand down," Gil said. "You're off the case. But tend to Steve."

Chad, who knew the rules, turned and gazed forlornly out over the lake for a few seconds, then shook his massive head, stifled a sob, and knelt at my side. As Chad applied a gauze dressing to my shattered rib, Gil barked a few words into his handheld radio.

"Troopers on the way," he said when he was finished. "They'll drive in to a cabin three miles west on the beach and head this way to cut Shoemaker off. Now let's get you to the hospital."

As Chad brought up the folding litter we kept in the Whaler, I passed out for the third time.

37

"I can't trust you to go out alone, either, can I?" said Ginny as I struggled out of the fog of anesthesia in a bed at Porcupine County Hospital. But she said the words softly and lovingly, with a cool hand on my cheek.

"It was supposed to be just a stakeout," I said weakly, still in defensive mode after her reaming-out the other day.

We'd taken a chance, a dangerous one, I knew. We had hoped Fourteen Mile Point would still be deserted after Chad and Fred had left the stakeout to join the search for Tommy. What could possibly happen in twenty-four hours if it had taken the cachers nearly all summer to locate their quarries? There is a corollary of Murphy's Law that deals with this kind of situation, and I tried to put it into words, but failed.

"Shush," Ginny said, kissing my forehead.

Night had fallen outside. I tried to sit up and fell back, groaning from the lightning in my side.

"You'll have to come live with me while I nurse you back to health," Ginny said.

"I can think of worse places to be," I said. Actually, there was nowhere I'd rather be than Ginny's house, and often I'd spend a night or two there. I had to be tough, though, or maybe I was just playing the macho game in a cloud of Vicodin. "But I can't impose on you."

"Nonsense," she said, stroking my cheek. "Maybe you'll get used to living with me. Think of it as practice, maybe." Her eyes twinkled and a small smile played at the edges of her mouth.

Tommy, who was standing on the other side of the bed, suddenly turned and looked out the window, his face a study in suppressed consternation. *Indians embarrass so easily,* I thought, *or maybe it's just because he's a kid.* I chuckled and gasped as my ribs shot me a painful reminder.

"Take it easy, Steve," said Doc Miller from the foot of the bed. "You're gonna be fine, but you're gonna hurt for a while. That bullet took out a hunk of one rib and cracked two others. I had to dig around in there and put in seventeen stitches to hold you together. You pay attention to Ginny, you hear? If you stay with her, you'll save the county a bunch of money in nursing home bills." Ever the practical man, Doc is.

Ginny bent and kissed me again. "The authorities want to talk to you," she said. "Tommy and I will be back tomorrow, and we'll take you home as soon as Doc lets you go."

Her home. Not mine. I'm fond of my cabin, but Ginny was right. I could get used to her place very easily. I squeezed her hand, and she and Tommy stepped out the door, to be replaced by the much less attractive countenance of the undersheriff.

"Did they get Shoemaker?" I asked.

"You bet," Gil said. "She just walked up to the troopers and gave in without a fight. She's talking. And how."

"How'd Shoemaker and Monaghan get to Fourteen Mile?"

"He and the girl drove out to a cabin four miles past the light, parked their car, and hiked down the beach."

"That's what I was afraid of," I said. "Anyway, what's the rest of the story?"

"Oh, it's quite a story," Gil said. "Stay right there. Don't move. I'll tell you all about it."

I was beginning to feel woozy again, and Doc Miller stepped in.

"Can it wait, Undersheriff?" he said. "The patient needs rest."

"Oh, sure," Gil said. "Nobody's going anywhere anyway. See you tomorrow, Deputy."

I passed out for the fourth time that day.

38

The next afternoon, my side still ached, but my head was clearer after a brief but loving visit from Ginny and Tommy. I had just put away a decent lunch when Gil knocked. Alex and Sergeant Sue Hemb followed him into the room, and the three pulled up chairs around my bed.

"Ready, Deputy?" the undersheriff said without preamble.

"Given the circumstances," I said, "maybe you could call me Steve."

Gil's expression remained set. Alex and Sue exchanged amused glances.

"That corpse on the North Country Trail?" Gil said. "Yeah, Monaghan cached it there, Shoemaker said. This is where things get really interesting. She said Monaghan had told her he and Kling had been roommates at Yale—we checked and she was right. All the way back at college, Monaghan had been the leader, Kling the follower. Sue?"

Sergeant Hemb nodded. "It's a common phenomenon with antisocial personality disorders," she said. "The mastermind and his loyal servant work together, until the mastermind decides the servant is no longer useful and does away with him."

"Yeah," Alex cut in, opening his notebook. "In the last couple of years, Monaghan and Kling had helped bankroll a couple of mortuaries, one in Jersey—that's the one that got busted last year—and one in Duluth. They both specialized in medical cadavers and harvested body parts for the legitimate market. At the Duluth mortuary, they got a crooked diener to cut out and sell illegal organs and alter the paperwork. Monaghan was the brains and Kling the bagman."

"Diener?" I asked.

"That's a mortuary worker responsible for handling, cleaning, and moving bodies. Sometimes he helps harvest organs."

"Go on."

"When the cops busted that ring in Jersey last year, Monaghan nearly got caught in the backwash. He and Kling decided to lie doggo with the Minnesota operation for a while until the heat blew over, but they had had so much fun and made so much money with harvesting cadavers in Minnesota that after a few months, they decided to start up again—but with the geocaching game."

"Whatever for?" I said.

"Just to keep their hand in," Gil said. "And we think they hoped to keep the diener happy by letting him make a few bucks selling the cadavers to the geocachers. It was probably just something to do until they could start peddling illegal organs and making big money again."

"Did Monaghan kill that hooker?"

"Shoemaker says he said he did."

"Just because he could?"

"Don't think so. The Duluth mortuary—it was raided and shut down last night—just didn't have a handy prepared cadaver that day for Monaghan to take. The diener is talking, by the way.

"Shoemaker also says Monaghan told her that he went out that night in Duluth, found a hooker, took her back to his motel room, had sex with her, then strangled her. Shoemaker said Monaghan told her in great detail how he stashed the body in his car, drove east into Wisconsin, cut her up in the woods, and tried to embalm her with formalin and a syringe. He buried the head and hands and carried the rest to the cache in Michigan."

"Alone?"

"Probably. Monaghan kept himself buff working out at a Bally's and had the beef to carry a heavy torso on his back two miles into the woods. What's more, Shoemaker said Monaghan told her he was doing the world a favor by ridding it of someone it would never miss."

"That's cold," I said.

"It's typical," Sergeant Hemb said.

"According to Shoemaker," Gil said, "that's what Arthur Kling told Monaghan, too, when he found the cache on the trail. It was stinking, and Kling guessed it wasn't a cadaver, but a vic done just to be a geocache. He called Monaghan in New York to complain that murder wasn't part of the game. Monaghan said he'd come out and meet Kling and talk over the matter. They agreed to meet at Page Falls at three P.M. August second. Shoemaker had told Kling about the place and even taken him there for a little sex.

"But now, if Shoemaker's story is right, Kling was badly worried. Somebody had been killed. He could be charged as an accessory to murder. But if he got rid of Monaghan, there would be no witness, either, that Kling was involved. That's what Shoemaker says he said."

"That explains why he had that varmint rifle in the motel," I said. "But why didn't he take it to Page Falls?"

"Bad timing. Shoemaker says Kling wanted to wait till after the meeting so he could hear Monaghan's side. He knew Monaghan hadn't yet been to the Fourteen Mile Point cache, and Kling was going to pick him off there and bury both Monaghan and the cache there in the woods. But Monaghan was waiting with a gun at Page Falls and got him first, then torched the car."

"Wait a minute," I said. "How come Sharon knows all this stuff? Why would Monaghan tell her anything?"

"If I may," Sue said quietly. Gil nodded.

"Sociopaths like to tell their victims all about their crimes, to impress them with how brilliant they are," she said. "Then they kill the people to whom they have allowed this knowledge, and in doing so, they symbolically bury the truth. It's how they live with themselves. And then they do it again and again."

"I'll be damned," I said.

"No, Steve," Gil growled. "*Monaghan* be damned."

I looked up at the use of my first name, but Gil's glower didn't change.

"Did Sharon say how she came to hook up with Monaghan?"

"She got into it with him when Kling wrote that fake phone number on Monaghan's business card after their, ah, encounter during Jerry and Adela's wedding dance. When Kling stopped calling and the phone number he gave her turned out to be bogus, she called Monaghan at his number on that business card to see if he knew where Kling might be. He told her he couldn't remember Kling, like he told you. But he got her phone number and after she gave you the card, he called her back."

"What for?" I asked.

"A little whoopee while he was out here hunting for caches and peddling corpses," Gil said. "Sharon decided she liked Monaghan better than Kling. He was rich and connected—and, *quote,* masterly, *unquote.* And he was, *quote,* great in the sack, *unquote.* She hoped he would take her away from this, *quote,* stupid backwater, *unquote.*" Gil unnecessarily pronounced "quote" and "unquote" in precise italics to make sure we knew they were her words, not his. The undersheriff never overestimated anybody's intelligence, least of all mine.

"Where was she when Monaghan did Kling?"

"Right there at Page Falls, watching from the woods. She said Monaghan stepped out when Kling drove up, said 'Artie?' and when Kling said 'Yes,' just popped him."

"That makes her an accessory."

"Right."

"What did she say she felt when that happened?"

"Glad," Gil said. "She said she hated Kling for running out on her."

"What's even worse is what Monaghan most likely planned to do with Sharon," I said. "Does she have any idea, Gil?"

"Not yet," the undersheriff said. "She says she thinks he planned to take her to New York with him."

I tried and failed to get my mind around the picture of a young urban sophisticate plunking a poor, uneducated, and unpolished woman from the backwoods into the drawing rooms of Wall Street society.

"Do you believe that?" I asked Sue.

"Not at all," she said. "When it was all over, Sharon would have become his third victim. I'm certain of it."

"How can any woman be that dumb?" I said.

"Bad boys attract women," Sue said. "Very bad boys attract stupid women."

At that, we all fell silent for a few beats.

"But something doesn't make sense," I finally said. "Monaghan must have known we were on to the geocaching scheme. He must have known we knew the corpse on the North Country Trail was a homicide, not a cadaver. And why did he come back to look for the last cache at Fourteen Mile?"

"In the simplest possible terms," Sue said, "sociopaths like to finish what they start. In shrink jargon, they're anal."

Alex snorted. "He probably thought he could get away with it. He probably thought a bunch of hayseed cops could never catch him."

"That's always their mistake, isn't it?" I said.

"Always," Sue said. "The sociopathic personality thinks he's figured out all the angles, but in reality he often leaves an important stone unturned. That's how we catch him."

Suddenly I groaned as pain knifed through the Vicodin and

laid open my side. Doc Miller stepped back into the room. "We're wearing Steve out," he said. "Let's give him the rest of the day off."

All night I tossed and turned, trying to find a comfortable position and drifting in and out of sleep.

39

The second morning in the hospital, I awakened still weary, but at last beginning to feel that I would survive my wound. I ate all the breakfast the nurse brought and was on my second cup of coffee when Gil again stuck his head in the door.

"I need your statement on what happened at Fourteen Mile Point," he said briskly, without even the customary how-are-you-feeling hello. "I'll tape it, type it up, and bring it for you to sign."

I took him through the events on the beach. Gil asked no questions, but simply listened carefully. When I was finished, he observed mildly, "What would you have done different if you were to do it all over again?" This is part of every postmortem discussion of a significant piece of police work.

"First, we should've assumed that somebody might have gotten to Fourteen Mile during those twenty-four hours Chad and Fred were away," I said. "We'd have beached the boat much farther down the shore from Fourteen Mile and walked to the lighthouse inside the tree line, staying out of sight. They wouldn't have gotten the drop on us that way."

"Right," Gil said. "You weren't thinking, were you?" His tone was gentle, not accusatory. He is a realist, but he is not cruel.

"No," I had to admit. "Nor was Eli, I guess. Our minds were on other things." The election. Our rivalry.

"That was *my* mistake," Gil said. "Somebody else should have gone on that stakeout."

I nodded. No argument with that.

"Second, I wouldn't have put my revolver in the rifle case. I'd have wrapped it in a plastic grocery bag and kept it in my holster on my belt."

"Would that have done any good?" Gil said skeptically. "The range was fifty yards. You'd have had a handgun, but he had a rifle with a scope."

"Yes, well," I said. "But I might have gotten lucky."

"You *did* get lucky, didn't you? You're alive."

"Yeah," I said. "Thanks to Eli."

"May God bless his soul," Gil said with feeling. I looked up in openmouthed astonishment. I had never before heard the undersheriff express a sentiment of any kind. He was full of surprises.

Gil stood and opened the door. Then he whirled back on his heel. "By the way, Steve, you're the sheriff now. The county board's voted to appoint you to the remainder of Eli's term, even though you're shot."

I looked up. "Does that mean you have to call me 'sir'?"

"Not right now. You haven't been sworn in yet." I could have declared that Gil smiled, but the grimace on his creased face, like a baby's, might have just been from gas.

In a few minutes, Ginny swept in, filling the room with the scent of the Vol de Nuit I loved but that she wore only on special occasions.

"Let's go home," she said.

40 Five days later, we buried Eli in grand style. More than a hundred cops drove in from all over Upper Michigan, Wisconsin, Minnesota, and even Iowa, Illinois, and Canada to pay their respects to one of their own who had fallen in the line of duty. Eli had been a sheriff for a long time and had been on speaking terms with just about every other law enforcement officer in five states and two Canadian provinces. He had been a good lawman and was now a renowned one.

All night at the Jones Funeral Chapel in downtown Porcupine City, an honor guard of four officers, one at each corner of the casket, stood gravely at attention as mourners passed in review. Every fifteen minutes the guard rotated, beginning with Porcupine County deputies and ending with Ontario Provincial Policemen.

I had stood my turn at watch, moving as gingerly as I could, unable to salute as briskly as my brother officers. Ginny had not wanted me to serve on the honor guard—she pushed me to rest another day at her home, where I'd gone after Doc Miller sprung me from the hospital two days after the shootout at Fourteen Mile Point. But standing sentinel over Eli's casket for a measly quarter of an hour was the least anybody could do for someone who had saved his hide. Tommy stood in the back of the room at the funeral parlor, ready to bring his foster mother to the rescue if I faltered. I didn't.

Those three quiet autumn days at Ginny's, spooning with her

by night under the warm quilt of her huge oaken bed and resting across from her by day in the leather recliner in her great room, carving the venison at dinner and quizzing Tommy on his homework, was the closest I had ever come to domesticity. It wasn't so bad, either. I was beginning to think I could get used to being an official part of a nuclear family.

The next morning, Eli's casket was driven to St. Matthew's Episcopal Church in downtown Porcupine City, and another honor guard took up its position in the church.

I had been to a dozen police funerals, most of them for retired cops who had died in their beds, but a few for those who had fallen on duty. With Ginny on my left and Tommy on my right, I took up my position in a front pew. Dorothy Garrow, who knew the healing power of a magnanimous gesture, had asked for our presence there. By rights I should have been one of the pallbearers—all of them were Porcupine County deputies, including Gil O'Brien—but my wound kept me from that honor.

The interior of St. Matthew's looked and smelled as if every florist within fifty miles of Porcupine City had been cleaned out for the occasion. Lilies and carnations flooded the altar and every corner of the church. Seemingly every police force in a radius of five hundred miles had sent a floral arrangement.

Dorothy, followed by a dozen of her children and grandchildren, walked slowly, chin held high, from the vestry and took her seat in the pew across from mine. Gil stepped away from the casket, snapped to attention before Dorothy, and gave her a smart white-gloved salute. Stooping, he gently folded into her hands Eli's six-pointed sheriff's star so that she would have a part of her husband to hold during the service, and he whispered something into her ear. She nodded, looked at her lap, and dabbed at her eyes with a handkerchief. My eyes widened and Ginny and I glanced at each other. *Gil* had a tender side?

As the opening hymn ended in a hush, Father Ted

McGillicuddy, St. Matthew's veteran rector and an immigrant
Scot, mounted the pulpit. "Elias Anthony Garrow is dead," Father
Ted began somberly in his soft burr. "The law enforcement community has lost a brother officer, and Porcupine County has lost a
fine citizen and protector."

Father Ted, a theatrical sort who affected scarlet vests and tar-
tan slacks around town, liked to scatter little rhetorical surprises in
his eulogies as well as his homilies and sermons. "But we will all
see our beloved sheriff again someday," he said happily. "This is
really a going-home party for Eli."

Even Dorothy smiled at that one.

"Let us celebrate his life."

Briskly, Ted took the congregation through the highlights of
Eli's colorful career as a law enforcement officer, a husband, and a
father—there were a remarkable lot of them, too—while skim-
ming over the peccadilloes. No need to spell them out. But Father
Ted was too honest not to acknowledge Eli's humanity.

"We don't shy away from the bad times," Father Ted said,
"because as fragile and sinful human beings, we make mistakes,
we hurt each other, and we don't do things right all the time. We
are not perfect. Neither was Eli. In God, it is never too late to ask
for forgiveness of those who have gone before us. In God, it is
never too late to forgive."

Whatever human flaws Eli had displayed during his long life,
I was perfectly willing to agree, were small and easily excused,
considering the manner in which he'd left that life.

And that expensive ad in *The Ironwood Globe* after I'd defeated
him in the primary? There was nothing dark and threatening about
that, as I had presumed. Eli, Dorothy said, had simply cashed in a
couple of government bonds he'd squirreled away as a small cush-
ion under what would have been a modest county pension.

"He just cared too much about being sheriff," Dorothy had
said during our long conversation when I'd phoned her to offer

my condolences. "I tried to talk him out of using that money. He was just too proud."

At the end, Father Ted said what we all expected him to say. We would have been indignant had he not said it. "Eli Garrow was a hero. In saving the life of another officer, he made the ultimate sacrifice."

The hush in the church deepened into dead silence as Father Ted continued.

"Eli Garrow has died. None of us has ever come back from the dead to tell the tale. And the Bible and the Church—indeed, all the religions of mankind—are not very consistent when it comes to defining exactly what it is we enter into at death. And even if they were consistent, they still would convey only matters of faith, rather than scientific proof. I too have no proof. All I can offer is hope."

A few more words, followed by communion, then we all stood for the Lord's Prayer and Father Ted's benediction. A bagpiper—George Haskell, who owned an ambulance service in Ironwood and had played at the funeral of every cop in three counties for decades—piped a mournful tune while the pallbearers bore the coffin out of the church past two lines of white-gloved officers standing at attention, holding their salute rigidly until Eli was placed gently into the hearse.

The procession to the cemetery, led by more than sixty police vehicles, was the longest in Porcupine County anybody could remember. Ginny, Tommy, and I, driven by Chad in a freshly washed cruiser just behind several limousines bearing the Garrow family and just ahead of those carrying Garner and the county commissioners, rolled slowly down U.S. 45 to the cemetery three miles south of town. Uniformed officers guarding every corner held salutes as the hearse passed by. So lengthy was the procession that the first vehicles arrived at the cemetery before the last ones had pulled out of the church parking lot and from the side streets surrounding it.

As we drove, I thought about the events of the day before. Alex had dropped by Ginny's to fill me in on the loose ends the investigative team had been able to tie up. All the remaining corpses had been recovered from their caches and transported to the Marquette lab for sampling in case a DNA match could be made sometime in the future, if ever. The police in Duluth said no prostitute had been reported missing, the homicide commander adding that he doubted one ever would be. Eventually the headless and handless bodies would be laid to rest in a potter's field, just like all those indigents from the Poor Farm so long ago.

"As for the other geocachers," Alex said, "we may never know who they are, either. We got four of them—Monaghan, Kling, Wilson, and Wilt—but the other three probably will never turn up. If they have any sense, they'll never set foot in Porcupine County again."

Because they had cooperated with us, I thought, Wilson and Wilt would receive light sentences—a year in county jail with time off for good behavior, perhaps a bit of community service afterward. Considering their crimes, I thought snarkily, a few hundred hours of picking up litter and mowing the lawns of county cemeteries would be appropriate. But neither man was a hardened criminal, just another lost and damaged soul who had fallen under the spell of a murderous Svengali. Having tried to cover his trail, Kling had been a harder case, but Monaghan was purely and simply evil. I wished I had learned more about him, what horrible events of his childhood had transformed him into an unredeemable sociopath. I felt no guilt over having relieved society of his presence, but the act of killing a fellow human being would stay with me for years to come, as had all the others.

Sharon Shoemaker would do time in state prison as an accessory to murder, although her sentence also would be lightened because she had cooperated. I didn't see much of a future for her after prison.

We'd keep the case open for a year or so, then, no new facts coming to light, the file would be moved from a cabinet in the sheriff's squad room to a dusty cardboard box in a dark corner of the archives at the Porcupine County Courthouse. And that would be that.

"Monaghan's uncle literally screamed bloody murder when word got to City Hall in Manhattan," Alex continued. "He said his nephew could never have done what we said he had, and he wanted the police commissioner to find and fire anybody on the New York City force who had helped us. The commish stood behind Franciscus. Rumor is that he's in line for a lieutenancy. And when the uncle told Garner he'd demand an official investigation into misconduct in the Porcupine County Sheriff's Department, Garner told him to go take a flying—"

"A flying what?" Ginny had said disingenuously as she walked in on us, causing Alex to blush violently and splutter. He can be *so* old-fashioned.

We arrived at the cemetery. With Ginny's cool palm in my left hand and Tommy's in my right, I strode to the grave, flinching as the wound in my side reminded me of its presence. I am not ashamed to admit that I hid behind the wince, for it camouflaged the emotions I felt. Despite my unchurchedness, funerals touch me deeply, and funerals for brother officers are almost unbearable. More than any other human rite, saying farewell to the dead is an ingathering of community, an acknowledgment of social kinship, a way of reaching out to others. We are all in this together, the ceremony declares, and together we shall survive even as some of us die.

Two hundred years ago, we Lakota constructed open-air scaffolds on which to place our dead and leave them to become one with the eagles and vultures, a rite that was every bit as holy and reverential as that performed today for a Christian burial. I doubted that any Lakota shaman would have found fault with Father Ted's closing words when it came time to scatter earth on the casket.

"We commend to Almighty God our brother Eli, and we commit his body to the ground; earth to earth, ashes to ashes, dust to dust. The Lord bless him and keep him; the Lord make his face to shine upon him and be gracious unto him, the Lord lift up his countenance upon him and give him peace. Amen."

As an army veteran, Eli was entitled to a military salute, and a team from the local Veterans of Foreign Wars raised their rifles, barking a rapid volley into the sky as we all twitched.

"In an important way," my pastor father had once told me, "the military salute is a reminder for the living of God's wrath."

The VFW tenderly handed its flag to Dorothy, then Garner stepped forward. "On behalf of a grateful county and state," he said, "we present you with this flag in remembrance of the ultimate sacrifice Eli made serving the residents of Porcupine County."

On his bagpipe, George Haskell skirled "Amazing Grace," the moment in a police funeral during which absolutely no eye can remain dry. Mine sure didn't. Ginny and Tommy both sobbed quietly beside me. As the last notes drifted into the sky, all the mourners burst into "Sheltered in the Arms of God" and loosed brightly colored balloons to float up into the sky, a singular touch I had been seeing at more and more Upper Peninsula funerals.

Gil spoke quietly into a handheld radio. We looked up past the slowly rising balloons as the drone of aircraft engines intruded on the hush. Four small planes approached from the north at a thousand feet in tight finger-four formation.

At the Number Two position, just behind a State Police Bonanza from Lansing, Doc Miller flew his Bird Dog. Numbers Three and Four were Cessnas from the Civil Air Patrol at Ironwood.

Just before the formation passed over the cemetery, the Bird Dog lifted skyward, climbing away in the classic Missing Man maneuver. The gesture had been my idea. Eli deserved it and Dorothy had welcomed it.

"I thought that was only for pilots," she had said.

"For one very important moment in my life, Dorothy," I had replied with feeling, "Eli was my wingman."

"He now guards the heavens," said Father Ted, who always comes up with just the right thing to say, as we all watched the Bird Dog ascend into the clouds. As the airplane disappeared into the mist, it was transfigured, in my Lakota mind's eye, into an eagle.

A Note to Geocachers

All the geographic waypoints given in this novel are real spots on Earth. But if you choose to go looking for these locations with your GPS, be aware that their surroundings are fictional.

THE AUTHOR